SHE LOVER OF DEATH

Also by Boris Akunin

Fandorin mysteries

The Winter Queen
The Turkish Gambit
Murder on the Leviathan
The Death of Achilles
Special Assignments
The State Counsellor
The Coronation

Sister Pelagia mysteries

Sister Pelagia and the White Bulldog
Sister Pelagia and the Black Monk
Sister Pelagia and the Red Cockerel

SHE LOVER OF DEATH

A FANDORIN MYSTERY

BORIS AKUNIN

Translated by Andrew Bromfield

The Mysterious Press
New York

First published in Great Britain in 2009 by Weidenfeld & Nicolson,
an imprint of the Orion Publishing Group.

First published in Russian as *Liubovnitsa smerti* by Zakharov Publications,
Moscow, Russia and Edizioni Frassinelli, Milan, Italy.

Published simultaneously in Canada
Printed in the United States of America

First Grove Atlantic hardcover edition: March 2020
First Grove Atlantic paperback edition: March 2021

Library of Congress Cataloging-in-Publication data available for this title.

ISBN 978-0-8021-4856-8
eISBN978-0-8021-4815-5

The Mysterious Press
an imprint of Grove Atlantic
154 West 14th Street
New York, NY10011

Distributed by Publishers Group West

groveatlantic.com

21 22 23 24   10 9 8 7 6 5 4 3 2 1

The author is grateful to Sergei Gandlevsky
and Lev Rubinstein, who helped the characters
in this novel – Gdlevsky and Lorelei Rubinstein –
to write their beautiful poetry

I. From the Newspapers

The Selfless Devotion of a Four-Legged Friend

Yesterday at shortly after two in the morning the inhabitants of the Goliath company's apartment building on Semyonovskaya Street were awoken by the sound of a heavy object falling to the ground, which was immediately followed by the protracted howling of a pointer dog belonging to the photographer S., who rented a studio in the attic. On hearing the noise, the yard keeper went outside and, looking up, he saw a lighted window with a dog standing on the window ledge and wailing in a most mournful, harrowing manner. A moment later the yard keeper noticed the motionless body of S. himself lying on the ground below the window. It was evidently the object that had made so much noise in falling. Suddenly, before the astounded yard keeper's very eyes, the pointer jumped down, landing close beside the body of its master and smashing itself to death against the cobblestones of the street.

Legends concerning canine fidelity are numerous, but selfless devotion that overcomes the very instinct of self-preservation and scorns death itself is extremely rare among animals, and cases of obvious suicide are encountered even less often among our four-legged friends.

The police initially proceeded on the assumption that S., who led a disorderly and not entirely sober life, had fallen from the window by accident: however, a note in verse discovered in the apartment indicated that the photographer had laid hands on himself. The motives underlying this act of desperation are unclear. S.'s neighbours and acquaintances assert that he had no reasons for settling his accounts with life: quite the contrary, in fact; in recent days S. had been in very high spirits.

L. Zh.
Moscow Courier, 4 (17) August 1900, p.6

Mystery of Fatal Junket Solved

Incredible details of the tragic events on Furmanny Lane

As we informed our readers two days ago, the name-day party to which grammar school teacher Soimonov invited four of his colleagues concluded in the most lamentable fashion possible, with the host and his guests all discovered seated, lifeless, around the well-laid table. An autopsy of the bodies revealed that the deaths of all five victims had been caused by a bottle of Castello port wine, which contained an immense dose of arsenic. This sensational news spread to every part of the city, and at the wine merchants' shops demand for the above-mentioned brand of port, formerly a great favourite with Muscovites, dried up completely. The police launched an inquiry at the Stamm Brothers' bottling plant, which supplies Castello to the wine merchants.

Today, however, we can state with absolutely certainty that the estimable beverage was not to blame. A sheet of paper bearing the following lines of verse was discovered in the pocket of Soimonov's frock-coat:

Song of Farewell

Loveless life is mere vexation!
Wary stealth, deliberation,
Hollow mirth, dissatisfaction
Blight and thwart my every
  action.
Deriders, you have had your fun,
Your time for mockery is done.
Help this valiant fellow now
Set the crown upon his brow.
To her who did reveal to me
The fearsome love that sets one
  free

2

I shall cry in that sweet hour:
'Pluck me like a pining flower!'

The meaning of this farewell missive is vague, but it is entirely clear that Soimonov intended to take his leave of this life and put the poison in the bottle himself. However, the motives for this insane act are not clear. The suicide was a reserved and eccentric individual, although he showed no signs of any mental illness. Your humble servant was able to ascertain that he was not much liked at the grammar school: among the pupils he had the reputation of a strict and boring teacher, while his colleagues decried his acrimonious and arrogant temperament, and several of them mocked his idiosyncratic behaviour and morbid meanness. However, all of this can hardly be considered adequate grounds for such an outrageous atrocity.

Soimonov had no family or servants. According to his landlady, Madam G., he often went out in the evenings and came back long after midnight. Numerous rough drafts for poems of an extremely sombre complexion were discovered among Soimonov's papers. None of his colleagues were aware that the deceased was in the habit of composing verse, and when some of those questioned were informed of the poetic efforts of this Chekhovian 'man in a case', they actually refused to believe it.

The invitation to the name-day party which ended in such a grisly fashion came as a complete surprise to Soimonov's colleagues at the grammar school. He had never invited anyone to visit him before, and those he did invite were the four people with whom he was on the very worst of terms and who, according to numerous witnesses, mocked him more than anyone else. The unfortunate victims accepted the invitation in the belief that Soimonov had finally determined to improve relations with his colleagues and also (as the grammar school superintendent, Mr Serdobolin, put it) 'out of understandable curiosity', since no one had ever been to the misanthrope's house before.

Now we know only too well what their curiosity led to.

It is perfectly clear that the poisoner had decided, not only to draw a line under his own miserable life, but also to take with him those who had affronted him the most, those same 'deriders' who are mentioned in the poem.

But what might be the meaning of the words about 'her who revealed the fearsome love'? Could there possibly be a woman behind this macabre story?

L. Zhemailo
Moscow Courier, 11 (24)
August 1900, p.2

Is a Suicide Club Active in Moscow?

Our correspondent conducts his own investigation and proposes a grim hypothesis!

The circumstances of an event that shook the whole of Moscow – the double suicide of latter-day Romeo and Juliet, 22-year-old Sergei Shutov and 19-year-old girl student Evdokia Lamm (see, *inter alia*, our article 'No sadder story in the world' of the 16th of August) – have been clarified. Newspapers reported that the lovers shot each other in the chest with two pistols simultaneously – evidently at some signal. Miss Lamm was killed outright and Shutov was seriously wounded in the region of the heart and taken to the Mariinskaya Hospital. It is known that he was fully conscious, but would not answer questions and only kept repeating, 'Why? Why? Why?' A minute before he gave up the ghost, Shutov suddenly smiled and said, 'I'm going. That means she loves me.' Sentimental reporters have discerned in this bloody story a romantic drama of love, however on closer consideration it appears that love had nothing at all to do with this business. At least, *not love between the two people involved in this tragedy*.

Your humble servant has ascertained that should the supposed lovers have wished to unite in the bonds of matrimony there were no obstacles in their path. Miss Lamm's parents are entirely modern people. Her father – a full professor at Moscow University – is well known in student circles for his progressive views. He is quoted as saying that he would never have stood in the way of his beloved daughter's happiness. Shutov had reached the age of consent and possessed a sum of capital that was not large, but nonetheless perfectly adequate for a comfortable life. And so it turns out that if they had wished, this couple could easily have married! Why, then, would they shoot each other in the chest?

Tormented by this question day and by night, we decided to make certain enquiries, which led to an extremely strange discovery. People who knew both of the suicides well are unanimous in declaring that the relationship between Lamm and Shutov was one of ordinary friendship and they did not entertain any ardent passion for each other.

Well now, we pondered, acquaintances can often be blind. Perhaps this young man and woman had grounds for carefully concealing their passion from everyone else?

Today, however, we came into possession (do not ask in what way – that is a professional journalist's secret) of a poem written by the two suicides shortly before the fatal volley was fired. It is a poetical work of a highly unusual nature and even, perhaps, without precedent. It is written in two hands – evidently Shutov and Lamm took it in turns to write one line each. What we have, therefore, is the fruit of a *collective* creative endeavour. The content of this poem casts an entirely different light, not only on the deaths of the strange Romeo and Juliet, but also on the string of suicides that have taken place in the old Russian capital during recent weeks.

He wore a white cloak. He
   stood on the threshold.
He wore a white cloak. He
   glanced in the window.
'I am love's emissary, sent to
   you from Her.'
'You are His bride and I am sent
   for you.'

Thus spoke he, reaching out
   his hand to me.
Thus spoke he. How pure and
   deep was his voice
And his eyes were dark and
   stern
And his eyes were light and
   gentle.
I said: 'I am ready. I have
   waited very long.'
I said: 'I am coming. Say that I
   am coming.'

Nothing but riddles from beginning to end. What does
the 'white cloak' mean?
Who has sent this emissary –
She or He? Where was he
actually standing, in the
doorway or outside the window? And what kind of eyes
did this intriguing gentleman
actually have – dark and
stern or light and gentle?

At this point we recalled
the recent and, at first glance,
equally motiveless suicides of
the photographer Sviridov
(see our article of the 4th of
August) and the teacher Soimonov (see our articles of
the 8th and 11th of August).
In each case a poem was left
as a suicide note, something
which, you must admit, is a
rather rare event in this prosaic Russia of ours!

It is a pity that the police
did not keep the note written
by the photographer Sviridov, but even without it
there is certainly more than
enough food for thought.

Soimonov's farewell poem
mentions a mysterious fe-
male individual who revealed
to the poisoner 'the fearsome
love that sets one free' and
later plucked him 'like a pining flower'. Shutov was visited by an emissary of love
from 'Her' – an unnamed
female individual; Lamm's
emissary was from a certain
bridegroom, who for some
reason also has to be mentioned with a capital letter.

Is it not, therefore, reasonable to assume that the face
filled with love that figures in
the poems of the suicides and
sets their hearts trembling so
reverently is the face of death
itself? Many things then become clear: passion urges the
enamoured individual, not
towards life, but towards the
grave – this is the love of
death.

Your humble servant is
no longer in any doubt that
a secret society of death-
worshippers has been established in Moscow, following

the example of several other European cities: a society of madmen – and women – who are in love with death. The spirit of disbelief and nihilism, the crisis of morality and art and, even more significantly, that dangerous demon who goes by the name of *fin de siècle* – these are the bacilli of the contagion that has produced this dangerous ulcer.

We set ourselves the goal of discovering as much as possible about the story of those mysterious secret societies known as 'suicide clubs', and this is the information that we have managed to glean.

Suicide clubs are not a purely Russian phenomenon, in fact they are not Russian at all. There have never previously been any of these monstrous organisations within the bounds of our empire. But apparently, as we follow Europe along the path of 'progress', we are also fated to suffer this malign pestilence.

The first mention in the historical annals of a voluntary association of death-worshippers dates back to the first century BC, when the legendary lovers, Antony and Cleopatra, established an 'academy of those who are not parted in death' for lovers 'who wish to die together: quietly, radiantly and when they choose'. As we know, this romantic undertaking concluded in less than idyllic fashion, since at the decisive moment the great queen actually preferred to be parted from her conquered Antony and tried to save herself. When it became clear that her much vaunted charms had no effect on the cold Octavian, Cleopatra eventually did take her own life, demonstrating a thoughtfulness and good taste truly worthy of antiquity: she deliberated at length over the best means of suicide, testing various different poisons on slaves and criminals, and eventually settled on the bite of the Egyptian cobra, which causes almost no disagreeable sensations apart from a slight headache, which is, in any case, rapidly replaced by 'an irresistible desire for death'.

But this is legend, you will object, or at least, these are

events of days long past. Modern man has his feet too firmly set on the ground, he is too materialistic and clings to life too tightly to set up any 'academy' of this sort.

Well then – let us turn to the enlightened nineteenth century, a period when suicide clubs flourished to an unprecedented degree: groups of people organised themselves into secret societies with one single goal: to depart from this life without publicity or scandal.

As early as 1802 in godless post-revolutionary Paris, a club was founded with a membership of twelve, which for obvious reasons, was constantly renewed. According to the club's charter, the sequence in which members left this life was determined by a game of cards. At the beginning of each new year a chairman was elected, and he was obliged to do away with himself when his term of office expired.

In 1816 a 'Circle of Death' appeared in Berlin. Its six members made no secret of their intentions – on the contrary, they attempted to attract new members by every possible means. According to the rules, the only 'legitimate' way to commit suicide was with a pistol. The 'Circle of Death' eventually ceased to exist, because all those who wished to join had shot themselves.

Later on, clubs whose members sought death ceased to be something exotic and became almost *de rigueur* for large European cities. Although, of course, persecution by the forces of law and order obliged these associations to maintain strict conspiratorial secrecy. According to information in our possession, 'suicide clubs' existed (and perhaps still exist to this day) in London, Vienna and Brussels, as well as in Paris and Berlin, as already mentioned, and even in the backwater of Bucharest, where the ultimate temptation of destiny was a fashionable amusement among rich young officers.

The most sensational reputation was earned by the London club, which was eventually exposed and disbanded by the police, but before that happened it had facilitated the despatch of about twenty of its members to the next world. These worshippers of death were only tracked down as a result of betrayal from within their own close-knit ranks. One of the aspirants was incautious enough to fall in love, as a result of which he became inspired with a rather poignant attachment to life and a violent aversion to death. This apostate agreed to testify. It emerged that this top-secret club only accepted as members those who could prove the seriousness of their intentions. The sequence of departure was determined by chance: the winner of a game of cards acquired the right to die first. The 'lucky man' was eagerly congratulated by everyone, and a banquet was arranged in his honour. In order to avoid any undesirable consequences, the death itself was arranged to look like an accident, with the other members of the brotherhood helping to organise it: they dropped bricks from roofs, overturned the chosen one's carriage and so on.

Something similar happened in Sarajevo in the Austro-Hungarian Empire, but there the outcome was more sombre. The suicide club in question called itself 'The Club of the Aware' and its membership numbered at least fifty. They gathered in the evenings to draw lots, each of them selecting a card from the pack until someone drew the death's head. The person who received the fateful card had to die within twenty-four hours. One young Hungarian told his comrades that he was leaving the club, because he had fallen in love and wanted to get married. They agreed to let him out on condition that he take part in the drawing of lots for one last time. In the first round the young man drew the ace of hearts – the symbol of love – and in the second round the death's head. As a man of his word, he shot himself. The inconsolable fiancée denounced 'The Aware' to the police, and as a result the whole business became public knowledge.

To judge from what has been happening in Moscow in recent weeks, our death-worshippers have no fear of public opinion and are not too concerned about publicity – at least, they do not take any measures to conceal the fruits of their activities.

I promise the *Courier*'s readers that the investigation will be continued. If a secret league of madmen who toy with death really has appeared in Russia's old capital, society must know of it.

Lavr Zhemailo
Moscow Courier, 22 August
(4 September) 1900, p.1,
continued on p.4

II. From Columbine's Diary

She arrived in the City of Dreams on a quiet lilac evening

Everything had been thought through in advance, down to the smallest detail.

After alighting from the Irkutsk train at the platform of Moscow's Ryazan station, Masha stood there for half a minute with her eyes squeezed shut, breathing in the smell of the city – the mingled scent of flowers, fuel oil and bagels. Then she opened her eyes and in a voice loud enough for the whole platform to hear, proclaimed the quatrain that she had composed two days earlier, on crossing the border between Asia and Europe.

> *Like a shipwrecked vessel foundering*
> *While the billows rage and roar*
> *No words or tears, regretting nothing,*
> *To fall, to soar aloft and fall once more!*

People glanced round over their shoulders at the young lady with the clear voice and thick plait – some in curiosity, some in disapproval, and one tradeswoman even twirled a finger beside her temple. Generally speaking, the first *public act* of Masha's life could be considered a success – and just you wait!

It was a symbolic step, marking the beginning of a new era, adventurous and uninhibited.

She had left quietly, without any public display. Left a long, long letter for papa and mama on the table in the drawing room. Tried to explain about the new age, and how unbearable the tedium of Irkutsk was, and about poetry. She had dropped tears all over every page, but how could they really understand? If it had happened a month earlier, before her birthday, they would have gone running to the police – to bring back their runaway daughter by force. But now, I beg your pardon, Marya Mironova has reached the age of majority and may arrange her life as she herself thinks fit. And she was also free to use the inheritance from her aunt as she thought best. The capital sum was not very large, but it would suffice for half a year, even with Moscow's famously high prices, and trying to see further than that was common and prosaic.

She told the cabby to drive to the Hotel Elysium. She had heard about it even in Irkutsk, and been captivated by the name that flowed like silvery mercury.

As she rode along in the carriage, she constantly looked round at the large stone buildings and signboards and felt desperately afraid. A huge city, with an entire million people, and not one of them, *not one*, had anything to do with Marya Mironova.

Just you wait, she threatened the city, you're going to hear about me. I'll make you gasp in delight and indignation, but I don't need your love. And even if you crush me in your stone jaws, it doesn't matter. There is no road back.

But her attempt to lift her spirits only made her feel even more timid.

And her heart fell completely when she walked into the vestibule of the Elysium, with its bronze and crystal all aglow with electric light. Masha shamefully inscribed herself in the register as 'Marya Mironova, company officer's daughter', although the plan had been to call herself by some special name: 'Annabel Gray' or simply 'Columbine'.

Never mind, she would become Columbine starting from tomorrow, when she would be transformed from a grey provincial moth to a bright-winged butterfly. At least she had taken an expensive room, with a view of the Kremlin and the river. What if a night in this gilded candy-box did cost a whole fifteen roubles! She would remember what was going to happen here for the rest of her life. And tomorrow she could find simpler lodgings. Definitely on the top floor, or even in an attic, so that no one would be shuffling their feet across the floor over her head; let there be nothing above her but the roof with cats gliding gracefully across it, and above that only the black sky and the indifferent stars.

Having gazed her fill through the window at the Kremlin and unpacked her suitcase, Masha sat down at the table, and opened a small notebook bound in morocco leather. She thought for a while, chewing on the end of her pencil, and started writing.

Everybody keeps a diary now, everybody wants to appear more important than they really are and, even more than that, they want to overcome their own death and carry on living after it, if only in the form of a notebook bound in Moroccan leather. This alone should have deterred me from the idea of keeping a diary for, after all, I decided a long time ago, on the very first day of the new twentieth century, *not to be like everyone else.* And yet here I am sitting and writing. But this will not be a case of sentimental sighs with dried forget-me-nots between the pages, it will be a genuine work of art such as there has never been before in literature. I am writing a diary, not because I am afraid of death or, let us say, because I wish to be liked by strangers I do not know, who will some day read these lines. What do I want with people? I know them only too well and despise them thoroughly. And perhaps I am not even slightly afraid of death either. Why be afraid of it, when it is a natural law of existence? Everything that is born, that is, which has a beginning, will come to an end sooner or later. If I, Masha Mironova, appeared in the world twenty-one years and one month ago, then the day is bound to come when I shall leave this world, and there is nothing unusual about that. I only hope that it happens before my face is covered in wrinkles.

She read it through, frowned and tore out the page.

What kind of work of art was that? Too vapid, boring, run-of-the-mill. She had to learn to express her thoughts (for a start, at least on paper) elegantly, fragrantly, intoxicatingly. Her arrival in Moscow ought to be described in a quite different fashion.

Masha thought again, this time chewing on the tail of her golden plait instead of the pencil. She leaned her head to one side like a grammar-school girl and started scribbling.

Columbine arrived in the City of Dreams on a lilac evening, on the final sigh of a long, lazy day that she had spent at the window of an express train as light as an arrow, which had rushed her past dark forests and bright lakes to her encounter with destiny. A following wind, favourable to those who slide across the silvery ice of life, had caught Columbine up and carried her on: long-awaited freedom beckoned to the frivolous seeker of adventures, rustling its lacy wings above her head.

The train delivered the blue-eyed traveller, not to pompous St Petersburg, but to sad and mysterious Moscow – the City of Dreams, resembling a queen who has been shut away in a convent to while away the years of her life, a queen whose empty-headed and capricious lord has bartered her for a cold, snake-eyed rival. Let the new queen hold sway in her marble halls with mirrors that reflect the waters of the Baltic. The old queen wept clear, transparent tears, and when her tears dried up, she was reconciled to her simple life. She passes her days in spinning yarn and her nights in prayer. My place is with her, abandoned and unloved, and not with the one who turns her pampered face to the wan sun of the north.

I am Columbine, frivolous and unpredictable, subject only to the caprices of my own whimsical fantasy and the fey wafting of the wind. Pity the poor Pierrot who will have the misfortune to fall in love with my candy-box looks, for my destiny is to become a plaything in the hands of the scheming deceiver Harlequin and be left lying on the floor like a broken doll with a carefree smile on my little porcelain face . . .

She read it through again and was satisfied, but did not carry on writing for the time being, because she started thinking about Harlequin – Petya Lileiko (Li-lei-ko – what a light, jolly name, like the sound of a sleigh bell or drops of meltwater in spring!). And he really had appeared in the spring, come crashing into the dreary life of Irkutsk like a red fox into a sleepy henhouse. He had cast a spell on her with the halo of fiery-red curls scattering across his shoulders, his loose-fitting blouse and intoxicating poems. Before then, Masha had only sighed over the fact that life was an empty, stupid joke, but he had commented casually – as if it were perfectly obvious – that the only true beauty is in fading, wilting and dying. And the provincial dreamer had realised how true that was! Where else could Beauty be? Not in life! What was there in life that could be beautiful? Marry a tax assessor, have a crowd of children and sit by the samovar in your mob-cap for sixty years?

Beside the arbour on the high riverbank, the Moscow Harlequin had kissed the swooning young lady and whispered, 'Out of pale and accidental life I have made a single endless thrill.' And then poor Masha really was completely lost, because she realised that was the whole point. To become a weightless butterfly fluttering your rainbow wings and giving no thought to autumn.

After the kiss beside the arbour (there had been nothing else) she had stood in front of the mirror for a long time, looking at her reflection and hating it: a ruddy, round face with a stupid thick plait. And those terrible pink ears that flamed up like poppies when she was even slightly flustered!

And then, when Petya's visit to his great-aunt, the deputy-governor's widow, was over, he had ridden away again on the Transcontinental and Masha had started counting the days until she came of age – it turned out to be exactly one hundred, just like Napoleon after the Elbe. She remembered she had felt terribly sorry for the emperor in history lessons – it was hard, to return to fame and glory for only a hundred days, but now she realised just how long a hundred days really was.

However, everything comes to an end sooner or later. When her parents handed their daughter her birthday present – a set of silver teaspoons for her future family home – they did not even suspect that the hour of their Waterloo was upon them. Masha had already cut out the patterns for unbelievably bold outfits of her own design. Another month of secret nights spent hunched over the sewing-machine (the time passed quickly then) and the Siberian captive was absolutely ready for her transformation into Columbine.

Through all that long week on the railway she imagined how astounded Petya would be when he opened the door and saw her there on the threshold – not the timid goose from Irkutsk in a boring little dress of white muslin, but the bold Columbine in a scarlet cape that fluttered in the breeze and a pearl-embroidered cap with an ostrich feather. Then she would give him a devil-may-care smile and say, 'A sudden blizzard from Siberia! Do with me what you will.' Petya of course, would choke in surprise at such audacious directness and the sensation of his own boundless power over this creature who seemed to be woven out of the very ether. He would put his arms round her shoulders, plant a passionate kiss on her soft, submissive lips and lead his uninvited guest into a boudoir enveloped in mysterious twilight. Or perhaps he would take her with all the passion of a rampant young satyr, right there on the floor of the hallway.

Her lively imagination had immediately painted for her a scene of passion in the company of umbrellas stands and galoshes. The traveller had frowned and trained her unseeing gaze on the spurs of the Ural mountains. She realised that she would have to prepare the altar for the forthcoming sacrifice herself, she could not rely on the whim of chance.

And that was when the miraculous word 'Elysium' had surfaced in her memory.

Well, she thought, the fifteen-rouble stage-setting was adequate for the sacred rites.

Masha – no, Masha no longer, Columbine – ran a caressing glance over the walls hung with lilac moiré satin, the deep-piled, bright-patterned carpet on the floor, the ethereally light furniture on curved legs, and frowned at the naked nymph in the sumptuous gold frame (that was going a bit too far).

Then she noticed an object of even greater luxury on the table beside the mirror – an absolutely genuine telephone! Her own personal apparatus, standing right there in her room! Just imagine!

And immediately an idea occurred to her that was even more dramatic than the first one of simply appearing in the doorway. Appearing was no problem, but what if he was not in when she did it? There was a whiff of provincial offhandedness about it too. And again, why make the journey if the fall (which was simultaneously a vertiginous flight) was to take place here, on this bed like a catafalque, with its carved columns and heavy canopy? But to telephone – that was modern, elegant, *metropolitan*.

Petya's father was a doctor, he was absolutely certain to have a telephone at home.

Columbine picked the stylish brochure entitled *Moscow Telephone Subscribers* up off the table and – would you believe it – she opened it straight away at the letter 'L'. There it was, now: 'Terentii Savelievich Lileiko, Dr of Medicine – 3128'. Surely this was the finger of fate?

She stood for a moment, facing the gleaming lacquered box with its metal circles and caps and focusing her will. She twirled the handle with desperate speed and when a brassy voice squeaked 'Central exchange' into her earpiece, she recited the four figures rapidly.

While she was waiting, she suddenly realised that the phrase she had prepared would not do for a telephone conversation. 'What sudden blizzard from Siberia?' Petya would ask. 'What sort of way is that to talk? And why should I do anything with you, madam?'

To bolster her courage, she opened the Japanese ivory cigarette case that she had bought at the station and lit the first *papirosa* of her life (the *pakhitoska* that Masha Mironova had once lit up in fifth class at school didn't count – back then she hadn't had the slightest idea that you were supposed to inhale the tobacco smoke). She propped her elbow on the little table, turned slightly sideways-on to the mirror and narrowed her eyes. Not bad, not bad at all, interesting and even rather enigmatic.

'Doctor Lileiko's apartment,' a woman's voice said in the earpiece. 'With whom do you wish to speak?'

The smoker was rather disconcerted – for some reason she had been certain that Petya would answer. She rebuked herself sternly. How stupid! Of course, he didn't live alone. His parents were there, and the servants, and possibly even some brothers and sisters. In fact, she didn't really know very much about him: only that he was a student, he wrote poems and spoke wonderfully well about the beauty of tragic death. And also that he kissed a lot better than Kostya Levonidi, her former future-fiancé, who had been decisively dismissed for being so tediously positive, reliable and humdrum.

'I'm a friend of Petya, Pyotr Terentsievich,' Columbine babbled in a highly trivial manner. 'A certain Mironova.'

A minute later she heard the familiar baritone voice with that enchanting Moscow drawl in the earpiece.

'Hello? Is that Mrs Mironova? Professor Zimin's assistant?'

By this time the inhabitant of the stylish hotel room had pulled herself together. She breathed a stream of dove-grey smoke into the bell mouth of the telephone apparatus and whispered: 'It is I, Columbine.'

'Who did you say?' Petya asked in surprise. 'So you're not Mrs Mironova from the faculty of Roman Law?'

She had to explain to the dimwit.

'Remember the arbour above the Angara. Remember how you called me "Columbine"?' and straight after that the phrase she had prepared on the way fitted in perfectly. 'It is I. Like a sudden blizzard from Siberia I have come to you. Do with me what you wish. Do you know the Hotel Elysium?' After that resounding word she paused. 'Come. I'm waiting.'

That got through to him! Petya started breathing rapidly and speaking in a thick voice – he must have put his hand over the mouthpiece.

'Masha, that is, Columbine, I am absolutely delighted that you have come . . .' he said rather formally. It was true that they had been on formal terms in Irkutsk, but now this way of talking seemed inappropriate, insulting even, to the seeker of adventures. 'Yes, indeed, just like a sudden blizzard out of nowhere . . . No, that is, it's simply marvellous! Only there's no way I can come to you now. I'm resitting an exam tomorrow. And it's late, mama will pester me with questions . . .'

And he went on to babble something absolutely pitiful about a failed examination and the word of honour he had given to his father.

The reflection in the mirror batted its eyelids and the corners of its mouth turned slowly downwards. Who could have imagined that the guileful seducer Harlequin had to ask leave from his mummy before setting out on an amorous escapade? And she suddenly regretted terribly the fifteen roubles that she had spent.

'Why are you here in Moscow?' Petya whispered. 'Surely not especially to see me?'

She laughed – it turned out very well, with a slightly husky note. She supposed that was because of the *papirosa*. So that he wouldn't get above himself, she said enigmatically, 'The meeting with you is no more than a prelude to another meeting. Do you understand?'

And she declaimed two lines from one of Petya's own poems:

To live life like a line of ringing verse
And write its full stop with no hesitation.

That time back at the arbour, foolish little Masha had whispered with a happy smile (it was shameful to recall it now): 'This must be true happiness.' The visitor from Moscow had smiled condescendingly and said: 'Happiness, Masha, is something quite different. Happiness is not a fleeting moment, but eternity. Not a comma, but a full stop.' And then he had recited the poem about the line and the full stop. Masha had flushed, torn herself out of his arms and stood at the very top of the cliff, with the dark water sighing down below. 'Do you want me to write that full stop right now?' she had exclaimed. 'Do you think I'll be too frightened?'

'You . . . Are you serious?' the voice in the telephone asked very quietly. 'Don't think that I've forgotten . . .'

'I'll say I'm serious,' she laughed, intrigued by the peculiar inflection that had crept into Petya's voice.

'A perfect fit . . .' Petya whispered incomprehensibly. 'Just when there's a vacancy . . . Fate. Destiny . . . All right, here goes. I tell you what, let's meet tomorrow evening at a quarter past eight . . . Yes, at a quarter past . . . Only where?'

Columbine's heart began beating very, very fast as she tried to guess what spot he would choose for the tryst. A park? A bridge? A boulevard? And at the same time she tried to calculate whether she could afford to keep the room in the Elysium for one more night. That would make thirty roubles, an entire month of living! Sheer folly!

But Petya said: 'Beside the Berry Market on the Marsh.'

'What marsh?' Columbine asked in astonishment.

'Marsh Square, it's near the Elysium. And from there I'll take you to an absolutely special place, where you'll meet some absolutely special people.'

The way he said it sounded so mysterious and solemn that Columbine didn't feel even a shred of disappointment. On the contrary, she felt that same 'endless thrill' again very clearly and realised that the adventures were beginning. Perhaps not exactly as she had imagined, but even so, coming to the City of Dreams had not been a waste of time.

She sat in the armchair by the open window until late at night, snuggled up in a warm rug, and watched the dark barges with their swaying lanterns floating down the Moscow river.

She was terribly curious about what these 'absolutely special' people could be like.

Roll on tomorrow evening!

Cleopatra's final moment

When Columbine woke up on the vast bed that had not, after all, become the altar of love, the evening still seemed a long way off. She lounged on the downy mattress for a while, phoned down to the ground floor to have coffee sent up, and in celebration of her new sophisticated life, drank it without cream or sugar. It was bitter and unpalatable, but it was bohemian.

In the foyer, after paying for the room and leaving her suitcase in the baggage closet, she leafed through the pages of announcements in the *Moscow Provincial Gazette*. She wrote out several addresses, selecting houses with at least three storeys, in which the flat on offer had to be at the very top.

She haggled for a while with the cabby: he wanted three roubles, she wanted to give him one, and they struck a deal for a rouble and forty kopecks. It was a good price, taking into account that for this sum the driver had agreed to drive the young lady round all four addresses, but the newcomer in town still paid too much anyway – she was so taken by the very first flat, right in the centre, in Kitaigorod, that there was no point in going any further. She tried to buy the driver off with a rouble (even that was a lot, for only fifteen minutes), but he was a good psychologist and he crushed the young provincial's resistance with the words: 'Here in Moscow a man might be a thief, but he still keeps his word.' She blushed and paid, but insisted that he had to bring her baggage from the Elysium and she stuck firmly to that.

The flat was a real sight for sore eyes. And the monthly rent wasn't high by Moscow standards – the same as one night at the Elysium. Of course, in Irkutsk you could rent an entire house with a garden and servant for that money, but then this wasn't the back of beyond in Siberia, it was Russia's Old Capital.

And then, who had ever seen buildings like this in Irkutsk? Six entire storeys high! The courtyard was all stone, not a blade of grass anywhere. It was obvious straight away that you were living in a real city and not a village. The side street that the windows of the room overlooked was as narrow as could be. If you stood on a stool in the kitchen and looked out through the small upper window frame, you could see the Kremlin towers and the spires of the Historical Museum.

The living space was not actually located in a garret or attic, as Columbine had been dreaming it would be, but it was on the top floor. Add to this that it was fully furnished, with gas lighting and an American stove. And the flat itself! Columbine had never in her life seen anything so delightfully absurd.

When you entered from the stairs there was a short corridor. The door on the right led into the living room (the only one), from that room you turned left and found yourself in the little kitchen, and there was another passage on the left, where there was a water-closet with a washbasin and a bath, and then the corridor led back out into the hallway. It was a kind of ludicrous circle, and it was impossible to understand what purpose anyone could have designed it for.

The room had a balcony, and the brand-new Muscovite fell in love with it immediately. It was wide, with fancy cast-iron railings and what's more – a point that was especially captivating because it was so fatuous – there was a gate in the railings. She couldn't guess what on earth it was for.

Perhaps the architect had been thinking of attaching a fire ladder to the outside of the balcony and then changed his mind?

Columbine drew back the stiff bolt, swung the heavy little gate open and glanced down. Far, far away, below the toes of her shoes, there were little carriages driving and little toy people creeping along. It was so wonderful that the new resident of the heavens actually burst into song.

On the opposite side of the street, but lower down, there was a gleaming metal figure: a well-fed angel with white wings, with a sign board swaying under his feet: 'MÖBIUS AND SONS INSURANCE COMPANY. With us there is almost nothing to fear.' How delightful!

There were also a few minuses, but they were insignificant.

It was all right that there was no elevator – it didn't take long to run up to the sixth floor.

But there was something else that had alarmed her. The landlord had warned her quite frankly that the appearance of mice or, as he called them, 'domestic rodents' was not entirely out of the question. For a minute or two Columbine had been quite upset – she had been afraid of mice ever since she was a child. Sometimes, when she heard the patter of those tiny little feet on the floor, she used to screw her eyes up so tight that she saw fiery circles behind her eyelids. But that was all in her past, unreal life now, she told herself straight away. Columbine was far too frivolous and reckless a creature to be frightened by anything. If the worst came to the worst, she could always buy some of that Antirattin Salami that was advertised in the *Gazette*.

That afternoon, when Columbine went to the market for provisions (oh, these Moscow prices!), she acquired another ally from the world of the night and the moon. She bought a young grass snake from some boys for eight kopecks. He was small and iridescent, and once in her basket he immediately curled up into a tight ring and lay there quiet.

Why did she buy him? Why, to drive Masha Mironova out

of herself as quickly as possible. That big ninny was even more afraid of snakes than of mice. Whenever she saw one anywhere on a forest path, she used to started screaming and squealing like a fool.

At home Columbine resolutely bit her lip and took the reptile into her hand. The little snake turned out not to be wet and slippery as you might have thought from looking at him, but dry, rough and cool. His tiny little eyes gazed up at the giantess in horror.

The boys had said: 'Put the snake in milk so it won't go sour, and when it grows a bit, it'll be good for catching mice.' Columbine, however, had a different idea, far more interesting.

First of all she fed the grass snake with curdled milk (after eating he immediately settled down to sleep); then she gave him a name – Lucifer; and after that she painted over the yellow spots on the side of his head with Chinese ink, so that what she had was not a grass snake, but some weird and mysterious reptile that might very well be deadly poisonous.

She undressed to the waist in front of the mirror, set the snake, still drowsy after feeding, on her bare breasts and admired herself. It was 'Cleopatra's final moment' to a tee.

A lucky ticket

She spent several hours preparing for her meeting with Harlequin and left the house in good time, in order to make her first gala promenade through the streets of Moscow without hurrying and give the city a chance to admire its new inhabitant.

The two of them – Moscow and Columbine – made a great impression on each other. On this overcast August evening the former was jaded, bored and blasé; the latter was wary and nervous, ready for any surprises.

For the Moscow premiere Columbine had chosen an outfit the like of which no one here could possibly have seen before. She didn't put on a hat, because that was a bourgeois prejudice; she let down her thick hair and tied it with a broad black ribbon, gathering it together at the side, below her right ear, with a magnificent bow. She put on a crimson waistcoat with silver stars over her lemon-yellow silk blouse with Spanish sleeves and a frilly jabot; her immense skirt of opalescent blue with countless pleats swayed like the waves of the ocean. An important detail of this daring costume was an orange sash with a wooden buckle. All in all, there was plenty for the Muscovites to look at. And certain individuals who looked really closely were in for yet another shock: on closer inspection, the black glittering ribbon on the neck of this breathtakingly spectacular stroller proved to be a live snake, which would occasionally turn its narrow head this way and that.

Accompanied by gasps and squeals, Columbine strode haughtily across Red Square and across the Moskvoretsky Bridge, and turned on to the Sofiiskaya Embankment, where the respectable public was out strolling. And here, in addition to showing herself off, she gazed around wide-eyed, gathering new impressions.

For the most part the Moscow ladies were dressed rather boringly: a straight skirt and white blouse with a necktie, or silk dresses in dreary dark tones. She was impressed by the size of the hats, which this season seemed especially luxuriant. She encountered hardly any extravagant ladies of any age, except for one, with a gauze scarf fluttering over her shoulder. And there was a horsewoman with pearly ash-grey hair under a veil, who rode past, holding a long amber cigarette holder with a *papirosa*. Stylish, Columbine thought, as she watched the woman ride away.

There proved to be no small number of young men in Moscow with smocks and berets and long hair, and a large bow on their chests: she even called out to one after mistaking him for Petya.

She deliberately arrived at the rendezvous twenty minutes late, for which she had to walk back and forth along the entire length of the embankment twice. Harlequin was waiting beside a fountain where the cabdrivers watered their horses and he looked exactly the same as in Irkutsk, but here among the granite embankments and closely crowded houses, Columbine felt that this was not enough. Why had he not changed in all these months? Why had he not become something bigger, or something new, or something else?

And somehow the way Petya behaved wasn't quite right either. He blushed and faltered. He was about to kiss her, but he couldn't bring himself to do it – instead he held his hand out in an absolutely fatuous manner. Columbine stared at his hand in jaunty incomprehension, as if she had never seen anything funnier in her life. Then he became even more embarrassed and thrust a bunch of violets at her.

'Why would I want these corpses of flowers?' she asked with a capricious shrug of her shoulders. She walked over to a cabby's horse and held the little bouquet out to her. The roan mare indifferently extended her large flabby lip over the violets and chewed them up in an instant.

'Quick, we're late,' said Petya. 'They don't like that in our set. The horse-tram stops over there, just before the bridge. Let's go!'

He glanced nervously at his companion and whispered.

'Everybody's looking at you. In Irkutsk you dressed differently.'

'Do I alarm you?' Columbine asked provocatively.

'What do you . . .' he exclaimed in fright. 'I'm a poet and I despise the opinion of the crowd. It's just really very unusual . . . Anyway, that's not important.'

Could he really be embarrassed by me? she wondered in amazement. Did harlequins even know how to be embarrassed? She glanced round at her reflection in a brightly lit shop window and flinched inwardly – it was a very impressive outfit indeed – but the attack of shyness was dismissed as disgraceful. That pitiful feeling had been left behind for ever beyond the branching Ural mountains.

In the tram, Petya told her in a low voice about the place where they were going.

'There isn't another club like it in the whole of Russia, even in St Petersburg,' he said, tickling her ear with his breath. 'Such people, you've never seen anyone like them in Irkutsk! We use special names, everyone invents his own. And some are given their names by the Doge. For instance, he christened me Cherubino.'

'Cherubino?' Columbine echoed in a disappointed voice, thinking that Petya really was more like a curly-haired page-boy than a self-confident, imperious Harlequin.

Petya misinterpreted the intonation of her voice and drew himself upright haughtily.

'That's nothing. We have more bizarre aliases than that. Avaddon, Ophelia, Caliban, Horatio. And Lorelei Rubinstein . . .'

'What, you mean Lorelei Rubinstein herself goes there?' the young provincial gasped. 'The poetess?'

There was good reason to gasp. Lorelei's sultry, shame-lessly sensual poems had only reached Irkutsk after a con-siderable delay. Progressive young ladies who understood modern poetry knew them off by heart.

'Yes,' said Cherubino-Petya, nodding portentously. 'Her alias in our group is the Lioness of Ecstasy. Or simply Lioness. Although, of course, everyone knows who she really is.'

Ah, what a sweet tightness she felt in her chest! Liberal-handed Fortune had flung open before her the doors into the most select possible society, and she looked at Petya far more affectionately now.

He continued. 'The leader of the club is Prospero. There aren't many men like him – not one in a thousand, or even a million. He's already getting on, his hair is completely grey. But you forget that straight away, he has such strength in him, such energy and magnetism. In biblical times the prophets were probably like him. And he is a kind of prophet, if you think about it. He's one of the old prisoners

27

from the Schliesselburg Fortress; he spent a long time in a cell for revolutionary activity, but he never talks about his former views, because he has abandoned politics completely. He says politics is for the masses, and nothing of a mass nature can be beautiful, for beauty is always unique and inimitable. Prospero looks rather severe and he is often abrupt, but in actual fact he is kind and magnanimous, everybody knows that. He secretly helps those aspirants who need money. He used to be a chemical engineer before he was in the fortress, but now he has been left an inheritance and is rich, so he can afford it.'

'Who are these "aspirants"?' she asked.

'That's what the members of the club are called. We're all poets. There are twelve of us, always twelve. And Prospero is our Doge. That's the same thing as a chairman, only a chairman is elected, and in this case it's the other way round: the Doge himself chooses who to accept as a member and who not.'

Columbine was alarmed.

'But if there always have to be twelve of you, what about me? That makes me superfluous.'

Petya replied mysteriously: 'When one of the aspirants marries, we can fill the place that is vacated with someone new. Naturally, the final decision is taken by Prospero. But before I take you into his home, you must swear that you will never tell anyone else what I have told you.'

Married? Vacated place? Columbine didn't understand a thing but, of course, she immediately exclaimed: 'I swear by sky, earth, water and fire that I shall say nothing!'

People on the seats nearby half-turned to look at her and Petya put one finger to his lips.

'But what do you do there?' asked Columbine, dying of curiosity.

The reply was triumphant.

'We serve the Eternal Bride and dedicate poems to her. And some fortunate Chosen Ones offer up to her the supreme gift – their own life.'

'And who is the Eternal Bride?'

His reply was a single short word, at the sound of which Columbine's mouth immediately went dry.

'Death.'

'But . . . but why is death a bride? After all, some of the aspirants are women – Lorelei Rubinstein, for instance. Why should she want a bride?'

'We just say that because in Russian "death" is a feminine noun. It goes without saying that for women Death is the Eternal Bridegroom. In general everything about the club is highly poetic. For the male aspirants Death is like *La Belle Dame sans Merci*, or the Beautiful Lady to whom we dedicate our poems and, if necessary our very lives. For the female aspirants Death is a Handsome Prince or an Enchanted Tsarevich, it's a matter of taste.'

Columbine wrinkled up her brow in concentration.

'And how is the rite of marriage performed?'

At that Petya glanced at her as if he were gazing at some wild savage with a bone through her nose. He narrowed his eyes incredulously.

'You mean to say you've never heard of the "Lovers of Death"? Why, all the newspapers write about it!'

'I don't read the newspapers,' she declared haughtily, 'It's too ordinary.'

'Good Lord! So you don't know anything about the Moscow suicides?'

Columbine shook her head cautiously.

'Four of our people have already become wedded to Death,' said Petya, moving closer, with his eyes gleaming. 'And a replacement was found for each of them straight away! And I should think so – the whole city's talking about us! Only no one knows where we are and who we are! If you came to Moscow to "write a full stop", then you really have been incredibly lucky. You've drawn the lucky ticket, so to speak. Gone straight to the person who can really help you. We have a chance to leave this life without any vulgar provincialism, not to die like a sheep in slaughterhouse, but poetically, meaningfully, beautifully! Perhaps we might even depart together, like Moretta and Lycanthrope.' His voice rang with inspiration. 'It's Moretta's place that I want to propose you for!'

'But who is this Moretta?' Columbine exclaimed rapturously, affected by his agitation, but still not understanding a thing.

She was aware of this shortcoming in herself – a certain slowness of wit. No, she did not think of herself as stupid (she was cleverer than many, thank God), it was just that her mind worked rather slowly – sometimes even she found it irritating.

'Moretta and Lycanthrope are the latest Chosen Ones,' Petya explained in a whisper. 'They received a Sign and shot themselves straight away, eleven days ago. Lycanthrope's place is already taken. Moretta's vacancy is the last one.'

Poor Columbine's head was spinning. She grabbed hold of Petya's arm.

'Sign? What sign?'

'Death gives his Chosen One a Sign. You must not kill yourself without the Sign – it's strictly forbidden.'

'But what is this Sign? What is it like?'

'It's different every time. There's no way to guess in advance, but it's quite impossible to mistake it . . .'

Petya looked keenly at his pale-faced companion. He frowned.

'Are you frightened? You should be, we're not playing games. Look, it's still not too late to go. Only remember the oath that you swore.'

She really was frightened. Not of death, of course, only that now he might change his mind and not take her with him. Appropriately enough, she recalled the signboard for the Möbius insurance company.

'I'm not afraid of anything with you,' Columbine said, and Petya beamed.

Taking advantage of the fact that she herself had taken him by the arm, he started stroking her palm with his finger, and Columbine was overwhelmed by the infallible presentiment that *it* would definitely happen today. She responded to his grip. And they rode on like that through the squares, streets and boulevards. After a while their hands started sweating and Columbine, who regarded this natural phenomenon as vulgar, freed her fingers. However, Petya had grown bolder now and he triumphantly placed his hand on her shoulder and stroked her neck.

'A snakeskin collar?' he whispered in her ear. 'Very *bon ton.*'

He suddenly gave a quiet cry.

Columbine turned her head and saw Petya's pupils rapidly expanding.

'There . . . there . . .' he whispered, unable to move a muscle. 'What is it?'

'An Egyptian cobra,' she explained. 'Live. You know, Cleopatra killed herself with one like that.'

He shuddered and pressed himself back against the window, clasping his hands against his chest.

'Don't be afraid,' said Columbine. 'Lucifer doesn't bite my friends.'

Petya nodded, with his eyes fixed on the moving black collar, but he didn't come close again.

They got off on a green street running up a steep incline, which Petya said was Rozhdestvensky Boulevard. Then they turned into a side street.

It was after nine and dark already, the streetlamps had been lit.

'There, that's Prospero's house,' Petya said in a quiet voice, pointing to a single-storey detached building.

All that Columbine could really make out in the darkness were six curtained windows filled with a mysterious reddish glow.

'What have you stopped for?' asked Petya, trying to hurry his companion along. 'Everyone's supposed to arrive exactly at nine, we're late.'

But at that precise moment Columbine was overcome by

an irresistible urge to run back on to the boulevard, and then down to the broad, dimly lit square, and on, and on. Not to that cramped little flat in Kitaigorod, to hell with it, but straight to the station and straight on to a train. The wheels would start to hammer, reeling the stretched thread of the rails back up into a ball, and everything would just be like it was before . . .

'You were the one who stopped,' Columbine said angrily. 'Come on, take me to these "lovers" of yours.'

Columbine hears the voices of the spirits

Petya opened the street door without knocking and explained: 'Prospero doesn't hold with having servants. He does everything himself – it's a habit from his time in exile.'

It was completely dark in the hallway, and Columbine couldn't make anything out properly, apart from a corridor that led on into the house and a white door. The spacious salon located behind the door proved to be not much brighter. There were no lamps lit, only a few candles on the table and, a little to one side, a cast-iron brazier with coals glowing scarlet. Crooked shadows writhed on the walls, the gilded spines of books gleamed on shelves, and the pendants of an unlit chandelier twinkled up under the ceiling.

It was only after Columbine's eyes had adjusted a little to the dim lighting that she realised there were quite a few people in the room – probably about ten, or even more.

The aspirants did not seem to regard Petya as a very significant individual. Some nodded in response to his timid greeting, but others simply carried on talking to each other. Columbine found this cool reception offensive, and she decided to maintain an independent line. She walked up to the table, lit a *papirosa* from a candle and, projecting a loud voice right across the room, asked her companion: 'Well, which one here is Prospero?'

Petya pulled his head down into his shoulders. It went

very quiet. But, noticing that the glances directed at her were curious, Columbine immediately stopped being afraid. She set one hand on her hip, just like in the advertisement for Carmen *papiroses*, and blew a stream of blue smoke up into the air.

'Oh come now, lovely stranger,' said a pasty-looking gentleman in a shantung cotton morning coat, with his hair combed across a bald spot in true virtuoso fashion. 'The Doge will arrive later, when everything's ready.'

He walked closer, stopped two paces away from her and began unceremoniously examining Columbine from top to bottom. She replied by looking at him in precisely the same way.

'This is Columbine, I've brought her as a candidate,' Petya bleated guiltily, for which he was immediately punished.

'Cherubino,' the new candidate said in a sweet voice. 'Surely your mama must have taught you that you should introduce the man to the lady, and not the other way round?'

The man in the morning coat immediately pressed his hand to his chest, bowed and introduced himself: 'I am Kriton. You have a quite insane face, Mademoiselle Columbine. It possesses a ravishing amalgam of innocence and depravity.'

The tone of his voice indicated that this was a compliment, but Columbine felt offended by the 'innocence'.

'Kriton – that's something chemical, isn't it?'

It was an attempt to mock, to show this shabby, well-worn individual that he was not dealing with some kind of *ingénue*, but a mature, self-confident woman. Unfortunately, it didn't work, it was even worse than that time in the literature exam when she called Goethe Johann-Sebastian instead of Johann-Wolfgang.

'It is from "Egyptian Nights", the man in shantung cotton replied with a condescending smile. 'Do you remember this?'

Tra-ta-ta-ta, the sapient youth,
Who life's sweet blandishments embraces,
Kriton, the bard of pleasure's truth,
Singer of Cupid and the Graces.

No, Columbine didn't remember that at all. She couldn't even remember who the Graces were.

'Do you like to make wild, abandoned love in the night, on the roof, to the hurricane's roar, with the teeming rain lashing your naked body?' Kriton enquired without lowering his voice, 'I truly love it.'

The poor Irkutsk girl was unable to find an answer to that. She looked round at Petya, but the rotten traitor moved away with a preoccupied air, striking up a conversation with a poorly dressed young man of very unattractive appearance: bright, bulging eyes, a wide, mobile mouth and blackheads scattered across his face.

'You must have a fine taut body,' Kriton surmised. 'Whiplash-lean, like a young predator. I can just see you in the pose of a panther prepared to pounce.'

What should she do? How should she answer?

According to the Irkutsk code of conduct, she ought to slap the impudent fellow across the face, but here, in this club of the elect, that was unthinkable – they would think her a hypocrite or, even worse, a prim and proper provincial. And what was so insulting anyway, Columbine thought to herself. After all, this man said what he thought, and that was more honest than striking up a conversation about music or the various ills of society with a woman who had taken your fancy. Kriton looked absolutely nothing like a 'young sage', but even so the audacious things he said made Columbine quite feverish – no one had ever spoken to her like that before. However, on looking more closely at the outspoken gentleman, she decided that he probably did bear a certain resemblance to the god Pan.

'I wish to teach you the terrible art of love, young Columbine,' the goat-hoofed seducer cooed and squeezed her hand – the same one that Petya had recently squeezed. Columbine stood there woodenly and submissively allowed him to knead her fingers. A long stub of ash fell from her *papirosa* on to the carpet.

But just then a rapid whispering ran across the salon, and everybody turned towards a tall leather-upholstered double door.

It went absolutely quiet and she heard measured footsteps approaching. Then the door swung open without a sound and a figure – improbably broad, almost square – appeared on the threshold. But the next moment the man stepped into the room, and it was clear that his build was absolutely normal, he was simply wearing a wide gown like those worn by European university professors or doctors of philosophy.

No greetings were pronounced, but it seemed to Columbine that the moment those leather doors opened soundlessly, everything around her changed in some elusive manner: the shadows became blacker, the fire became brighter, sounds were suddenly more subdued.

At first she thought the man who had come in was really old: he had grey hair, cut in an old-fashioned style, the same length all round. Turgenev, Columbine thought. Ivan Sergeevich Turgenev. He looks just like him. Exactly like the portrait in the grammar-school library.

However, when the man in the gown halted beside the brazier and the crimson glow lit up his face from below, the eyes were not those of an old man at all – they were a refulgent black, and they glowed even brighter than the coals. Columbine made out a thoroughbred aquiline nose, thick white eyebrows and fleshy cheeks. *Venerable* – that's what he is, she said to herself. Like in Lermontov: 'The venerable grey-haired sage', Or was it really Lermontov? Well, it didn't matter.

The venerable sage ran his gaze slowly round the assembled company and it was clear immediately that not a single detail or, perhaps, secret thought could possibly escape those eyes. The calm gaze rested on Columbine for just a moment, no longer, and she suddenly swayed and trembled all over.

Without even realising it, she pulled her hand away from the 'teacher of terrible love' and pressed it to her breast.

Kriton whispered in her ear in a derisive tone: 'And this is from Pushkin.

> *Not only in youth's downy cheek*
> *And curly locks of tender brown*
> *Will passion its true object seek.*
> *The furrowed brow and elder's frown*
> *May fire beauty's imagination*
> *With a consuming conflagration.*

'Those "curly locks of tender brown" are yours, are they?' the young lady snapped back, stung. 'And anyway, who needs you and your Pushkin!'

She stomped off ostentatiously and stood beside Petya.

'That's Prospero,' he told her in a low voice.

'I guessed that without you.'

Their host cast a brief glance at the two whisperers, and immediately absolute silence fell. The Doge reached out one hand to the brazier, so that he looked like Mucius Scaevola in the fourth-class history book. He sighed and uttered a single word: 'Dark.'

And then everybody gasped as he placed a red-hot coal on his palm. He really was Scaevola!

'I think it will be better like this,' Prospero said calmly, raising the lump of fire to the large crystal candelabra and lighting the twelve candles one after another.

The light revealed a round table, covered with a dark tablecloth. The darkness retreated to the corners of the room and now that she could finally examine the 'lovers of death' properly, Columbine began turning her head in all directions.

'Who will read?' their host enquired, seating himself on a chair with a high carved back.

All twelve of the other chairs set around the table were simpler and lower.

Several people immediately volunteered.

'The Lioness of Ecstasy will begin,' Prospero declared.

Columbine stared wide-eyed at the famous Lorelei Rubinstein, She didn't look as she might have been imagined from her poems: not a slim, fragile lily with impulsive movements and huge black eyes, but a rather substantial lady in a shapeless robe that hung down to her heels. The Lioness looked about forty, but that was in the semi-darkness.

She cleared her throat and said in a rumbling voice: ' "The Black Rose". Written last night.'

Her plump cheeks quivered with emotion, her eyes darted upwards, towards the rainbow sparkling of the chandelier, her eyebrows knitted together dolefully.

Columbine gave Lucifer a gentle slap to stop him distracting her by slithering round her neck, and she became all ears.

The celebrated poetess declaimed wonderfully, intoning with real passion.

> *When will Night come, rapturous and enticing,*
> *When will he make his entrance through my door,*
> *Entering swiftly, without knocking,*
> *This darling Guest that I am waiting for?*
>
> *How luminous, in jail or roaming free,*
> *The flame with which my chosen lover glows*
> *But in the sacred darkness here with me*
> *His eye will not descry the lone black rose.*
>
> *And then the sonorous Word shall be proclaimed*
> *Sundering the dense silence like a pall.*
> *Let it be so: what is not fated*
> *Will then be gone once and for all.*

Just think of it, she had heard a new poem by Lorelei Rubinstein, one she had only just written! She and these few chosen ones were the first!

Columbine began applauding loudly, but immediately

broke off, realising that she had committed a *faux pas*. Applause was apparently not the done thing here. Everybody – including Prospero – looked at the enraptured young woman without saying a word. She froze with her hands parted and blushed. She had muffed it again!

The Doge cleared his throat and said to Lorelei in a quiet voice: 'Your usual shortcoming: elegant, but unintelligible. But that black rose is interesting. What does the black rose mean to you? No, don't tell me. I'll guess for myself.'

He closed his eyes and lowered his head on to his chest. Everybody waited with bated breath, and the poetess's cheeks flushed bright crimson.

'Does the Doge write poems?' Columbine asked Petya quietly.

He put a finger to his lips, but she knitted her brows angrily and he whispered back almost silently: 'Yes, and they are works of genius, for certain. No one understands poetry better than he does.'

She found this reply strange.

' "For certain"?'

'He doesn't show his poems to anyone. He says that they're not written for people to read and he will destroy everything he has written before his departure.'

'What a shame!' she exclaimed rather more loudly than was necessary.

Prospero glanced at his new guest again, but once more he said nothing.

'I have it,' he said, giving Lorelei an affectionate, sad smile. 'I understand.'

Lorelei beamed and the Doge turned to a spruce, quiet little man with a pince-nez and a Van Dyke beard.

'Horatio, you promised to bring some poems today at last. You know there's nothing to be done about it – the Bride accepts only poets.'

'Horatio's a doctor,' Petya told Columbine. 'That is, he's a dissector – he cuts up bodies in the anatomy room. He took Lancelot's place.'

'And what happened to Lancelot?'

'He departed. And he took some companions with him,' Petya replied obscurely, but this was no time to ask questions – Horatio was ready to recite.

'This is actually the first time I have tried my hand at poetry . . . I studied a manual on versification, made a great effort. And this, mmm, as it were, is the result.'

He cleared his throat in an embarrassed manner, straightened his tie and took a folded piece of paper out of his pocket. When he was just about to begin, he evidently decided that he had not explained enough: 'The poem is about my professional, so to speak, line of work . . . there are even a few special terms in it. The rhyme has been simplified, just the second and fourth lines, it's very hard when you're not used to it . . . After our esteemed, mmm . . . Lioness of Ecstasy, of course, my efforts in verse will seem even less accomplished . . . But anyway, I offer them up for your strict judgement. The poem is called "Epicrisis".

> *The girl swallowed a hundred needles*
> *To still her heart's torment and pain.*
> *Slicing neatly into her abdomen*
> *The scalpel brings them to the light again.*
>
> *'You do not know if you should laugh or cry,*
> *It's like a hedgehog in the rain,*
> *The way the human stomach shudders,*
> *Flabbily trembling over and again.*
>
> *'The young cadet condemned himself to death*
> *After his visit to a whore.*
> *You neatly open up his brain pan*
> *To find what you are looking for.*
>
> *'And you will find the piece of lead you seek*
> *Among the grey necrotic mush,*
> *Glinting dully like some precious pearl*
> *Lodged in the epithalimus.*

The reader broke off, crumpled up the sheet of paper and put it back in his pocket.

'I wanted to describe the lungs of a woman who has drowned as well, but I couldn't manage it. I only made up one line: "Among the dove-grey spongy mass", but I just couldn't carry on . . . Well gentlemen, was it very bad?'

Nobody spoke, waiting for the verdict of the chairman (he was the only one there still sitting in his original pose).

' "Epicrisis" – I believe that is the conclusion of a medical diagnosis,' Prospero said, slowly and thoughtfully.

'Yes indeed,' Horatio agreed eagerly.

'A-ha,' Prospero drawled. 'Well, this is *my* epicrisis for you: you cannot write poetry. But you are genuinely entranced by the multiplicity of the faces of death. Who is next?'

'Teacher, let me!' said a large strapping fellow with broad shoulders, raising his hand. He had childlike, naive blue eyes that looked strange in his coarse face. What does he want with the Eternal Bride? Columbine thought in surprise. He should be floating rafts of timber down the Angara river.

'The Doge dubbed him Caliban,' Petya whispered, and then felt it necessary to explain. 'That's from Shakespeare.' Columbine nodded: so it was from Shakespeare. 'Nowadays he works as an accountant in some loan company or other. He used to be a bookkeeper in a merchant-shipping line, sailing the oceans, but he was shipwrecked and only survived by a miracle, so he doesn't go to sea any more.'

She smiled, pleased with her skill in reading faces – she hadn't been so very far wrong with those rafts of timber.

'As far as intellect goes, he's a complete nonentity, an amoeba,' Petya gossiped and then added enviously, 'but Prospero gives him special treatment.'

Stamping loudly, Caliban walked out into the centre of the room, cocked his hip and started bawling out extremely strange verse in a stentorian voice:

The Island of Death

Where blue waves murmur to the sky
And seabirds ride the ocean swell
There is a solitary isle
Where only ghosts and phantoms dwell.

'Some of them lie there on the sand
And over them the crabs do crawl
Others in mournful sorrow wander,
Bare skeletons, no flesh at all.

'The rattling of their bones I hear,
I see them walk, oh horrid sight!
It fills me with such dreadful fear,
I cannot get to sleep at night.

'My teeth do knock, my hands do shake
Even by the bright light of day.
I long to be there with the wraiths
On that dread island far away.

'Then we shall blithe and merry be,
Rejoicing as we did before,
Luring the vessels from the sea
On to the jagged cliffy shore.

At the beginning Columbine almost snorted out loud, but Caliban declaimed his ungainly doggerel with such feeling that she soon stopped wanting to laugh, and the final verse sent cold shivers down her spine.

She glanced at Prospero without the slightest doubt that the severe judge who had dared to criticise Lorelei Rubinstein herself would demolish these shoddy efforts utterly.

But he didn't!

'Very good,' the Doge declared. 'Such expression! You can hear the sound of the ocean waves and see their foaming crests. Powerful. Impressive.'

Caliban's face lit up in a smile of happiness that completely transformed his square-cut features.

'I told you, he's the favourite,' Petya muttered in her ear. 'What on earth does he see in this primitive amoeba? Aha, this is Avaddon, he's at university with me. He's the one who brought me here.'

Now it was the turn of the ill-favoured youth with blackheads who had been talking to Petya earlier.

The Doge nodded patronisingly.

'Very well, Avaddon, we are listening.'

'He's going to read "Angel of the Abyss",' Petya told her. 'I've already heard it. It's his best poem. I wonder what Prospero will say.'

This was the poem:

Angel of the Abyss

The abyss has been unsealed,
Releasing its hot dry gloom.
See the locust horde set free
Spreading pain and doom.

'See them flourish their sharp barbs
And those they choose to sting
Never knew the Grief Divine,
Living this life of sin.

'Silver hooves trample the ground
And with their tortured breath
All those who are smitten down
Invoke their own swift death.

'But all that was just a dream.
There is no death, no hope.
The dark angel Avaddon
Gazes through the smoke.

Columbine liked the poem very much, but she was no longer sure what she ought to think about it. What if Prospero thought it was mediocre?

Their host paused for a moment and then said: 'Not bad, not bad at all. The last stanza is good. But "flourish their sharp barbs" is no good at all. And the rhyme "death" and "breath" is very hackneyed.'

'Nonsense,' a clear, angry voice exclaimed. 'There are almost no rhymes for the word "death", and they can no more be hackneyed than can Death itself! It is the rhymes for the word "love" that have been mauled by sticky hands until they are banal, but no dross can stick to Death!'

The person who had called the opinion of the master 'nonsense' was a pretty-looking youth who seemed hardly more than a boy – tall and slim, with a capriciously curved mouth and a feverish bloom on his smooth cheeks.

'It is not a matter of the freshness of the rhyme, but of its precision,' he continued somewhat incoherently. 'Rhyme is the most mysterious thing in the world. Rhymes are like the reverse side of a coin! They can make the exalted seem ludicrous and the ludicrous seem exalted! Hiding behind the swaggering word "king" we have the banal "thing" and behind the gentle "flower" we have "power"! There is a special connection between phenomena and the sounds that denote them. The person who can penetrate to the heart of these meanings will be the very greatest of discoverers.'

'Gdlevsky,' Petya sighed with a shrug. 'He's eighteen, hasn't even finished grammar school yet. Prospero says he's as talented as Rimbaud.'

'Really?' Columbine took a closer look at the irascible boy, but failed to see anything special about him. Except that he was good-looking. 'And what's his alias?'

'He doesn't have one. Just "Gdlevsky". He doesn't want to be called anything else.'

The Doge was not at all angry with the troublemaker – on the contrary, he smiled paternally as he looked at him.

'All right, all right. You're not really very strong on

theorising. Since you got so steamed up over the rhyme, I expect you have "breath" and "death" too?'

The boy's eyes flashed, but he said nothing, from which it was possible to conclude that the perspicacious Doge was not mistaken.

'Well then, recite for us.'

Gdlevsky tossed his head, sending a strand of light hair tumbling down across his eyes and declared:

Untitled

I am a shadow of shadows, one of the reflections,
Wandering blindly through this earthly maze,
But midnight with its sacred incantations
Unfurls the starry scrolls before my gaze.

'The time will come when I draw my last breath,
And summon the disastrous heavenly fire –
Go soaring upwards with my sister Death,
My premonitions leading ever higher.

'The Poet is not ruled by happenstance
His destiny is the prophetic rhyme.
Mysterious and magic circumstance
Compose the link of prophecy with time.

This was Prospero's commentary. 'Your writing gets better and better. You should think less with your head, listen more to the voice sounding within you.'

After Gdlevsky no one else volunteered to recite a poem. The aspirants began discussing what they had heard in low voices, while Petya told his protégée about the other 'aspirants'.

'They are Guildenstern and Rosencrantz,' he said, pointing to a pair of rosy-cheeked twins who kept together. 'Their father is a confectioner from Revel and they are studying at the Commercial College. Their poems are never any good – nothing but *"herz"* and *"schmerz"*. They're both very serious

44

and thoroughgoing, they joined the aspirants out of some complicated philosophical considerations and they are sure to get what they want.'

Columbine shuddered as she imagined what a tragedy this Teutonic single-mindedness would produce for their poor 'mutti', but then immediately felt ashamed of this philistine thought. After all, only recently she had written a poem which asserted the following:

> Only the reckless and impetuous
> Can drain life's goblet till it's dry
> Our home, our parents, what are these to us?
> Give us the glitter of the sparkling wine!

One of the other people there was a short, stout man with dark hair and a long nose that looked completely out of place on his plump face. He was called Cyrano.

'He's not particularly subtle,' said Petya, pulling a face. All he does is copy the manner of Rostand's Bergerac: "Into the embraces of she who is dear to me I shall fall at the end of this missive." An inveterate joker, a buffoon. Absolutely desperate to get to the next world just as soon as possible.'

This last remark made Columbine look closely at the follower of the famous Gascon wit. While Caliban was declaiming his terrifying work about skeletons in a thundering bass, Cyrano had listened with an exaggeratedly serious expression, but when he caught the new visitor's glance, he made a skull-face by sucking in his cheeks, opening his eyes in a wide stare and moving his eyes together towards his impressive nose. Taken by surprise, Columbine tittered slightly and the prankster bowed to her and resumed his air of intent concentration. Absolutely desperate to get to the next world? This jolly, tubby man was obviously not so very simple after all.

'And that is Ophelia, she holds a special position here. Prospero's main assistant. When we're all dead, she'll still be here.'

Columbine had not noticed the young girl until Petya mentioned her, but now she found her more interesting than the other members of the club. She took envious note of the clear white skin, the fresh little face, the long wavy hair which was so blonde that in the semi-darkness it appeared white. A perfect angel from an Easter card. Lorelei Rubinstein didn't count – she was old and fat, and an Olympian figure in any case, but in Columbine's opinion, this nymph was clearly superfluous. Ophelia had not uttered a single word the whole time. She just stood there as if she couldn't hear the poems or the conversations and was listening to something completely different; her wide-open eyes seemed to look straight through the other people there. What sort of 'special position' could she have? the new visitor thought jealously.

'She's strange, somehow,' said Columbine, delivering her verdict. 'What does he see in her?'

'Who, the Doge?'

Petya was about to explain, but Prospero raised his hand imperiously and all talking ceased immediately.

'Now the mystery will begin, but there is a stranger among us,' he said, without looking at Columbine (her heart skipped a beat). 'Who brought her?'

'I did, Teacher,' Petya replied anxiously. 'She is Columbine. I vouch for her. She told me several months ago that she is weary of life and definitely wishes to die young.'

Now the Doge turned his magnetic gaze to the swooning damsel and from feeling cold, Columbine turned feverish. Oh, how his stern eyes glittered!

'Do you write poetry?' Prospero asked.

She nodded without speaking, afraid that her voice would tremble.

'Recite one verse, any will do. And then I shall say if you can stay.'

I'll muff it straight away, I know I will, Columbine thought mournfully, batting her eyelids rapidly. What shall I recite? She feverishly ran through all of her poems that she

could remember and chose the one she was most proud of –
'The Pale Prince'. It was written on the night when Masha
read Rostand's *Distant Princesses* and then sobbed until the
morning.

> *The Pale Prince seared me with the gaze*
> *Of his eyes of effulgent green*
> *And now we shall never see the day*
> *Of the wedding that might have been.*

The 'Pale Prince' was Petya, the way he had seemed to her
in Irkutsk. At that time she had still been a little bit in love
with Kostya Levonidi, who had been planning to propose to
her (how funny it was to remember that now!) and then
Petya, her dazzling Moscow Harlequin, had appeared. The
poem about the 'pale prince' had been written to make
Kostya understand that everything was over between them,
that Masha Mironova would never be the same again.

Columbine hesitated, afraid that one quatrain was not
enough. Perhaps she should recite a little more, to make the
meaning clearer? The poem went on like this:

> *We shall never stand at the altar*
> *To make our wedding vows*
> *The Pale Prince came riding to me*
> *And called me to Moscow town.*

But thank God that she didn't recite that part, or she would
have spoiled everything. Prospero gestured for her to stop.

'The Pale Prince, of course, is Death?' he asked.

She nodded hastily.

'A pale prince with green eyes . . .' the Doge repeated.
'An interesting image.'

He shook his head sadly and said in a quiet voice: 'Well
now, Columbine. Fate has brought you here, and fate will
not be gainsaid. Stay, and do not be afraid of anything.

47

"Death is the key that opens the doors to true happiness."
Guess who said that.'

She glanced in bewilderment at Petya, who shrugged.

'It was a composer, the very greatest all composers,'
Prospero prompted her.

Bach was the gloomiest of all the composers that Columbine knew, and so she whispered uncertainly: 'Is it Bach?'
And then, remembering her unfortunate gaffe with Goethe,
she explained: 'Johann-Sebastian, wasn't it?'

'No, it was the radiant Mozart who said it, the creator of
the *Requiem*,' the Doge replied and turned away.

'That's it, now you're one of us,' Petya murmured behind
her back. 'I was so nervous for you!'

He looked just as if it was his birthday. Obviously he
thought that now the candidate he had proposed had passed
the examination, his own status among the 'lovers' would be
enhanced.

'Well then,' said Prospero, gesturing invitingly towards
the table. 'Please be seated. Let us listen to what the spirits
will tell us today.'

Ophelia took the seat to the right of the Doge. The others
also sat down, placing their hands on the tablecloth so that
their little fingers touched each other.

'This is a spiritualist figure,' Petya explained. 'It's called
"the magic wheel".'

Spiritualist seances were known even in Irkutsk. Columbine had done a little table-spinning herself, but that had
been more like a jolly game of Yuletide fortune-telling: there
was always someone tittering, gasping or giggling, and
Kostya always tried to squeeze her elbow or kiss her cheek
under the cover of darkness.

But here everything was deadly serious. The Doge extinguished the candles, leaving only the dull glow of the brazier,
so that the faces of everyone sitting there were red below
and black above – as if they had no eyes.

'Ophelia, your time has come,' their chairman said in a

48

deep, resonant voice. 'Give us a sign when you hear the Beyond.'

So that's who Ophelia is, Columbine realised. A genuine medium, and that's why she seems so much like a sleepwalker.

The blonde nymph's face was still and absolutely expressionless, her eyes were closed and only her lips were trembling slightly, as if she were soundlessly whispering some incantation.

Suddenly Columbine felt a tremor run across her fingers and a cold draught blow on her cheeks. Ophelia raised her long eyelashes and threw her head back, and her pupils were so wide that her eyes were completely black.

'I see you are ready,' the Doge declared in the same solemn tone. 'Summon Moretta to us.'

Columbine remembered that was the name of the girl whose vacancy she had filled. The poor creature who had shot herself together with that other one, Lycanthrope.

Ophelia was absolutely still for a few seconds, and then she said: 'Yes . . . Yes . . . I hear her . . . She is far away, but coming closer every moment . . . It is I, Moretta. I have come. What do you want to know?' she suddenly said in a quite different voice – a low, breathy contralto.

'That's Moretta's voice!' Lorelei Rubinstein exclaimed. 'Do you hear?'

The people at the table stirred and their chairs creaked, but Prospero shook his head impatiently and everyone was still again.

'Moretta, my girl, have you found your happiness?' he asked.

'No . . . I don't know . . . It all feels so strange . . . It's dark here, I can't see anything. But there is someone beside me, someone who touches me with his hands and breathes in my face . . .'

'It is he! The Eternal Bridegroom!' Lorelei whispered passionately.

'Quiet!' the bookkeeper Caliban bellowed at her.

The Doge's voice was gentle, almost unctuous.

'You are not yet accustomed to the World Beyond, it is hard for you to speak. But you know what you must tell us. Who will be next? Who should expect the Sign?'

The silence was so intense that they could hear the coals crackling in the brazier.

Ophelia didn't say anything. Columbine noticed that Petya Lileiko's little finger was trembling rapidly – he was sitting on her right – and she suddenly started trembling herself: what if the spirit of this Moretta were to name her, the new aspirant? But her sense of grievance was stronger than her fear. How unjust that would be! Before she had really even become a member of the club, before she had really understood anything properly. There, take that!

'A . . . A-a-a . . . A-va . . . Avaddon . . .' Ophelia said very quietly.

Everyone turned towards the unhandsome student, and the people beside him – the anatomist by the name of Horatio and one of the twins (Columbine couldn't remember which one it was) involuntarily jerked their hands away. A bewildered smile appeared on Avaddon's face, but he was looking at Prospero, not the medium.

'Thank you, Moretta.' the Doge said. 'Return to your new dwelling place. We wish you eternal happiness. Send Lycanthrope to us.'

'Teacher . . .' Avaddon said with a gulp, but Prospero jerked his chin peremptorily.

'Be quiet. This does not mean anything as yet. We shall ask Lycanthrope.'

'I am already here,' Ophelia responded in a hoarse young man's voice. 'Greetings to the honest company from the newly-wed.'

'I see you are still a joker, even there,' the Doge chuckled.

'Well why not, this is a jolly place. Especially looking at you lot.'

'Tell us who should be next,' Prospero told the spirit sternly. 'And no jokes.'

'Ah, yes, that's no joking matter . . .'

Columbine was gaping wide-eyed at Ophelia. It was incredible! How could this delicate girl's lips speak in such a confident, natural baritone?

Lycanthrope's spirit said quite clearly: 'Avaddon. Who else?' And then he concluded with a laugh: 'The wedding bed is already made up and waiting . . .'

Avaddon cried out, and the strange guttural sound roused the medium from her trance. Ophelia shuddered, fluttered her eyelids and rubbed her eyes, and when she took her hands away, her face was as it had been before: absent-minded and illuminated by a faint, timid smile. And her eyes were no longer black, but quite normal – bright and moist with tears.

Someone lit the candles and soon the chandelier was lit too, making the drawing room very bright.

'What's his real name?' Columbine asked, unable to take her eyes off the Chosen One (in fact, everyone else had eyes only for him).

'Nikisha. Nikifor Sipyaga,' Petya murmured in confusion.

Avaddon got up and looked at the others with a strange expression on his face, a mixture of fear and superiority.

'Straight in off the red!' he laughed, then sobbed and laughed again.

'Congratulations!' Caliban exclaimed with sincere feeling, shaking the condemned man firmly by the hand. 'Phoo, your hand's covered in cold sweat. Turned coward? Eh, the fools have all the luck!'

'What . . . What now?' Avaddon asked the Doge, 'I can't seem to gather my thoughts . . . my head's spinning.'

'Calm down,' said Prospero, going over and putting a hand on his shoulder. 'We know the spirits like to play tricks on the living. Without the Sign all this means absolutely nothing. Wait for the Sign, and make sure you don't do anything stupid . . . That is all, the meeting is over. Leave now.'

He turned his back to the aspirants and one by one they made their way to the door.

Shaken by what she had seen and heard, Columbine

watched Avaddon's unnaturally straight back as he left the room first.

'Let's go.' said Petya, taking her by the hand. 'There won't be anything else.'

Suddenly they heard a low, imperious voice.

'Let the new girl stay!'

Columbine immediately forgot about Avaddon and Petya. She turned round, afraid of only one thing – that she might have misheard.

Without looking round, Prospero raised one hand and beckoned with his finger for her to approach.

Petya, the false Harlequin, looked plaintively into Columbine's face and saw it was flushed with happiness. He shuffled his feet, sighed and meekly walked out.

A minute later, Columbine was left alone with the master of the house.

A discarded chrysalis

This is how it was. The wind was howling outside the windows, bending down the trees. The metal sheeting of the roof was clattering. Nature was rampaging in the grip of titanic passions.

The same passions were raging in Columbine's soul. Her little heart alternately stood still and fluttered wildly, as rapidly as a moth beating its wings against the glass.

But he – he slowly approached and put his hands on her shoulders and throughout the entire mystical ritual he did not utter another word. There was no need to speak, this evening belonged to silence.

He grasped Columbine's slim wrist and drew her after him into a dark series of rooms. The captive felt as if, passing through these rooms, she underwent a series of transformations, like a butterfly.

In the dining room she was still a larva – moist and timid, curled up, helpless; in the study she became rigid with fear, a blind, motionless chrysalis; but on the bearskin that was spread out in the bedroom, she was destined for transformation into a butterfly with bright-coloured wings.

No words can even come near to describing what happened. Her eyes were wide open as her innocence was sacrificed, but they saw nothing except shadows slipping across the ceiling. And as for sensations . . . No, I do not remember any. Alternating immersion first in cold, then in heat, then in cold – that is probably all.

There was none of the pleasure that is described in French novels. Nor any pain. There was the fear of saying or doing something wrong – what if he should pull away contemptuously and the ritual was interrupted, left incomplete? And so Columbine said nothing and did nothing, merely submitted to his gentle but astonishingly masterful hands.

One thing I know for certain: it did not last long. When I walked back through the drawing room, alone, the candles were not even burned halfway down.

Oh no, he did not stand on ceremony with his obedient puppet. First he took her, never doubting his right for a moment, then he stood up and said: 'Leave'. One word, only one.

Stunned and confused, Columbine heard the rustle of retreating footsteps and the quiet creak of a door: the rite of initiation was over.

The clothes lying on the floor even looked like a discarded chrysalis. Ah, a discarded chrysalis is nothing at all like an abandoned doll!

The new-born butterfly got up and fluttered her white arms like wings. She spun round on the spot. If she must leave, she must leave.

She walked along the deserted boulevard on her own. The wind threw leaves torn from the trees and fine rubbish into her face. Ah, how fiercely the night rejoiced in its new convert, exulted that the fall from light into darkness had finally been accomplished!

Apparently there is pleasure even in this – wandering through the empty streets at random, without knowing the way. A strange, incomprehensible city. A strange, incomprehensible life.

But a genuine one. Absolutely genuine.

Columbine re-read the entry in her diary. She crossed out the paragraph about pleasure as too naive. She hesitated over the silence throughout the mystical ritual – that was not entirely true. When Prospero started unfastening the buttons of her lemon-yellow blouse as they walked along, silly little Lucifer had snapped at the aggressor's finger with his infant fangs (he must have feeling jealous) and that had spoiled everything a little bit. The Doge had cried out in surprise and insisted that the reptile must be imprisoned in a jug during the ritual, and he had spent at least two minutes rubbing the bite – two tiny indentations in his skin – with alcohol. Meanwhile Columbine had stood there with her blouse unbuttoned, not knowing what to do – button the blouse up again or take it off herself.

No, she hadn't written about that petty, annoying trifle – what would be the point?

Afterwards she sat down in front of a mirror and studied herself for a long time. Strange, but she couldn't see any particular changes, any new maturity or sophistication, in her face. They would come, but obviously not straight away.

One thing was clear: she would not be able to sleep on this great night.

Columbine sat down in the armchair by the window and tried to spot a star, even the very tiniest, in the murky sky, but she couldn't. She felt rather upset, but then she told herself that it was all right. The thicker the darkness, the better.

She did fall asleep after all. And she only realised she had been sleeping when she was woken by loud knocking.

Leave

When she opened her eyes, she saw the sun already high in the sky outside the window and heard the sounds of the street: hooves clopping over cobblestones, a knife-grinder crying his trade. And then she heard that insistent knocking again: rat-a-tat-tat, rat-a-tat-tat!

She realised it was late morning and someone was knocking on the door, perhaps they had already been knocking for a long time.

But before she went to open the door, she checked to make sure there were no creases or indentations on her face after her sleep (there weren't), ran a comb through her hair, straightened her dressing gown (cut Japanese-style, with Mount Fujiyama on the back).

The knocking on the door continued. Then she heard a muffled call: 'Open up! Open up! It's me!'

Petya. Well, of course, who else? He had come to make a jealous scene. She shouldn't have given him her address yesterday. Columbine sighed, pulled her hair across her left shoulder on to her breasts and tied it with a scarlet ribbon.

Lucifer was lying on the bed in a neat spiral. He was probably hungry, poor thing, so she poured some milk into a bowl for the little snake and only then let the jealous rival in.

Petya burst into the hallway, pale-faced, with his lips trembling. He cast a surreptitious glance at Columbine (at least, that was how it seemed to her) and immediately turned his eyes away. She shook her head in amazement at herself. How could she have taken him for Harlequin? He was Pierrot, an absolutely genuine Pierrot, and that was his real name, after all, Pyotr, Petya.

'What are you doing here at the crack of dawn?' she asked severely.

'But it's midday already,' he babbled and sniffed. His nose was wet and red. Had he caught a cold? Or had he been crying?

It proved to be the latter. The disgraced Harlequin's face contorted, his lower lip worked up and down, tears gushed from his eyes and he started blubbing in grand style. He spoke haltingly, incomprehensibly, and not about what Columbine had been expecting.

'I went round this morning, to his flat . . . He rents one, on Basmannaya Street, in the Giant company building . . . Like yours, on the top . . . So we could go to lectures together. And I was worried after yesterday. I caught up with him and walked him home.'

'Who?' she asked. 'Speak more clearly.'

'Nikisha. You know, Nikifor, Avaddon.' Petya sobbed. 'He wasn't himself at all, he kept repeating: "It's been decided, it's over, now I just have to wait for the Sign." I said to him: "Maybe there won't be any Sign, eh, Nikisha?" "No", he said, "There will, I know there will. Goodbye, Petushok. We won't see each other again. Never mind" he said, "it's what I wanted" . . .'

At this point the story was interrupted by another fit of sobbing, but Columbine had already guessed what was wrong.

'What, there was a Sign?' she gasped. 'A Sign of Death? The choice was confirmed? And now Avaddon will die?'

'He already has!' Petya sobbed. 'When I got there, the door was wide open. The yard keeper, the owner of the house, the police. He hanged himself!'

Columbine bit her lip and pressed one hand to her breast, her heart was pounding so hard. She listened to the rest without interrupting.

'And Prospero was there too. He said he hadn't been able to get to sleep during the night, and just before dawn he quite clearly heard Avaddon calling him, so he got up, got dressed and went. He saw that the door was half-open. He went in, and there was Nikifor, that is, Avaddon, in the noose. He was already cold . . . Of course, the police don't know anything about the club. They decided that Prospero and I were simply acquaintances of the deceased.' Petya squeezed his eyes shut, obviously recalling the terrible scene. 'Nikisha was lying on the floor, with a blue furrow round his neck and his eyes bulging out, and his tongue was huge and swollen, too big to fit in his mouth. And there was an appalling smell!'

Petya started shaking and his teeth chattered

'So there must have been a Sign . . .' Columbine whispered and raised her hand to cross herself (not out of piety, of course, but from childish habit), and only caught herself just in time. She had to pretend to tuck away a lock of hair.

'Who can tell now?' Petya asked with a fearful shudder. 'The poem doesn't say anything about a Sign.'

'What poem?'

'The death poem. It's a custom of ours. Before you marry Death, you have to write a poem, it's essential. Prospero calls it the "epithalamium" and also the "moment of truth". He gave the constable fifty kopecks, and he allowed him to make a copy. I copied it out for myself too . . .'

'Give it to me!' Columbine demanded.

She grabbed the crumpled, tear-stained piece of paper out of Petya's hands. At the top, in big letters, she read 'A Riddle'. That was obviously the title.

But she simply couldn't read the epithalamium with Petya there. He burst into sobs again and started telling the whole story for a second time.

So Columbine took hold of him by the shoulders, pushed him towards the door and said just one word: 'Leave'.

She said it in exactly the same way as Prospero had to her the night before, after everything was over. Only she pointed with her finger for greater emphasis.

Petya looked at her imploringly, wavered on the spot for a while, sighed several times and walked out, like a beaten puppy dog. Columbine frowned. Surely she hadn't looked as pitiful as that the night before?

Petya's expulsion gave her a distinctly wicked pleasure. I definitely have what it takes to be a femme fatale, Columbine told herself, and sat down by the window to read the poem by the ugly individual who in life had borne the ugly name of Nikifor Sipyaga.

A Riddle

A nervous night, a hostile night,
The bed clatters its teeth,
Arching its back in wolfish spite.
I dare not sleep.

I fear sleep. In my waking trance
The wall-eyed windows show
Blue ash-tree skeletons that dance.
They creak, they groan.

I am still in this world, still here,
Warm, quivering, afraid.
The wind, knowing the Beast is near,
Taps on the pane.

The sated Beast will still be here,
The wind will sob and sigh
But I shall not be in this world.
Oh where am I?

Columbine suddenly felt quite unbearably afraid – afraid enough to make her want to go running after Petya and ask him to come back.

'Oh, dear mother,' whispered the femme fatale. 'What Beast is this?'

III. From the 'Agents' Reports' File

To His Honour Lieutenant-Colonel Besikov
(Private and confidential)

Dear Lieutenant-Colonel,

Ever since our latest exchange of opinions I have been reproaching myself for failing to display the firmness of character required to answer you in the appropriate manner. I am a weak man, and you possess the strange ability to stifle my will. The most disgusting thing of all is that I experience a strange pleasure in submitting to you, for which I hate myself afterwards. I swear that I shall drive this base, voluptuous servility out of myself!

Alone with a sheet of paper, it is easier for me to say what I think of your outrageous demand!

I think that you are abusing my goodwill and my readiness to assist the authorities voluntarily and render entirely disinterested assistance in eradicating this deadly cancer that is consuming society. For after all, it was I who informed you about my family tragedy, about my dearly beloved brother who became obsessed with the idea of suicide. I am a principled opponent of evil, and not some 'collaborator' as you call paid informers in your department. And if I have agreed to write you these letters (do not dare to call them 'reports'), it is not at all out of fear of being exiled for my former political views (as you once threatened), but only because I have realised just how truly malign spiritual nihilism is and come to fear it. You are absolutely right – materialism and inflated concern for the rights of the individual are not the Russian way, I am in complete agreement with you on that, and I believe I have already demonstrated quite adequately the sincerity of my enlightenment. It would appear, however, that you have decided to make it impossible for me to remain a decent human being! That is going too far.

I hereby declare categorically and irrevocably that I will not tell you the real names of the members of the club (in fact, I do not even know most of them), indeed, I will not even tell you the absurd aliases that they use among themselves, for that would be dishonourable and it smacks of simple informing.

Be merciful. I yielded to your insistent requests and agreed to find the secret society of potential suicides and insinuate myself into it, because you saw a political background to this sinister movement, like the medieval Arab order of assassins, fanatical killers who placed no value at all on human life – neither other people's nor their own. You must admit that I carried out your difficult assignment quite excellently, and now you receive reliable first-hand information about the 'Lovers of Death'. And I have had enough of you. Do not ask me to do anything more.

It has become absolutely clear to me that the Doge and his followers have no connection whatever with terrorists, socialists or anarchists. And what is more, these people have no interest whatever in politics and they despise all social concerns. You may put your mind at rest there – none of them will throw themselves under the wheels of the governor-general's carriage with a bomb. They are the perverted and world-weary children of our decadent era – affected and sickly, but in their own way very beautiful.

No, they are not bombers, but for society, and especially for young, immature minds, the 'lovers' are very, very dangerous indeed – precisely because of their pale, intoxicating beauty. The ideology and aestheticism of the lovers of death undeniably contain a poisonously attractive temptation. They promise their followers an escape into a magical world far removed from the humdrum greyness of everyday life – the very thing for which exalted and sensitive souls yearn.

And the main danger, of course, is represented by the Doge himself. I have already described this terrible character to you, but his truly satanic grandeur is revealed more clearly to me every day. He is a ghoul, a vampire, a basilisk! A genuine fisher of souls who is so artful in subordinating others to his will that I swear to God even you cannot compare with him.

Recently a new member appeared – a funny, touching young girl from somewhere in Siberia. Naive and rapturous, with her head full of all sorts of foolishness that is fashionable among today's young people. If she had not found her way into our club, in time she would have grown out of all this and become like everyone else. The usual story! But the Doge instantly snared her in his web and turned her into a walking automaton. It happened before my very eyes, in a matter of minutes.

Undoubtedly, an end must be put to all of this, but ordinary arrest will not suit here. Arrest will only make the Doge into a tragic figure, and it is frightening to think what a public trial would be transformed into! This man is picturesque, imposing, eloquent. Why, after his address to the court, 'lovers' would appear in every one of our district towns!

No, this monster has to be unmasked, trampled underfoot, displayed in a pitiful and monstrous light, so that his poisonous sting can be drawn once and for all!

And for what offence could you actually arrest him? After all, it is not a crime to set up poetry clubs. There is only one way out: I must uncover some *corpus delicti* in the Doge's activities and prove that this gentleman, with deliberate intent and malice aforethought, encourages frail souls to commit the terrible sin of suicide. Only when I manage to obtain reliable evidence will I give you the Doge's name and address. But not before then, not before.

Fortunately, I am not suspected of playing a double game.

I deliberately make myself out to be a jester, and even derive a certain morbid satisfaction from the frankly scornful looks that certain of our smart alecks, including the Master himself, give me. Never mind, let them think me a pitiful worm, that is more convenient for my purposes. Or am I really a worm? What do you think?

Very well, let us leave that aside. The convulsions of my wounded vanity are of no importance. I am tormented by something quite different: after Avaddon's terrible death we have another 'vacancy', and I am waiting anxiously to see what new moth will come flying to singe its wings on this infernal flame . . .

Yours affronted, but with genuine respect,

ZZ
28 August 1900

CHAPTER 2

I. From the Newspapers

Lavr Zhemailo Meets the High Priest of the 'Lovers of Death'

And so, it has come to pass! Your humble servant has succeeded in infiltrating the holy of holies of the highly conspiratorial suicide club which set everyone talking after the recent death of S., a 23-year-old student at Moscow University. The story of how I managed to overcome all the cunning barriers and insuperable obstacles in order to attain my goal would make the plot of a thrilling novel. However, bound by my word, I shall remain silent, and let me state immediately for the benefit of the gentlemen of the police that *Lavr Zhemailo will never, under any circumstances, even under threat of imprisonment, betray his helpers and informants.*

My meeting with the high priest of the sinister sect of worshippers of death commenced in a dark and gloomy cellar, the location of which has remained a mystery to me since my *cicerone* delivered me there with a blindfold over my eyes. I could smell damp earth, several times cobwebs dangling from the ceiling brushed across my face and once a bat flew past with a loathsome squeak. After this prelude, I felt sure I would see some appalling vault with slimy walls, but when the blindfold was removed, there was a rather pleasant disappointment in store for me. I was standing in a spacious, superbly furnished room that resembled the drawing room of a rich house: a crystal chandelier, bookcases, chairs with carved backs, a round table like those that are used for spiritualist seances. The person I spoke to told me to call him 'Doge'. Naturally, he was wearing a mask, so that I could see only his long, snow-white hair, small grey beard and exceptionally keen, or rather, I should say, *piercing* eyes. The Doge's voice proved to be resonant and beautiful, and at times quite spellbinding. There can be no doubt that he is a talented and exceptional individual.

'I know you, Mr Zhemailo, as a man of honour, and that is the only reason I have agreed to meet you.' Thus did my mysterious companion begin the conversation. I bowed and promised once again that the 'Lovers of Death' need not fear any indiscretion or foul play on my part.

My reward for this promise was an extensive lecture, delivered by the Doge with such exceptional eloquence that I was enthralled even against my own will. I shall try here to convey the content of this eccentric sermon in my own words.

The venerable Doge asserts that man's true native land is not the planet Earth or the condition which we call life, but in fact the absolute opposite: Death, Blackness, Non-existence. This is the true homeland of all of us. That is where we formerly dwelt, and where we shall soon return. For a brief, insubstantial moment, we are doomed to dwell in the light, in life, in existence. Precisely doomed, that is, punished, expelled from the bosom of Death.

All of the living, without exception, are winnowed chaff, dross, criminals condemned to the daily torment of life for some crime that we have forgotten, but which must be extremely grave. Some of us are less guilty and therefore condemned only to a short sentence. Such individuals return to Death when they are still infants. Others, who are guiltier, are condemned to hard labour for seventy, eighty or even a hundred years. Those who live to extreme old age are the most evil of wrongdoers and unworthy of any indulgence. But nonetheless, sooner or later, Death in its infinite mercy forgives everyone.

At this point your humble servant, unable to restrain himself, interrupted the orator.

'A curious assertion. And so the length of our lives is not set by God, but by Death?'

'Let it be God – use whatever name you wish. Only the judge whom people have called God is by no means the Lord Almighty, but merely an acolyte in the service of Death.'

'What an appalling image!' I exclaimed.

'Not at all,' the Doge reassured me. 'God is stern, but Death is merciful. Out of benevolence Death has endowed us with the instinct of self-preservation, so that we will not feel oppressed by the walls of our prison and will fear any attempt to escape from them. And Death has also granted us the gift of oblivion. We have no memory of our true homeland, of our lost Eden. Otherwise not one of us would be willing to bear the torment of imprisonment

and there would be a genuine orgy of suicides.'

'What is so bad about that, from your point of view? After all, surely you actually exhort the members of your circle to commit suicide?'

'Unauthorised suicide is an escape from prison, a crime that is punishable by a new term of imprisonment. No, it is not permissible to flee from this life. But it is possible to earn pardon – that is, a reduction in the sentence.'

'In what way, if I might enquire?'

'Through love. One must love Death with all one's soul. Entice and summon her to you, like your own dearly beloved. And wait, wait meekly for her Sign. When the Sign is manifested, you not only may, but should, die by your own hand.'

'You speak of Death as "she", as your dearly beloved, but there are both men and women among your followers.'

'In Russian, Death is a feminine noun, but that is a convention of grammar. In German, as we know, the word is masculine – *der Tod*. For a man Death is the Eternal

Bride. For a woman he is the Eternal Bridegroom.'

Then I asked the question that had been bothering me from the very beginning of this strange dialogue: 'When you talk it is clear that you have unshakeable confidence in the truth of what you say. How do you know all this, if Death has denied man any memory of his previous existence, that is – I beg your pardon – Non-existence?'

The Doge replied with a triumphant air.

'There are some people – rare individuals – from whom Death has decided to take away the gift of forgetting, so that they are able to perceive both worlds, Being and Non-being. I am one of these people. After all, a prison administration needs a steward from among the prisoners in the cell. It is the steward's duty to keep an eye on those in his care, to instruct them and recommend those who deserve leniency to the Governor. That is all, no more questions. I have nothing more to say.'

'Just one. The very last!' I exclaimed. 'Do you have many wards in your "cell"?'

'Twelve. I know from the newspapers that many times that number would like to join us, but our club only opens its doors to the select few. To become a Lover of Death is a precious lot, the highest possible reward for anyone alive . . .'

I was blindfolded from behind and led towards the door. The conversation with the Doge, the high priest of the suicide sect, was over.

As I was plunged into darkness, I could not help shuddering at the thought that I was descending forever into the Blackness so dear to the 'lovers'.

No, gentlemen, I thought to myself when I was back in the bright sunshine under the blue sky, I may be a condemned criminal, but I do not desire any leniency – I prefer to serve my 'sentence' to the end.

But what would you prefer, dear reader?

Lavr Zhemailo
Moscow Courier, 29 August
(11 September) 1900, p.2

II. From Columbine's Diary

Her slippers barely even touch the ground

Poor Columbine, brainless puppet, dangling in mid-air. Her satin slippers barely even touch the ground, and if the deft puppet-master pulls on the slim strings, the puppet throws up its arms or doubles over in a bow: sometimes crying, sometimes laughing.

I think about one and the same thing all the time now: the meaning of the words that he spoke; the tone in which he said them; the way he looked at me; why he didn't look at me at all. Oh, my life is so full of strong feelings and experiences!

For example, yesterday he said: 'You have the eyes of a cruel child.' For a long time afterwards, I wondered if that was good or bad – a cruel child. From his point of view, probably good. Or bad?

I have read that old men (and he's very old, he knew Karakozov, who was hanged thirty-five years ago) feel a burning passion for young girls. But he's not lascivious at all. He's cold and indifferent. Since that first, tempestuous union, when the trees outside the windows were bowing before the hurricane's onslaught, he has only told me to stay once. That was the day before yesterday.

Without a single word, with only gestures, he ordered me to throw off my clothes, lie on the bearskin and not move. He covered my face with a white Venetian mask – a dead, stiff disguise. All I could see through the narrow eye-slits was the ceiling, looking light-coloured in the twilight.

I lay there for a long time without moving. It was very quiet, all I could hear was the quiet crackling of the candle flames. I thought: He's looking at me, defenceless, with no covering, without even a face. This is not me, this is nameless female flesh, simply a rubber doll.

What did I feel?

Curiosity. Yes, curiosity and the sweet thrill of uncertainty. What would he do? What would his first touch be like? Would he press his lips to mine in a kiss? Or lash me with a whip? Would he scorch me with hot drops of candle wax? I would have accepted anything at all from him, but time passed and nothing happened.

I started feeling cold, my skin was covered with goosepimples. I said plaintively: 'Where are you? I'm frozen!' Not a single sound in reply. Then I took off the mask and sat up.

There was no one else in the bedroom, and this discovery set me trembling. He had disappeared! This inexplicable disappearance set my heart beating faster than even the most ardent of embraces.

I thought for a long time about what this trick could mean. For a whole night and a day I searched desperately for the answer. What was he trying to tell me? What feelings did he have for me? Without a doubt, there was passion. Only not fiery, but icy, like the polar sun, which scorches no less for being cold.

I am only writing this in my diary now, because I have suddenly understood the meaning of what happened. The first time he possessed only my body. The second time he possessed my soul. The initiation is complete.

Now I am his thing. His property, like a key-ring or a glove. Like Ophelia.

There is nothing between them, I am sure of that. That is, the girl is in love with him, of course, but he only needs her as a medium. I cannot imagine any man being inflamed with passion for this sleep-walker. A strange, innocent smile constantly trembles on her face, her eyes

68

have a gentle but abstracted look. She hardly ever opens her mouth – except during the seances. But during those minutes of communication with the World Beyond, Ophelia is completely transformed. As if somewhere deep inside her fragile little body a bright lamp suddenly lights up. Pierrot says that she is actually half-insane and she should be put in a clinic, that she lives in a dream. I don't know. I think, on the contrary, that she is only alive and fully herself when acting as a medium.

I myself find it hard to distinguish dreams from reality now. The dream is getting up late in the morning, break-fast, all the shopping that has to be done. Waking life only begins as evening approaches, when I try to write poems and get ready to go out. But I only come fully awake after eight, as I walk quickly along Rozhdestvenka Street, with its bright streetlamps, towards the boulevard. The world bears me along on waves of energy, the blood pulses in my veins. My heels clatter along so quickly, so single-mindedly that people turn round to look at me as they walk by.

Evening is the culmination and the apotheosis of the day. Later, after midnight already, I come home and artificially prolong the magic by writing down the details of everything that happened in a Moroccan leather notebook.

Today many things happened.

From the very beginning he behaved quite differently from usual.

But no, I mustn't write like that – always he, he. I am not writing for myself, but for art.

Prospero was not the same as always – he was lively, almost agitated. Nearly as soon as he joined us in the drawing room, he started talking.

'Today a man approached me in the street. Handsome, elegantly dressed, very self-confident. He spoke strange words with a slight stammer: "I know how to read faces. You are the one I need. Fate has s-sent you to me."

' "But I can read nothing in your face," I replied hostilely, since I cannot bear undue familiarity. "I am afraid, sir that you have made a mistake. No one can send me anywhere, not even fate."

' "What is that you have there?" he asked, taking no notice of my harsh words and pointing to my coat pocket. "What is m-making that bulge? A revolver? Give it to me."

'You know that I never leave home without my Bulldog. The stranger's behaviour was beginning to intrigue me. Without further words I took the weapon out and handed it to him – to see what would happen.'

At this point Lorelei exclaimed: 'But he is obviously insane! He could have shot you! How reckless you are!'

'I am used to trusting in Death,' Prospero said with a shrug. 'She is wiser and kinder than we are. And then, tell me, good Lioness, what would I have lost if the mad stranger had put a bullet through my forehead? It would been an elegant conclusion . . . But listen to the rest.'

And he went on with his story: 'The stranger opened the revolver and shook out four bullets into the palm of his hand, leaving the fifth in the gun. I observed his actions with curiosity.

'He spun the drum hard, then suddenly put the barrel against his temple and pressed the trigger. The hammer clicked loudly against an empty chamber, and not a single muscle twitched in the amazing gentleman's face.

' "Now will you talk to me seriously?" he asked.

'I didn't answer, I was rather shaken by this performance. Then he spun the barrel again and set the gun against his temple again. I tried to stop him, but I was too late. The trigger clicked again – and again he was lucky.

' "Enough," I explained. "What is it that you want?"

'He said: "I want to be with you. You are the person I t-take you to be, are you not?"

'Apparently he had been searching for the "Lovers of Death" for a long time in order to become one of them. Naturally, he had not guessed who I was from my face –

that had been said simply for the sake of effect, in order to make an impression on me. In actual fact, he had pursued a cunning investigation that had led him to me. What do you make of that? He is an extremely interesting individual – I know people. He composes poetry, in the Japanese style. You will hear it, it is quite unlike anything else. I told him to come today. After all, Avaddon's place is still free.'

I envied this unknown gentleman who had managed to make such an impression on our impassive Doge, although I was not listening to the story very carefully, because something else was bothering me. I was going to read a new poem that I had worked on throughout the previous night and I was hoping that I had finally managed to get it right, and that Prospero would criticise this cry from the soul less severely than my previous efforts, which . . . Never mind, I have already written about that more than once, I will not repeat myself here.

When my turn came, I read out:

> *You'll forget her, won't you,*
> *This doll with hempen curls*
> *And eyes of misty blue*
> *Enchanted by your spells?*
>
> *'It's clear you do not care*
> *That she is a martyr*
> *To the doting worship*
> *Of her celluloid heart.*
>
> *'Then should I pray to God,*
> *Offer up this drama?*
> *The former touch-me-not*
> *Weeps quietly: ma-ma!*

There was another stanza, which I particularly liked (I even shed a few teardrops over it) – about how a puppet has no god but the puppet-master.

But heartless Prospero waved his hand dismissively for me to stop, and frowned as he said: 'Stodgy semolina!'

My poems do not interest him at all!

Afterwards Gdlevsky, whom Prospero always praises exorbitantly, read his verse, and I quietly left the room. I stood in front of the mirror in the hallway and started to cry. Or rather, I started howling. 'Stodgy semolina!'

It was dark in the hallway, and all I could see in the mirror was my own stooped figure with a stupid bow in my hair, which had slipped right over to the left. Lord, how unhappy I felt! I remember I thought: If only the spirits would summon me today, I would gladly leave you all and go to the Eternal Bridegroom. But there was not much hope. Firstly, just recently the spirits had either not appeared at all or had simply babbled some sort of nonsense. And secondly, why would Death choose such a worthless, untalented woodlouse for a bride?

Then there was a ring at the door. I hurriedly straightened my bow, dried my eyes and went to open it.

There was a surprise in store for me.

Standing on the doorstep was the same gentleman I had seen when I took the forget-me-nots to Avaddon.

The appearance of Prince Genji

On that day when the tearful Petya-Cherubino had shown up at the small flat under the roof and frightened its occupant with the news of Avaddon's death, and then with the Chosen One's final poem, Columbine had sat in the armchair for a long time, reading the mysterious lines over and over again.

She had cried a little bit, of course. She felt sorry for Avaddon, even if he was a Chosen One. But then she had stopped crying, because what point was there in crying if someone had been granted what he was yearning for? His wedding with his Eternal Betrothed had been celebrated. In such cases one should not sob and weep, but feel glad.

And Columbine had set out to the newly-wed's flat to congratulate him. She had put on her very smartest dress (white and airy, with two silver streaks of light sewn along the bodice), bought a bouquet of delicate forget-me-nots and gone to Basmannaya Street. She had taken Lucifer with her, only not on her neck, like a necklace (black would not have been appropriate on a day like this) but in her handbag – so that he would not be bored at home alone.

She found the Giant company's building – a new, five-storey stone structure – with no difficulty. She had been planning simply to leave the flowers at the door of the flat, but the door was not sealed, in fact it was even half-open. She could hear muffled voices inside. If other people can go inside, then why can't I, the bearer of congratulations, she reasoned, and walked in.

It was a small flat, no larger than her own in Kitaigorod, but quite remarkably neat and tidy and far from squalid, as she would have expected it to be from the late Avaddon's shabby clothes.

Columbine stopped in the hallway, trying to guess where the room in which the Bridegroom had met his Bride would be.

The kitchen seemed to be on the left. She heard a man speaking in it, with a slight stammer.

'And what d-door is this? The rear entrance?'

'Precisely so, Your Excellency,' replied another voice, husky and obsequious. 'Only the gentleman student never used it. The back door is for servants, and he managed for himself. Because he was dog-poor, if you'll pardon the expression.'

She heard a bump and a clang of metal.

'So he d-didn't use it, you say? Then why are the hinges oiled? And very thoroughly too?'

'I couldn't say. I suppose someone must have oiled them.'

The man with a stammer sighed and said: 'A reasonable s-supposition.' There was a pause in the conversation.

He must be a police investigator, Columbine guessed and

started back towards the door to avoid trouble – he might start pestering her with questions: who was she, why was she here, what did the forget-me-nots mean? But before she could withdraw, three men walked out of the short corridor into the hall.

The first, ambling along and occasionally glancing round, was a bearded yard keeper in an apron, with his metal badge on his chest. Following him at a leisurely pace and tapping his cane on the floor, came a tall lean gentleman in a beautifully tailored frock-coat, snow-white shirt with immaculate cuffs and even a top hat – a perfect Count of Monte Cristo – and the yard keeper had called him 'Excellency', hadn't he? The similarity to the former prisoner of the Château d'If was reinforced by the pale well-groomed face (which, she had to admit, was most impressive) and romantic black moustache. And the dandy was about the same age as the Parisian millionaire – she could see grey temples under the top hat.

Bringing up the rear was a squat, solidly built Oriental in a three-piece suit and a bowler hat pulled so far forward that it almost covered his eyes. But they weren't really eyes – he stared out at Columbine from under the black felt through two narrow slits.

The yard keeper waved his arms at the young lady as if he were shooing away a cat.

'You can't come in here, get out! Go away!'

But Monte Cristo looked keenly at the smartly dressed girl and said laconically: 'Never mind, it's all right. Here, take this as well.'

He handed the yard keeper a banknote, and the bearded man doubled over in delight and called his benefactor 'Your Highness' instead of 'Your Excellency', from which she concluded that the handsome man with the stammer was not a count and most definitely not a policeman. Who had ever heard of policemen flinging rouble notes at yard keepers? Another curious outsider, Columbine decided. He must have read about the 'Lovers of Death' in the newspapers, and now he'd come to gape at the lodgings of the latest suicide.

The handsome gentleman doffed his top hat (in the process revealing that only his temples were grey, and the rest of his coiffure was still quite black), but he didn't introduce himself, he merely asked: 'Are you an acquaintance of Mr Sipyaga's?'

Columbine refused to favour the Count of Monte Cristo with a glance, let alone a reply. The feeling of excitement and exultation had returned, she was not in the mood for idle conversation.

Then the persistent dark-haired gentleman lowered his voice and asked: 'You must b-be from the "Lovers of Death", I suppose?'

'What makes you think so?' she asked with a start, glancing at him in fright.

'Why, it's quite clear.' He leaned on his cane and started bending down the fingers of one hand in a close-fitting grey glove. 'You walked in without ringing or kn-knocking. So you must have come to see someone you know. That is one. You see strangers here, but you don't ask after the occupant of the flat. So you already know that he is dead. That is two. But that didn't stop you coming here in an extravagant dress with a f-frivolous bouquet. That is three. Who could regard a suicide as cause for congratulation? Only the "Lovers of Death". That is four.'

The Oriental joined in the conversation. He spoke Russian rather briskly, but with an appalling accent.

'Not onry ruvers,' he protested energetically. 'When Prince Asano's nobur samurai receive permission commit hara-kiri, everyone congraturate them too.'

'Masa, we can d-discuss the story of the forty-seven faithful vassals some other time,' said Monte Cristo, interrupting the short Oriental. 'At the moment, as you can see, I am talking to a lady.'

'You may be talking to the lady,' Columbine snapped. 'But the lady is not talking to you.'

'His Highness' shrugged, discouraged, and she turned into the doorway that led to the right, beyond which there were two small rooms. The first one contained nothing but a cheap writing desk and the one beyond it was the bedroom. Her eye was caught by the divan bed, one of the new-fangled kind, with a central section that folded out, but it was very shabby and crooked. The top section didn't fit properly against the bottom and the divan seemed to be grinning with a dark mouth.

Columbine remembered a line from Avaddon's final poem, and muttered: 'The bed clatters its teeth.'

'What's that?' She heard Monte Cristo say behind her. 'Poetry?'

Without turning round, she recited the entire quatrain in a whisper.

> *A nervous night, a hostile night,*
> *The bed clatters its teeth,*
> *Arching its back in wolfish spite.*
> *I dare not sleep.*

There really was something wolfish about the divan's curved back.

The windowpane trembled (it was windy, like the evening before), Columbine gave a chill shudder and recited the final lines of the poem:

> *The wind, knowing the Beast is near,*
> *Taps on the pane.*
>
> *'The sated Beast will still be here,*
> *The wind will sob and sigh*
> *But I shall not be in this world.*
> *Oh where am I?*

And she sighed. Where are you now, Chosen One Avaddon? Are you happy in the World Beyond?

'That is Nikifor Sipyaga's d-death poem?' the quick-witted dandy stated rather than asked. 'Interesting. Very interesting.'

The yard keeper told them: 'There was a beast howling, really. The tenant on the other side of the wall told me. The walls here are flimsy, Your Excellency, nothing to them really. When the police left, the tenant next door came down to see me, out of curiosity. And he told me: at night, he says, someone started howling, eerie it was, going up and down, like he was calling someone or threatening them. And it went on right until dawn. He even banged on the wall – he couldn't sleep. Thought as Mr Sipyaga had got a dog. Only there wasn't any dog here.'

'An interesting little flat,' said the man with dark hair. 'I can hear some k-kind of sound too. Only not howling, it's more like hissing. And this intriguing sound is coming from your handbag, Mademoiselle.'

He turned to Columbine and looked at her with his blue eyes – she couldn't tell if their expression was sad or happy.

Never mind, they'll be frightened in a moment, Columbine thought mischievously.

'From my handbag? Are you sure?' she asked, feigning surprise. 'But I can't hear anything. Well now, let's take a look.'

She deliberately lifted up her bag so that it was right under the arrogant stranger's nose and clicked open the little lock.

Lucifer didn't let her down. He stuck out his narrow little head just like a jack-in-a-box, opened his jaws and gave such a hiss! He'd obviously got bored in his dark, cramped lair.

'Holy Mother of God!' the yard keeper howled, banging the back of his head against the doorpost. 'A snake! It's black! And I haven't drunk a drop!'

But what a pity – the handsome gentleman wasn't in the least bit frightened. He inclined his head to one side to take a good look at the snake and said approvingly: 'A fine little g-grass snake. You're fond of animals, Mademoiselle? Very laudable.'

And then he turned back to the yard keeper, as if nothing had happened.

'So, you say the unknown b-beast was howling until dawn. That's the most interesting thing of all. What's the neighbour's name? The one who lives on the other side of the wall. What does he d-do for a living?'

'Stakhovich. He's an artist.' The yard keeper kept glancing warily at Lucifer and rubbing the bruise on the back of his head. 'Young Miss, is he safe? He won't bite?'

'Of course he will!' Columbine replied haughtily. 'Not half he will.' And she told the Count of Monte Cristo. 'You're a grass snake. This is an Egyptian cobra.'

'A Co-bra, very well,' he drawled absentmindedly, not really listening.

He stopped by the wall where there was clothing hanging on nails – evidently Avaddon's entire wardrobe: a pitiful, patched greatcoat and a worn student's uniform jacket, obviously second-hand.

'So Mr Sipyaga was very p-poor?'

'As poor as a church mouse. Never even tipped a kopeck, not like Your Grace.'

'And yet the flat is not at all bad. Probably thirty roubles a month?'

'Twenty-five. Only it wasn't him that rented it, how could he have? It was Mr Blagovolsky, Sergei Irinarkhovich, who paid.'

'Who's he?'

'I couldn't say. That's what it says in the accounts book.'

As she listened to this conversation, Columbine turned her head this way and that, trying to guess exactly where the wedding with Death had taken place. And eventually she found it. There was a severed rope-end hanging from the hook of the curtain rod.

She gazed at the crude piece of metal and the tattered piece of hemp in awe. Lord, how pitiful, how wretched are the gates through which the soul escapes from the hell of life into the heaven of Death!

'Be happy, Avaddon!' she thought to herself and put the bouquet down on top of the skirting board.

The Oriental came across and clicked his tongue disapprovingly: 'Brue frowers no good! Brue for when drowned. When hanged, should be daisy.'

'Masa, you ought to give the "Lovers of Death" lectures on how to honour suicides,' Monte Cristo remarked with a serious air. Tell me now, what colour should the bouquet be, for instance, when someone has shot himself?'

'Red,' Masa replied just as seriously. 'Roses or poppies.'

'And if he poisoned himself?'

The Oriental didn't hesitate for a second.

'Yerrow chrysanthemums. If no chrysanthemums, can be buttercups.'

'And what if his stomach was slit open?'

'White frowers – because white corow most nobur.'

The Oriental folded his short-fingered hands as if in prayer and his friend nodded in approval.

'A pair of clowns,' Columbine exclaimed scornfully. She cast a final glance at the hook and walked towards the door.

Who could have imagined that she would see the dandy from Avaddon's flat again and, of all places, at Prospero's house!

He looked almost exactly the same as he had at their previous meeting: elegant, with a cane, only the frock-coat and the top hat were ash-grey instead of black.

'Good evening, m-madam,' he said with his characteristic slight stammer. 'I'm here to see Mr Blagovolsky.'

'Who? There's no one here by that name.'

In the semi-darkness he couldn't make out Columbine's face, but she recognised him immediately – there was a gas lamp burning under the canopy of the door. She was terribly surprised. Had he got the wrong address? What a very strange coincidence that would be!

'Ah, yes, I b-beg your pardon,' said her chance acquaintance, bowing jokingly. 'I meant to say Mr Prospero. Indeed, I was warned most strictly that it is not the d-done thing to use one's own name here. So you must be Zemfira, say, or Malvina?'

'I am Columbine,' she replied coolly. 'But who are you?'

Once he walked into the hallway he was able to see who it was that had opened the door for him. He recognised her, but gave no sign of being surprised.

'Hello, mysterious stranger. Well, it's a small world, as they say.' Lucifer was dozing on the girl's neck and he stroked the snake's head. 'Hello there, little one. Allow m-me to introduce myself, Mademoiselle Columbine. Mr Blago . . . that is, Mr Prospero and I agreed that here I will be known as Genji.'

'Genji? What a strange name!'

She simply couldn't understand what this mysterious appearance could mean. What had this gentleman with a stammer been doing at Avaddon's flat? And what did he want here?

'In olden times there was a Japanese p-prince by that name. A seeker of thrills such as myself.'

She rather liked the unusual name – Genji. *Japonisme* was so refined. So, it was not 'Your Excellency' but actually 'Your Highness'. Columbine chuckled sarcastically, but she had to admit that the dandy really was remarkably like a prince, if not Japanese, then at least a European one, like in Stevenson.

'Was your companion Japanese?' she asked, struck by a sudden insight. 'The one I saw on Basmannaya Street? Is that why he kept talking about samurais and cutting out stomachs?'

'Yes, he is my valet and closest friend. By the way, you were wrong to call us cl-clowns.' Genji shook his head reproachfully. 'Masa has great respect for the institution of suicide. As, indeed, do I. Otherwise I would not be here, would I?'

She rather doubted the sincerity of that last assertion – the tone in which it was made was far too flippant.

'You don't look as if you were particularly keen to leave

this world,' Columbine said mistrustfully, looking into the visitor's calm eyes.

'I assure you, Mademoiselle Columbine, that I am a desperate man, c-capable of the most extreme, quite inconceivable actions.'

Once again he spoke in a way that made it impossible to tell if he was serious or joking. But then she suddenly remembered the Doge's story about 'a highly interesting character'. He wasn't like any of the other aspirants. In fact, she had never seen anyone of his type before.

'Well, now you're here, let's go,' she said coolly, so that he wouldn't get too high an opinion of himself. 'You still have to pass the test.'

They entered the salon just as Gdlevsky was completing his recitation and Rosencrantz was preparing for his performance.

Telling the twins apart had turned out to be quite easy. Guildenstern spoke quite faultless Russian (he had studied at a Russian grammar school) and his disposition was noticeably more cheerful. Rosencrantz was always writing something down on a thick notepad and he sighed frequently. Columbine often caught his doleful Baltic glance on her, and although her own response was uncompromising, she enjoyed this silent adoration. It was a pity that the young German's poetry was so appallingly bad.

This time he had taken up that solemn pose again: feet in position three, the fingers of the right hand spread out like a fan, his eyes fixed on Columbine.

The pitiless Doge interrupted him after the very first stanza.

'Thank you, Rosencrantz. You can't say "weeping with a sighfully pure tear" in Russian, but you did do a little better today. Ladies and gentlemen! Here is the candidate for Avaddon's place,' he said, introducing the newcomer, who had halted in the doorway and was surveying the drawing room and the people gathered in it with a curious glance.

Everyone turned towards the candidate and he gave a light bow.

'It is our custom to hold a kind of poetic examination,' the Doge told him. 'I only need to hear a few lines of a poem written by a candidate and I can tell immediately if his way lies with us or not. You write verse that is unusual for our literature, with no rhymes or rhythm, and so it is only fair if I ask you to extemporise on a theme that I set.'

'By all means,' Genji replied, not disconcerted in the least. 'What theme would you l-like to suggest?'

Columbine noticed that Prospero addressed him in a rather formal tone, which was unusual in itself. This formidable gentleman had obviously made quite an impression.

The chairman paused for a long moment. Everyone held their breath and waited: they knew that in a moment he would dumbfound the self-confident novice with some paradox or sudden surprise.

And so he did. Flinging back his lacy cuff (today the Doge was dressed as a Spanish grandee, which suited his beard and long hair very well), Prospero took a red apple out of a bowl and sank his firm teeth into it with a crunch. He chewed, swallowed and glanced at Genji.

'There is your subject.'

They all looked at each other. What kind of subject was that?

Petya whispered to Columbine: 'He did that on purpose. Now he'll shoot him down, just you see.'

'A b-bitten apple, or an apple in general?' the probationer enquired.

'That is for you to decide.'

Prospero smiled contentedly and sat on his throne.

With a shrug of his shoulders, as if this was all the merest of trifles, Genji recited:

> *The apple is beautiful,*
> *Not on the branch or in the stomach*
> *But in the moment of its fall.*

82

Everybody waited for the continuation. But none came. Then Cyrano shook his head and Kriton giggled rather loudly, although Gdlevsky nodded approvingly and the Lioness of Ecstasy even exclaimed: 'Bravo!'

Columbine had been about to pull a disdainful face, but instead she assumed a thoughtful air. If the two leading luminaries had seen something in Prince Genji's outlandish composition, it couldn't be entirely irredeemable. But of course, the important opinion was the Doge's.

Prospero walked up to Genji and shook him firmly by the hand.

'I was not mistaken in you. Precisely so: the essence lies neither in dreary existence nor in decay following death, but in the catharsis that transforms one into the other. Precisely so! And so terse, not a single superfluous word! So help me, the Japanese have something to teach us.'

Columbine squinted sideways at Petya. He shrugged – like her, he had clearly failed to find anything exceptional in the aphorism he had just heard.

The new aspirant strolled across the salon and declared in a tone of surprise: 'I was certain that the interview with the high priest of the suicide club p-printed in the *Courier* was a stupid hoax. However, the description of the way the room is furnished was exact, and the worthy Doge himself seems to have been drawn from the life. Is such a thing really possible? Did you meet with a c-correspondent, Mr Prospero? But what for?'

There was an awkward silence for, without knowing it, Genji had touched on a sore point. The calamitous article, which had expounded Prospero's views rather precisely and even directly quoted some of his favourite maxims, had caused a real storm in the club. The Doge had formally interrogated every one of them in an attempt to discover if one of his followers had been too open with outsiders, but he had failed to identify the informant.

'I didn't talk to any correspondent!' Prospero said angrily and gestured round the aspirants. 'There's a Judas here, among my own disciples! Either out of vanity, or for a few silver pieces, one of them has held me and our society up to the mockery of the crowd. Genji, to be quite honest, I have special hopes for you. You impressed me with your remarkable analytical abilities. With only a few scattered crumbs of information to go on, you unerringly followed the trail to the "Lovers of Death" and identified me as the leader of the club. So perhaps you will assist me to expose the mangy sheep that has insinuated itself into my flock?'

'I expect that will not be difficult,' said Genji, glancing round at the faces of the hushed 'lovers'. 'But first I shall have to g-get to know these ladies and gentlemen a little better.'

No one liked the sound of these words at all, they sounded far too menacing.

'Only hurry,' Kriton laughed. 'The acquaintance might prove to be short, since we stand on the edge of a gaping grave.'

Cyrano wrinkled up his monumental nose and declaimed with a sneer:

> Set the secret police to work
> Make the cunning rogue confess
> Send the rascal to the block
> To edify and scare the rest.

Even prim, starchy Horatio, the bard of the anatomist's art, who did not open his mouth very often, was outraged: 'The last thing we need here is detectives and informers!'

Columbine suddenly felt afraid. This was a genuine revolt. Well, now the troublemakers would get what they deserved! Prospero would unleash the withering force of his wrath against the rebels.

But the Doge did not cast any thunderbolts or wave his arms in the air. His face took on a sad expression and his head sank down on to his chest.

'I know,' Prospero said in a quiet voice. 'I have always known. One of you will betray me.'

And with that he got up and walked out of the door without saying another word.

'Teacher! As long as I'm here, you have nothing to fear!' Caliban roared furiously and looked at Kriton, who was standing beside him, with an expression of such intense hatred that the goat-hoofed preacher of amorous passion recoiled in horror.

Columbine's heart was aching with compassion. She would have gone dashing after Prospero, if only she dared. Then he would know that she at least would never betray him!

But the door slammed shut adamantly. Columbine knew only too well what lay beyond it: a sparsely furnished dining room, then a large study crowded with massive furniture, and after that – the bedroom that she dreamed about so often at night. You could get straight out of the study into the corridor and then into the hallway. That was the inglorious route that Columbine herself had followed twice as she left those sacred halls, crushed and confused . . .

'Vill zere be no zeance?' Rosencrantz asked, fluttering his white eyelashes. 'But ze Toge said today voz a perfect evening for talking vith ze spirits of ze dead. A starry sky, a fat moon. It is a shame to miss zuch a shance!'

'What do you say, dear?' the Lioness of Ecstasy asked Ophelia gently, as if she were a little child. 'After all, we really have been waiting so long for the full moon. What can you feel? Will we be able to establish contact with the World Beyond today?'

Ophelia smiled in confusion and babbled in her thin little voice: 'Yes, today is a special night, I can feel it. But I can't do it on my own, someone has to lead me. I need a calm, confident pair of eyes so that I don't lose my way in the fog. Only Prospero has eyes like that. No, ladies and gentlemen, I simply can't do it without him.'

'So we're going home then?' asked Guildenstern. 'That's

stupid. The time's just been wasted. I'd have been better off studying. The exams are soon.'

Some people were already on their way to the door, but the new member walked over to Ophelia, took her by the hand, looked straight into her face and said quietly: 'Well now, my d-dear young lady, look into my eyes. That's right. Good. You can trust me.'

God only knows what Ophelia saw in his eyes, but she suddenly became calm, the wrinkles disappeared from her clear little forehead, and her smile was no longer confused, but radiant.

'Yes,' she said with a nod. 'I trust you. We could try.'

Columbine almost choked on her indignation. A spiritualist seance without Prospero? Unthinkable! Just who did this svelte gentleman think he was? He was an impostor, an upstart, a usurper! And this would be an even worse betrayal of the Doge than careless talk with a newspaper reporter!

However, the others did not appear to share her sense of outrage, in fact they seemed intrigued. Even Caliban, the Doge's devoted minion, asked Prince Genji in an almost obsequious voice: 'Are you sure it will work? Will you be able to summon the spirits? And will they name the next Chosen One?'

Genji shrugged.

'Why, naturally it will work. They'll show up, as meek as lambs. And we'll find out soon enough what they have to t-tell us.'

He calmly seated himself on the chairman's throne and all the others rushed to take their places, with their fingers spread out wide.

'What are you doing?' asked Petya, turning to look at the outraged Columbine. 'Sit down. Without you there's a link missing.'

And so she sat down. It was hard to go against everyone else all on your own. And of course, she felt curious as well – would it really work?

86

Genji clapped his hands rapidly three times and it suddenly went very quiet.

'Look only at me, Mademoiselle,' he told Ophelia. 'You must shut down the other f-four senses and leave only hearing. Listen to the silence. And you, gentlemen, do not distract the medium with extraneous sounds.'

Columbine looked at him in absolute amazement. How quickly this man, who had only just appeared in the club, had imposed his authority on all the others! No one had even attempted to dispute his leadership, and yet he hadn't done anything special, and he had spoken no more than a few words. Then the recent grammar-school girl remembered how in one lesson their history teacher, Ivan Ferdinandovich Segiur (all the girls in seventh class were in love with him), had told them about the role of strong personalities in society.

There were two types of strong personalities: the first was full of energy, highly active, he would out-shout anyone, override and bedazzle them and drag them after him, even against their own will; the second was taciturn and at first glance seemed rather inactive, but he conquered the crowd with an aura of calm, confident power. The strength of leaders of this kind, wise Ivan Ferdinandovich had asserted, with the glint of his pince-nez fascinating the female pupils, derived from a natural psychological defect – they felt no fear of death. On the contrary, everything they did seemed intended to tempt or summon death to them: quickly, come and take me. Grammar-school girl Mironova's breast had heaved under her white apron and her cheeks had blazed bright red, she found what her teacher said so exciting.

Now, thanks to Segiur, she realised why a person like Prince Genji had wanted to join the 'Lovers of Death'. He really must be an exceptional personality, truly desperate and capable of acting in extreme ways.

'Are you ready?' he asked Ophelia.

She was already in a trance: her eyelashes were drooping, her face was blank, her lips were moving faintly.

'Yes, I'm ready,' she replied, still speaking in her normal voice.

'What was the n-name of the last Chosen One, the one who hanged himself?' Genji asked quietly, turning to Guildenstern, who was sitting beside him.

'Avaddon.'

Genji nodded and said to Ophelia: 'Summon the spirit of Avaddon.'

For about a minute nothing happened. Then Columbine felt the familiar cold breeze that always took her breath away blow over the table. The flames of the candles fluttered and Ophelia threw her head back as if it had been pushed by some invisible force.

'I'm here,' she said in a hoarse, muffled voice that sounded very like the voice of a man who had hanged himself. 'It's hard to talk. My throat's crushed.'

'We won't torment you for long.' It was strange, but as he talked to the spirit, Genji stopped stammering completely. 'Avaddon, where are you?'

'Between.'

'Between what and what?'

'Between something and nothing.'

'Ask what he's feeling now,' the Lioness whispered excitedly.

'Tell me, Avaddon, what feelings are you experiencing now?'

'Fear . . . I'm afraid . . . very afraid . . .'

Poor little Ophelia started shaking all over, her teeth even started chattering, and her pink little lips turned purple.

'Why did you decide to leave this life?'

'I was sent a Sign.'

Everybody held their breath.

'What Sign?'

The spirit didn't answer for a long time. Ophelia opened and closed her mouth without making any sound, her forehead wrinkled up as if she was trying very hard to listen to something, her nostrils distended. Columbine felt afraid now that the medium would start talking meaningless gibberish, as she had during all the latest seances.

'Howling . . .' Ophelia exclaimed hoarsely. 'A terrible, eerie howling . . . A voice calling me . . . It's a Beast . . . She has sent a Beast for me . . . I can't bear it! One more line, just write the last line, and then no more, no more, no more. Oh, where am I? Oh, where am I? Oh, where am I?'

After that the words became unintelligible. Ophelia was shaking all over. She suddenly opened her eyes, and there was such inexpressible horror in them that several people cried out.

'Go back! Go back immediately!' Genji exclaimed abruptly. 'Go in peace, Avaddon. And you, Ophelia, come to me. This way, this way . . . Calmly now.'

She gradually came round. She shuddered and started sobbing. The Lioness hugged her, kissed her on the top of her head and murmured something reassuring.

But Columbine sat there, overwhelmed by the blood-chilling revelation. A Sign! The Sign of the Beast! Death had sent a Beast to Avaddon, her Chosen One! 'The Beast is near!' 'The sated Beast!' It wasn't a metaphor, not just a figure of speech!

At that moment she glanced round and saw Prospero standing in the doorway that led from the drawing room into the hallway and watching everyone who had taken part in the seance. There was a strange, lost expression frozen on his face. She suddenly felt so sorry for him – no words could have expressed it! In Christ's twelve disciples, there had only been one Judas, but here every one of them had betrayed and abandoned their teacher.

She jumped to her feet impetuously and walked over to Prospero, but he didn't even glance at her – he was looking at Ophelia and slowly shaking his head, as if he couldn't believe what he saw.

The aspirants started to leave, talking among themselves in low voices.

Columbine waited for them all to go. Then she would be left alone with the Doge and she would show him that there were such things as true devotion and love in the world. Today she would not be his submissive puppet, but his genuine lover. Their relationship would be changed once and for all! Never again would he feel betrayed and alone!

Then Prospero spoke those cherished words, but they were not addressed to Columbine.

He beckoned to Ophelia with one finger and said in a quiet voice: 'Stay. I'm worried about you.'

Then he took her by the hand and led her after him into the depths of the house.

She trotted along behind submissively – small, pale and exhausted after associating with the spirits. But her little face was aglow with joyful surprise. Well, she might be half-witted, but she was still a woman! Unable to bear the sight of that idiotic smile, Columbine stamped her foot, dashed headlong out of the house, and then strode backwards and forwards in front of the porch, not really sure what to do or where to go.

Just then Genji came out, glanced thoughtfully at the distressed young lady and bowed.

'The hour is late. Will you allow m-me to see you home, Mademoiselle Columbine?'

'I'm not afraid of wandering through the night alone,' she answered in a faltering voice and then couldn't go on as the sobs rose in her throat.

'Nonetheless, I will escort you,' Genji said resolutely.

He took her by the arm and led her away from that cursed house. She didn't have the strength to argue or refuse.

'Strange,' Genji said pensively, seeming not to notice the state his companion was in. 'I always used to think that spiritualism was a f-fraud or, at best, self-deception. But Mademoiselle Ophelia does not seem like a liar or a hysterical girl. She's an interesting specimen. And what she t-told us is also extremely interesting.'

'Really?' Columbine asked, squinting sideways at the Japanese prince and sniffing inelegantly.

A melancholy thought came to her: Even this one finds Ophelia more interesting than me.

She was found by a boatman

She was found by a boatman. The hem of her dress had caught on one of the piers of the Ustinsky Bridge, where the Yauza joins the River Moscow. She was swaying there, in the murky green water, her loose hair rippling like waterweed in the current. It was Genji who told me, he knows everything and he has connections everywhere. He even has informers in the police.

First she disappeared, and Prospero didn't gather us together for two days, because the seances were impossible without her in any case.

During those days, I didn't know what to do with myself. I went to the general shop once and bought half a pound of tea and two *baumkuchen* pastries for four kopecks each. I nibbled on one, but didn't even touch the other. I went out to have lunch at the small local restaurant, read the entire menu and only ordered Seltzer water. The rest of the time I simply sat on the bed and looked at the wall. I wasn't there. I didn't feel hungry at all. Or sleepy.

It was as if the doll had been put back in her dusty box, and she just lay there, staring at the ceiling with her glass eyes. There was no reason to go anywhere. I tried writing a poem, but I couldn't. Apparently I can't manage any longer without our meetings, without Prospero. I can't manage at all.

Pierrot came and talked about some nonsense or other, I hardly even listened. He took my hand and squeezed it and kissed it for a long time. It tickled, and then I got fed up of it, and I pulled my hand away.

Yesterday the Lioness of Ecstasy unexpectedly came to call and stayed for a long time. I was flattered by this visit. She's talkative, with broad, sweeping gestures, and she smokes *papirosas* all the time. She's amusing to be with, only she seems unhappy somehow, although she claims that she lives a full life. She thinks of herself as a great connoisseur of men. She said that Prospero was probably once badly hurt or humiliated by a woman and so he's afraid of them, he doesn't let them get close to him and prefers to torment them. Then she looked at me expectantly, waiting to see if I would offer any revelations. But I didn't. Then the Lioness started making confessions of her own. She has two lovers, both well-known men (she said it with the meaning of 'too well-known') – the editor of a newspaper and a certain Great Poet. They adore her immeasurably, but she toys with them as if they were pet dogs. 'The secret of handling men is simple,' the Lioness lectured me. 'If you don't know this secret, they become dangerous and unpredictable. But they're basically primitive and easy to manage. No matter how old he might be or what high position he might hold, deep in his heart every one of them is a boy, an adolescent. You have to treat a man like a one-year-old bulldog – the foolish creature's teeth have already grown, so it's best not to tease him, but you must not be afraid of him. Flatter them a little, intrigue them a little, scratch them behind the ear every now and then, do not torment them too long, otherwise their attention will be caught by another bone that is more accessible. Deal with them like this, my child, and you will see that a man is the very dearest of creatures: undemanding, useful and very, very grateful.'

Lorelei lectured me in this way for a long time, but I sensed this was not what she had come for. And then, evidently having taken a decision, she said something that set me quivering with excitement.

Here are her precise words: 'I have to share this with someone,' the Lioness murmured, interrupting her own peroration in mid-word. 'With one of us, and it has to be a woman. But not with Ophelia! And anyway, no one knows where she's got to. That only leaves you, dear

Columbine . . . Of course, I ought to keep quiet about it, but I'm absolutely bursting. Here I've been telling you all sorts of nonsense about my lovers. They're just baubles, pitiful surrogates who help to fill at least a part of the hole in my soul. I don't need them any longer.' She lowered her voice and clutched the mother-of-pearl watch hanging round her neck in a plump hand spangled with rings. 'I think I have been chosen,' she told me in a terrible whisper. 'And without any seances. The Tsarevich Death has sent me a sign. "But in the sacred darkness his eye will not descry the lone black rose", that's what I wrote. But he did notice it and he has made it clear to me in no uncertain terms. The Sign has already been given twice! There can hardly be any more doubt!'

Of course, I started showering her with questions, but she suddenly fell silent and her plump face contorted in fright.

'Oh Lord, what if he's offended with me because I gossip about it? What if there won't be a third Sign now?'

And she ran out, all flustered, leaving me to be devoured by envy – which has been my entire lot just recently.

How I had envied Ophelia! How I had hated her. How I had wanted to be in her place!

But it had turned out that her place was the murky water under the Ustinsky Bridge, where rubbish floats on the surface and fat leeches wriggle in the silt.

Genji rang the doorbell at four minutes to five – I was lying on the bed and watching the face of the clock for want of anything better to do.

'She's b-been found,' he said when I opened the door.

'Who?' I asked.

'Who?' he repeated in surprise. 'Ophelia!'

One of his acquaintances in the police had told him about a drowned woman found in the Yauza whose description matched the missing girl. Genji had already been to the morgue, but he hadn't been able to provide a positive identification; after all, he had only seen her in a dark room, and her face had changed.

'I went to Prospero's house, but he wasn't at home,' said Genji. 'You're the only aspirant whose address I know, and that's only b-because I happened to walk you home once. Let's go, Columbine . . .'

And so we went . . .

Yes, it was Ophelia, without the slightest doubt. The attendant jerked back the dirty grey sheet with its sickening blotches and I saw the skinny little body stretched out on a narrow zinc-covered table, the sharp features of the little face, the familiar half-smile frozen on her bloodless lips. Ophelia was lying there completely naked: I could see her thin collarbones and ribs and her sharp hips through her bluish skin; her hands were clenched into tiny little fists. For a moment I thought the body looked like a plucked chicken.

If the Eternal Bridegroom chooses me, will I lie there like that too – naked, with glassy eyes, and will the drunk attendant hang an oilcloth number on my foot?

I had a fit of genuine hysterics.

'She didn't want to die! She shouldn't have died!' I shouted, sobbing on Genji's chest in an absolutely pitiful fashion. 'She wasn't even a real aspirant! He couldn't have chosen her!'

'Who is he?'

'Death!'

'Then why say "he", instead of "she"?'

I didn't explain to the slow-witted dunce about *der Tod*: instead I surprised even myself by showering him with reproaches.

'Why did you bring me to this dreadful place? You're lying when you say you couldn't identify her! She hasn't changed all that much! You deliberately wanted to make me suffer!'

And then he said quietly, but very clearly: 'You're right. I wanted you t-to see her like this.'

'But . . . but why?' I asked, choking on my indignation.

'To wake you up. To make you realise that this insanity has to be stopped,' said Genji, nodding towards the blue body of the drowned woman. 'No m-more deaths. That's why I joined your society.'

'So you don't want to be Death's Bridegroom, then?' I asked stupidly.

'I have already played that p-part once, many years ago,' he replied with a sombre air. 'I thought I was marrying a beautiful young woman, but instead I married death. Once is enough.'

I didn't understand this allegory. In fact, I couldn't understand anything at all.

'But you fired the revolver!' I exclaimed, remembering. 'And twice! Prospero told us. Or was that some kind of trick?'

He shrugged one shoulder, seeming slightly embarrassed.

'Something of the kind. You see, Mademoiselle Columbine, in some ways, I'm quite a rare phenomenon: I always win at any game of chance. I don't know how to explain this anomaly, but I came to terms with it a long time ago and sometimes make use of it for practical purposes, as I did during my meeting with Mr Prospero. Even if there had been b-bullets in four out of the five chambers, I would quite certainly have got the empty one. But one chance of death against four of life is simply a joke.'

I didn't know how to take this bizarre explanation. Was it plain ordinary bragging or did he really have some special relationship with fate?

Genji said: 'Do not forget what you have seen here. And for God's sake, don't do anything stupid, no matter what miraculous signs may be manifested to you. I shall destroy this loathsome temple of corpse worship. Oh yes, I haven't told you yet – a messenger brought me a note from Prospero. You're certain to get one t-today as well. The meetings are to recommence. We are expected tomorrow at nine, as usual.'

I immediately forgot about Genji and his plans for destruction, and even about the cold mortuary, with its stench of decay.

Tomorrow! Tomorrow evening I shall see him again! I shall awake and start to live again.

She thought him magically handsome

Today I shall present to you the very finest of my inventions!' the Doge declared, as he swept into the dimly lit drawing room.

Columbine thought him magically handsome in his crimson velvet blouse with a cambric frill, a beret tilted on one side of his head and short suede boots. A genuine Mephistopheles! The resemblance was emphasised by the dagger glittering with precious stones hanging at his side.

A brief gust of air followed him in through the door and the candles on the table fluttered and went out, leaving only the uncertain light of the brazier.

The Doge drew his dagger from its sheath, touched each candle with it in turn and – wonder of wonders – they lit up again, one after another.

Then Prospero glanced round at the assembled company, and everyone's eyes lit up just as the candles had done a moment earlier. Columbine felt the usual effect of that hypnotic glance. She was suddenly feverish and found it hard to breathe; she felt that she was finally waking up at last, emerging from a hibernation that had lasted for three whole days while there had not been any evening meetings.

Columbine and also, she assumed, all the others, were swept away by the most magical and wonderful feeling that anyone can experience – the anticipation of a miracle.

The sorcerer halted by the table, and it was only then that

most of those present noticed that all the chairs except one, the chairman's, had disappeared, and there was something covered with a patterned shawl lying in the middle of the table: something large, high and round, like a wedding cake.

'I used to be an engineer and, so they say, quite a good one,' said the Doge, smiling slyly into his grey moustache. 'But I assure you, none of my inventions can compare with the brilliant simplicity of this one. Ophelia has been united with the Eternal Bridegroom. We are glad for her, but now who will help us to maintain contact with the World Beyond? I have racked my brains over this problem and found an answer. What informs a man most clearly and unambiguously of the attitude that fate takes toward him?'

He waited a moment for an answer, but none of the eleven seekers spoke.

'Come now!' Prospero encouraged them. 'It was one of you who gave me the idea of the solution – Prince Genji.'

Everybody looked at Genji. He was frowning at the Doge, as if suspecting some cunning trick.

'Blind chance,' Prospero declared triumphantly. 'Nothing has keener sight than blind chance! It is the will of the Supreme Judge. A spiritualist seance is an unnecessary affectation, an entertainment for bored, hysterical ladies. But here everything will be simple and clear, without words.'

And, so saying, he jerked the shawl off the table. Something brightly coloured and round glinted with a hundred brilliant points of light. A roulette wheel! An ordinary roulette wheel, the kind to be seen in any casino.

However, when the seekers crowded round the table and examined the wheel more closely, it transpired that this wheel of fortune had one unusual feature: where the double zero ought to have been, there was a white skull and crossbones.

'This invention is called the "Wheel of Death". Now everyone will be able to ascertain his own relationship with the Eternal Bride,' said Prospero. 'And here is your new medium.' He opened his hand, and there, glittering on his palm, was a small golden ball. 'This whimsical piece of metal, which at first glance would not appear to be subject to anybody's will, will become the messenger of love.'

'But surely messages can be sent by other means too?' the Lioness of Ecstasy asked in anxious alarm. 'Or can it now only be through the roulette wheel?'

She's worried about her Signs, Columbine guessed. After all, the Lioness and the Tsarevich have established their own secret relationship. I wonder what it is. What kind of Signs does he send her?

'I am not Death's personal interpreter,' the Doge said in a stern, sad voice. 'I do not have absolute mastery of her language. How would I know what means she might choose to inform her Chosen Ones that their feelings are reciprocated? But this means of communicating with fate appears irrefutable to me. It is similar to the means used by the ancients to elicit from the oracle the will of Morta, the Goddess of Death.'

The Lioness of Ecstasy seemed completely satisfied with this answer, and she walked away from the table with an air of superiority.

'Every one of you will have an equal chance,' Prospero continued. 'Anyone who feels ready, whose spirit is sufficiently strong, may try his or her luck today. The lucky player who throws the ball so that it lands on the death's head is the Chosen One.'

Cyrano asked: 'What if everyone tries their luck and no one wins? Do we carry on spinning the wheel all night long?'

'Indeed, the probability of success is not very high.' Prospero agreed. 'One chance out of thirty-eight. If no one is lucky, then Death has not yet made her choice and the game will be continued the next time. Agreed?'

The first to respond was Caliban.

'An excellent idea, Teacher! At least everything will be fair, with no favourites. That Ophelia of yours couldn't stand me. I'd have been waiting till the end of the century with her seances. And by the way, some people who arrived after me have already scooped the prize. But now everything will be fair. Fortune can't be duped! Only you ought to let us keep on trying our luck until we get a result.'

'It will be as I have said,' the Doge interrupted him sternly. 'Death is not a bride who can be dragged to the altar by force.'

'But surely only someone who is morally prepared can throw the ball? Participation in the game is not compulsory?' Kriton asked in a quiet voice. When the Doge nodded in agreement, he declared in relief: 'I'd really had quite enough of all that spiritualist wailing. The roulette is quicker, and there are no doubts.'

'I think the idea of this game of chance is vulgar,' Gdlevsky said with a shrug. 'Death is not a croupier in a white shirt-front. Her Signs must be more poetic and exalted. But we can spin the little ball round and round to titillate our nerves. Why not?'

Lorelei exclaimed passionately: 'You are right, my radiant boy. This device does belittle the majesty of Death. But there is one thing you have not taken into account. Death is no snob, and he will talk to anyone who is in love with him in a language that she can understand. Let them spin their wheel, what does that matter to you and me?'

Columbine noticed that Caliban, who envied both of the poetical luminaries and was jealous of their relationship with the Doge, cringed at these words.

The anatomist Horatio cleared his throat, adjusted his pince-nez and enquired in a businesslike voice: 'Very well, let us assume that one of us has landed on the skull. Then what? What action, so to speak, is taken after that? Does the lucky winner immediately go dashing off to hang himself or drown himself? Surely you agree that performing this act requires a certain degree of preparation? But if it is postponed until the next morning, then weakness may stir in a person's soul. Would it not be an insult to Death and all of us if her Chosen One were to . . . mmm . . . leave her standing at the altar? Pardon me for being so direct, but I am not entirely sure of all our members.'

'Are you . . . Are you alluding to me?' Petya cried out in a trembling voice. 'How dare you! Just because I have been in the club for a long time and am still alive, it doesn't mean that I am avoiding it or playing the coward. I have been waiting for a message from the spirits! And I'm willing to spin the roulette wheel first!'

Petya's emotional outburst took Columbine by surprise – she had imagined that the anatomist's thrust was directed against her. But if the cap fits . . . She had just that moment imagined that she would have to die today, and the thought had been so unbearable that she had started trembling in fear.

Prospero raised his hand to call for silence.

'Do not be concerned, I have taken care of everything.' He pointed to the door. 'Through there, in the study, there is a glass of malmsey. And dissolved in the wine is cyanide, the most noble of poisons. The Chosen One will drain the wedding cup, then walk along the street to the boulevard, sit on a bench, and a quarter of an hour later he or she will fall into a quiet sleep. It is a good way to depart. With no pain and no regrets.'

'That's a different matter,' said Horatio, chewing on his lips. 'In that case I'm in favour.'

The twins exchanged glances and Guildenstern spoke for both of them: 'Yes, we like this method better than spiritualism. Mathematical *Wahrscheinlichkeit*[1] is more serious than the voices of the spirits.'

Someone touched Columbine's elbow. Turning round, she saw Genji.

'How do you like Prospero's invention?' he asked in a low voice. 'You're the only one who hasn't s-said anything.'

'I don't know. I feel like all the others.'

1. Probability

It was strange – never before had she felt so alive as during these moments that might be the last before her death.

'Prospero is a genuine magician,' Columbine whispered excitedly. 'Who else could fill our souls with this tremulous, all-embracing rapture of existence? "All that threatens ruin is fraught with delight for the mortal heart." Oh, how true that is! "Perhaps the pledge of immortality"!'

'You mean to say that if your ball lands on the skull, you will d-dutifully drink that lousy muck?'

Columbine imagined the treacherous wine flowing in a rivulet of fire down her throat and into her body, and she shuddered. And the most terrible thing would be to get through those final fifteen minutes, with your heart still beating and your mind still wakeful, but with no way back, because you are already a living corpse. Who would find the dead body on the bench, and when? And what if it was sitting there slumped over with its eyes goggling and saliva dribbling from its open mouth?

She imagined it so vividly that it set her lips trembling and her eyelashes fluttering.

'Don't be afraid,' Genji whispered, squeezing her elbow to reassure her. 'You won't land on the skull.'

'Why are you so sure?' she asked, offended. 'Do you think that Death could not choose me? That I am unworthy to be her lover?'

He sighed.

'Ah indeed, our Russian soil is not yet ready for Mr Prospero's teachings, that much is clear from basic grammar. What was that you just said? "*Her* lover". That smacks of perversion.'

Columbine realised that he was trying to cheer her up and she attempted to smile, but it came out forced.

Genji repeated what he had said, speaking in a perfectly serious voice.

'Don't be afraid. You won't have to drink poison, because *I* am certain to land on the p-precious skull.'

'But you're afraid yourself!' she guessed, and her own fear

immediately receded to make way for gloating. 'So much for your desperate personality – you're afraid too! You're only playing the part of a superman, but actually you're afraid of the end, just like everyone else.'

Genji shrugged.

'I t-told you about my special relationship with Fortune.'

And he walked away.

Meanwhile everything was ready for the ritual.

The Doge raised one hand in the air, calling the aspirants to silence. He was holding the small ball between his fore-finger and thumb and it sparkled and flashed like a bright little golden star.

'And so, ladies and gentlemen. Who feels ready? Who is the first?'

Genji immediately threw up his hand, but his rivals' response was more energetic.

Caliban and Rosencrantz, Columbine's timid admirer, exclaimed in chorus: 'Me! Me!'

The bookkeeper glared at his rival as if he wanted to tear him to pieces. But Rosencrantz gave Columbine a haughty smile and was rewarded with a gentle smile of approval.

Neither they nor Prospero had noticed Genji's reserved gesture.

'Boy!' Caliban fumed. 'How dare you? I'm first! I'm older, and I've been a member of the club for longer!'

But the quiet little German lowered his head like a bull and was obviously not prepared to give way.

Then Caliban appealed to the Doge.

'What is all this, Teacher? A Russian can't breathe in his own country any longer! Whichever way you spit, there's nothing but Germans and Polacks and Yids and Caucasians! And they not only prevent us from living, they even try to jump the queue to the next world! You decide for us!'

Prospero said sternly: 'You should be ashamed, Caliban. Surely you do not think that the Eternal Beloved attaches any importance to nonsensical trifles such as nationality or creed? As punishment for your rudeness and impatience you shall be second, after Rosencrantz.'

The former ship's bookkeeper stamped his foot angrily, but he didn't dare to argue.

'I beg your pardon,' Genji put in, 'but I raised my hand even before these gentlemen put in their bids.'

'This is not an auction at which you can signal with gestures,' the Doge snapped. 'You should have stated your intention out loud. You will be third. If, that is, your turn comes.'

That was the end of the discussion. Columbine noticed that Genji was very annoyed and even slightly alarmed. She recalled the threat he had made the day before to disband the club of 'Lovers of Death' and wondered how he could do it. After all, the aspirants didn't meet here under compulsion.

Rosencrantz took the ball from the Doge, looked at it closely and suddenly crossed himself. Columbine was so startled by this unexpected gesture that she gasped in compassion. The Baltic German span the roulette wheel and then played a trick that was entirely unlike him: looking straight at his young female sympathiser, he gave the ball a quick kiss before tossing it resolutely on to the rim of the wheel.

While it was spinning – and it went on for an eternity – Columbine moved her lips in a prayer to Death, Fate and God (she did not know whose) for the boy's throw not to land in the fatal pocket.

'Twenty-eight,' Prospero announced dispassionately and everyone sighed in chorus.

Pale-faced Rosencrantz declared with dignity: '*Schade*.'[2]

He walked away from the wheel. He didn't look at Columbine any more, evidently feeing that he had already made enough of an impression. And in all honesty, he had. She thought that desperate kiss had made Rosencrantz look terribly sweet. But alas, Columbine's heart belonged to another.

2. A pity

'Come on, give me that,' Caliban said impatiently, grabbing the ball. 'I have a feeling I'm going to be lucky.'

He spat three times over his left shoulder, span the roulette wheel with all his strength and tossed the little ball so that it went skipping across the pockets and almost flew over the edge.

Everybody froze as they watched the spinning wheel gradually slow down. When its impetus was spent, the ball landed on the skull! A howl of triumph erupted from the bookkeeper's chest, but the next moment the little golden sphere tumbled across the dividing line as if attracted by some strange force, and settled in the next pocket.

Someone giggled hysterically – Columbine thought it was Petya. Caliban stood there as if he had been struck by lightning.

Then he croaked, 'I'm not forgiven! I'm rejected!' And he dashed towards the door, sobbing desolately.

Prospero sighed and said: 'As you can see, Death informs us of her will unambiguously. Well now, would you care to try your luck?'

The question was addressed to Genji, who nodded politely and performed the necessary procedure quickly and efficiently, with no affectation: he span the roulette wheel gently, casually dropped in the ball and then didn't even watch it, but looked at the Doge.

'The skull!' squealed the Lioness.

'Ha! That's quite a trick!' Gdlevsky declared in a ringing voice.

Then everyone started shouting and talking at once and Columbine involuntarily groaned: 'No!'

She didn't understand why herself.

No, perhaps she did.

This man whom she had only known for such a short time radiated an aura of calm, confident strength. When she was with him the world somehow felt bright and clear, it was if she were transformed from Columbine, who had strayed into the dark wings of the stage, back into the old Masha

Mironova. But there was clearly no way back – Genji's fatal throw was the proof of that.

'Please accept my congratulations,' Prospero said solemnly. 'You are a lucky man and we all envy you. Goodbye until tomorrow, my friends. Let us go, Genji.'

The Doge turned away and walked slowly through into the next room, leaving the doors open.

Before he followed him, Genji turned towards Columbine and smiled – as if he were trying to comfort her.

But he failed.

She ran out into the street, choking on her sobs.

III. From the 'Agents' Reports' File

To His Honour Lieutenant-Colonel Besikov
(Private and confidential)

Dear Lieutenant-Colonel,

An entirely new side has been revealed to the story of the 'Lovers of Death' and the part played by the Doge in all of these events.

I am writing this letter at night, with recent impressions still fresh in my mind. I have just returned from the Doge's apartment, where I was witness to truly astounding events. Oh, how easy it is to be mistaken about people!

I beg your pardon for a certain degree of incoherence – I am still very excited. Let me try to set everything out in the correct order.

Today the society resumed its regular meetings, which had been interrupted by the disappearance of the medium. I must confess that I had expected the loss of our Vestal Virgin to throw the Doge into disarray and deprive him of his most dangerous weapon, but he has proved extremely enterprising and inventive. The substitute that he has found for spiritualism is brilliantly simple: a roulette wheel on which one of the divisions is marked with a skull and crossbones. If anyone lands on this grim symbol of death, he has to drink poison prepared by the Doge in person.

I felt encouraged when I heard all this, since I decided that the man whom I regarded as the devil incarnate had finally abandoned his habit of caution and now it would be possible to catch him red-handed.

I was lucky. Today, on the very first evening of this game,

which is certainly the most hazardous known to mortal man, there was a winner – the very same Stammerer concerning whom I have already had the honour of reporting to you, and whom you, for some reason, found so very interesting. He is a most unusual individual, I have seen and heard enough to be quite sure of that, but how could you know him? A mystery.

However, I must not deviate from my subject.

When all the other members had left, I hid in the hallway and then went back into the drawing room, where the candles and the brazier had already been extinguished. It was very helpful that for certain reasons of principle the Doge does not believe in having servants.

My plan was very simple. I was counting on obtaining direct proof of the Doge's guilt. To do that, it was sufficient to slip through the dining room, open the door into the study slightly (all the doors in the house are upholstered with soft leather, and so they do not close tightly) and wait for the master of the house to offer the Stammerer the cup of poisoned wine with his own hands. After painful deliberations, I had come to the conclusion that the Stammerer would have to be sacrificed for the sake of the cause – there was nothing that could be done about that. In the final analysis, I reasoned, the life of one man does not outweigh the chance to avert a threat to dozens, or perhaps even hundreds, of immature souls.

I was going to wait for the Stammerer to drink the poison and go out to die on the boulevard (that was the arrangement reached earlier) and then call the constable who always stands on Trubnaya Square. The death by poisoning would be recorded by a representative of authority, and if the Stammerer had not lost consciousness by the time the policeman appeared, and if he had even a shred of conscience, he would still be able to testify against the Doge, and his testimony would be incorporated in the report. But even without this testimony, I thought, the very fact of the death and my evidence would still be enough. The constable and I would immediately set out for the Doge's apartment and detain the criminal at the scene of his crime. He would be unlikely to have already washed the glass, and there would still be traces of cyanide on it. And in addition there would be a live witness – me. And also the roulette wheel with the skull.

You must admit that it was rather a good plan. At the very least, the Doge's part in everything would have been revealed in a most unattractive light: he had organised a deadly dangerous game at his own home, but he himself did not take part; he had prepared the poison and served it to the victim himself. And there would have been the result of all these actions – a body that was still warm. This is quite obviously a serious criminal offence. At the same time, I had reason to hope that I would be able to persuade two, if not three, of the least convinced 'lovers' to give evidence for the prosecution if the case went as far as court proceedings.

But now let me tell you what actually happened.

I managed to open the door slightly without making a sound, and since it was quite dark in the drawing room I could not only hear, but also see what was happening in the study without any risk of being discovered.

The Master was sitting in his chair at the desk with a triumphant, almost majestic air. Glinting on the polished surface of the desk was a crystal goblet, containing a liquid the colour of pomegranate juice.

The Stammerer was standing by the desk, and so the scene was rather reminiscent of the artist Ge's picture *Peter the Great Questioning the Tsarevich Alexei*. How often I have imagined myself as the captive Tsarevich: I stand in front of the formidable Peter, wholly and completely in his power, and my heart is wrung by a sweet feeling in which the awareness that I am absolutely defenceless, the fear of punishment and the hope of paternal mercy are all mingled together. But then, unlike the Tsarevich, the Stammerer was gazing straight at the seated man without the slightest sign of fear. I could not help being amazed at such presence of mind in a man who was destined to depart from this life in a matter of only a few minutes.

Neither of them spoke, and the pause seemed to go on forever. The Stammerer was looking hard straight into the Doge's eyes, and the Doge started to seem a little bewildered.

'I really do feel quite sorry,' he said, sounding slightly embarrassed, which in ordinary circumstances is not typical of him at all, 'that this lot has fallen to you.'

'Why so?' the Stammerer asked in a steady voice. 'After all, this is the greatest good fortune, is it not?'

Seeming even more embarrassed, the Doge hastily agreed: 'Yes, yes, of course. I am certain that all the other seekers – or almost all of them – would be glad to be in your place . . . All I meant to say was that I regret parting with you so soon. You intrigue me, and we still haven't had a chance for a heart-to-heart talk.'

'Well, then,' the Stammerer said, in the same even voice. 'Let's have a heart-to-heart talk now. I'm not in any hurry. Are you?'

I had the impression that the Doge was glad to hear these words. 'Excellent, let us talk,' he said. 'I couldn't really understand why a mature and apparently self-sufficient individual like you was so eager to become one of my disciples. In fact, the more I thought about it, the stranger it seemed. By character you are an individualist, and not at all like the seeker who recently hanged himself. If you have serious reasons to wish to die, you could quite easily have managed without all these ceremonies.'

'But the ceremonies you invent are so amusing. And I, sir, am a very curious man.'

'Ah, yes,' the Doge mused, looking up at the other man. 'You certainly are a curious man.'

'Oh, no more so than yourself, Mr Blagovolsky,' the Stammerer said.

Later it will become clear to you why I now consider it possible to reveal to you the Doge's real name (by the way, in the club he goes by the name of 'Prospero'). But then, I should also say that I had not known his name previously and heard it spoken for the first time by the Stammerer.

The Doge shrugged. 'Well, so you have made enquiries about me and found out my real name. Why did you need to do that?'

'I had to find out as much about you as possible. And I managed to do it. Moscow is my city. I have many acquaintances here, some of them in the most surprising places.'

'Then what have your acquaintances who inhabit the most surprising places discovered about me?' the Doge enquired ironically, but I could see that he was uneasy.

'A lot. For instance, that while you were serving a seventeen-year sentence in the Schliesselburg Fortress, you tried to end your own life on three occasions. The first time, in 1879, you went on hunger strike in protest against the conditions imposed on your comrades, who had been deprived of the right to take exercise outside their cells by the prison authorities. There were three of you on the strike. On the twenty-first day you, and only you, agreed to take food. The other two remained intransigent and died.'

The Doge cringed against the back of his armchair, but the Stammerer continued implacably: 'The second time was even worse. In April 1881 you attempted to commit self-immolation after the prison commandant sentenced you to an exemplary flogging for replying disrespectfully to an inspector. Somehow you managed to obtain matches, pour the kerosene out of a lamp and impregnate your prison robe with it, but you couldn't bring yourself to ignite the blaze. After you were subjected to corporal punishment, you wove a noose out of threads, hung it from one of the bars on the window and were on the point of hanging yourself, but once again at the last moment you changed your mind and did not wish to die. When you were already floundering in the noose, you grabbed hold of the window ledge and started calling loudly for help. The jailers took you down and sent you to the punishment cell . . . From that time until you were released on the occasion of the coronation of His Majesty the Emperor, you caused no more trouble and made no more attempts at suicide. Your relations with the Death whom you adore seem rather strange, Sergei Irinarkhovich.'

I assume, Vissarion Vissarionovich, that it will not be difficult for you to check the correctness of the information adduced by the Stammerer through your own professional connections, but I do not have the slightest doubt concerning its authenticity – it was enough for me to see the Doge's response. He covered his face with his hands, sobbed several times and generally looked pitiful in the extreme. If the aspirants had been shown their godlike Teacher at that moment, it would have caused a real furore. I remember thinking: It is beyond all understanding how Death could choose a sniveller like this as her instrument! Surely a more worthy helper could have been found? I even felt sorry for her, the poor noseless creature.

There was another lengthy pause. The Doge carried on sobbing and blowing his nose, and the Stammerer waited for him to pull himself together. Eventually Blagovolsky (how strange it feels for me to call him that) said: 'Are you from the police? Yes, of course, how else could you have found out . . . But then, no, you can't be from the police – you wouldn't have toyed with Death so lightly when you spun the drum of the Bulldog. It's my revolver, after all, and the bullets in it were real, I ought to know. Who are you? By the way, would you like to sit down?' He indicated a heavy oak armchair facing the desk.

The Stammerer shook his head, laughed and said: 'Well, let's just say that I represent the secret club of "Lovers of Life". Consider that I have been sent to inspect your establishment – to see if you are breaking any of the rules, not playing fair. I am resolutely opposed to suicide, with the exception of certain special cases when to leave this life is not really suicide at all. At the same time, unlike the fathers of the Christian church, I believe that every man is free to do as he wishes with his own life, and if he has decided to destroy himself, then that is his right. But only if, Sergei Irinarkhovich, the fatal decision was really taken independently, with no urging or compulsion. It is quite a different matter when someone else soaps the noose for an individual who is highly impressionable or easily influenced, especially someone very young, or helpfully hands them the revolver, or sets out the cup of poison.'

'Oh, how mistaken you are about me!' the Doge cried out in extreme agitation, interrupting the Stammerer (who, as it happens, had not stammered even once in the course of the above speech). 'I am a weak, sinful man! Yes I am terribly afraid of Death, she petrifies me! More than that, I hate her! She is my very worst enemy. I am scorched and poisoned forever by the foul stench that she has breathed into my face three times. No doubt you were only speaking figuratively about the "Lovers of Life", but if such an organisation really did exist, I would be its most fanatical member!'

The Stammerer shook his head incredulously. 'Really? Then how am I to explain your activities?'

'By this very thing, my dear sir! Explain them by this very thing! I have entered into single combat with the cruel, ravenous monster that has been abducting the purest and most precious of society's children. In recent times how many people, mostly young and unspoiled, have been taking their own lives! This is a terrible degenerative disease of the soul, a gift to us from a jaded and faithless Europe. I do not destroy my disciples, as you imagined on the basis of external appearances. I do not kill tender young souls, I try to save them!' He jerked his chin nervously. 'Listen, would you not like to sit down? I have arthritis, it's devilish uncomfortable for me to hold my head back all the time.'

'You chose a strange way of saving delicate young souls,' said the Stammerer, sitting down in the armchair.

'Certainly it is strange! But effective, very effective. My club, the "Lovers of Death" is a kind of clinic for the mentally ill, and I am like the psychiatrist. After all, I do not accept

as members romantically inclined youths who have succumbed to fashionable influences and simply wish to appear
interesting to their friends, but only those who are genuinely
obsessed with the idea of death, who have already set the
revolver to their temple. I catch them at this dangerous
moment, engage their morbid attention and try to lead
them away from taking the fatal step. First of all, I free the
potential suicide from his isolation and the feeling of his own
infinite loneliness. A desperate man sees that there are many
others like him and there are people whose suffering is
possibly even worse than his own. This is extraordinarily
important! That is the way we are all made – in order to
survive we need to know that there is someone in the world
who is less fortunate than ourselves. The second major
component of my "treatment" is the resurrection of *curiosity*.
The near-suicide has to stop being concerned only with
himself and start looking in amazement at the world around
him. To this end all means are good, even those that use
quackery. I shamelessly dupe the seekers with all sorts of
cunning tricks and impressive trumpery.'

The Doge pointed casually to his Spanish beret and medieval dagger.

The Stammerer nodded: 'Oh yes, like lighting candles with
a knife-blade that has been smeared with phosphorous.
That's an old trick.'

'Or holding a burning coal on a hand that has been rubbed
with a mixture of egg-white, resin and starch, which protects
the skin from burning,' the Doge put in. 'Anything that
impresses them and makes them submit to your will is
useful . . . Oh, don't smile in that shrewd fashion! You think
I have given myself away by mentioning submission. Believe
me, I am only too well aware of my weaknesses. Of course,
apart from the main goal, I also derive a lot of pleasure from
this game. I won't try to pretend that I don't enjoy having
power over people's souls, I find their adoration and boundless trust intoxicating, but I swear to you that I never use the
power I have acquired for evil! I invent all these complicated

and basically ludicrous rituals only in order to mesmerise the potential suicide, to distract him, to stimulate interest in the eternal mystery of existence! For my observations suggest that people most often arrive at the idea of self-destruction not out of grief or hopelessness, but out of a lack of any interest in life, out of boredom! But if the true cause of the suicidal impulse lies only in poverty (which also happens quite often), then I try to help the seeker concerned with money – as far as possible in some discreet way that is not humiliating for these morbidly proud individuals.' At this point the Doge hesitated and spread his arms in a gesture of helplessness. With one finger he caught the cover of a bronze inkwell in the form of a heroic Russian warrior, raised the helmet that had been lying open, and started stroking it nervously. 'But I am not all-powerful. There are too many neglected, incurable cases. My disciples die one after another, and every one lost costs me years of my life. But still, I can see that some are close to being cured. You must have noticed from the way the seekers behaved today that some of them no longer wish to die at all. I shall not be surprised if some are frightened by the dispassionate roulette wheel and do not come here again, and that will be a genuine victory for me. I would have saved many more of my wards, if only . . .

'If only what?' the Stammerer asked, urging him on and getting up out of his chair. I believe he was just as astounded by what he had heard as I was. In any case, he had listened to the Doge very attentively, without interrupting.

But the Doge hesitated, and his face turned whiter and whiter before my very eyes. He seemed to be trying to decide if he could reveal himself completely to the other man.

Finally he made up his mind: 'If only . . . Oh, do sit down!' The Stammerer shook his head impatiently and the Doge started looking around. I saw that his face was contorted into a mask of genuine terror. 'If only I had not failed to take into account . . . that Death really does exist!'

'That is indeed a most important discovery,' the Stammerer remarked demurely.

'Don't laugh! You understand perfectly well what I mean. And if you don't, then you're not as intelligent as you seem. Death exists, not only as the end of physical existence, but as an animated substance, as an evil force that has accepted my challenge and entered into battle with me for the souls of my disciples.'

'Listen, Blagovolsky, keep all that for the Lioness of Ecstasy,' the Stammerer said with a frown.

The Doge gave a bitter smile.

'Oh, I used to be just as much a sceptic as you are. Only very recently.' He suddenly leaned forward bodily and grabbed hold of the other man's hand. He looked almost insane, and his voice dropped to a loud whisper. 'Have you not heard about the Signs? It was I who invented this additional complication, so that the aspirants would not take poor Ophelia's ululations too seriously. It was a clever idea: a summons from the spirits is not enough, you also have to receive a mystical summons from Death. And they did receive them!' the Doge shouted out, so loudly that I banged my head against the door in surprise. Thank God the moment was too tense for the two talkers to pay any attention to that dull sound.

The Doge started jabbering deliriously: 'They all received them, every one! Ophelia only had to name the next Chosen One and he immediately started receiving Signs!'

'Nonsense,' the Stammerer retorted. 'That's not possible.'

'Nonsense?' The Doge laughed darkly and his bloodshot eyes glittered. 'First there was Raven, a quiet drunk, a photographer by trade. One evening Ophelia named him as the Chosen One, and that night he jumped out of the window. I bought his farewell poem from the policeman, it talks in rather vague terms about "a vision, by means of which the call from beyond was reinforced". It's a terrible poem, simply appalling, but that's not the point. What was that vision? Who can answer that now?'

'Who knows what he might have thought he saw in his cups?' the Stammerer objected quite reasonably. 'No doubt after the spiritualist revelation your photographer celebrated his selection rather energetically.'

'It's possible, I won't deny it!' the Doge said, with a shake of his head, 'I didn't attach any importance to that line myself at first. But then, the letter had a postscript, addressed to me: "For P. No doubts remain! I am happy. Goodbye and thank you!" Thank you, eh? How do you think it felt for me to read that? But just listen to what happened next! A few days later Ophelia said in Raven's voice: "Now it is the turn of the one for whom Death's envoy will come swathed in a white cloak. Wait." I immediately felt reassured – what damned envoy, I thought, where is he going to come from? But that very night, do you hear, *that very night*' – the Master dropped his voice from a shout to a hiss again – 'two of the searchers had a vision: someone in a white cloak came to them and summoned them to unite with Death. One was a student, a very gloomy character, a hypochondriac, who called himself Lycanthrope. The other was quite different – a wonderful, pure young girl – I thought that she would soon abandon this nonsensical obsession with suicide! Tell me, Doubting Thomas, how often does it happen that two entirely different people have the same dream at the same time?'

'It can happen. If the mention of an envoy in a white cloak produces a strong impression on both of them . . .'

'Too strong an impression!' the Doge exclaimed, waving his arms in the air. 'Lycanthrope and Moretta told us about their "good fortune" at the next meeting. I tried to dissuade them. They pretended to agree with me and said they were in no hurry to commit suicide, but they colluded with each other. They left this life together, but not out of love for each other – out of love for Death . . . Before he died, Avaddon heard the voice of some Beast. And what happened to Ophelia is a complete mystery. I was with her only shortly before her terrible end. Believe me, doing away with herself was the last thing she was thinking of. Quite the opposite . . .'

He cleared his throat in embarrassment. I have already told you that this old satyr is voluptuous and eagerly exploits the blind adoration of the female seekers – they are all in love with him. They say that the late Moretta was also acquainted with his bedroom. However, that has nothing to do with the matter at hand.

'And our Lioness of Ecstasy!' he continued. 'Today this lady whispered to me that "Tsarevich Death" was courting her more gallantly than any of her numerous admirers, and sending her miraculous gifts. And this is a famous poetess, who has seen a great deal of the world, not some silly little girl who is ga-ga over decadence.'

'Mass insanity?' the Stammerer suggested with a frown. 'Some kind of infectious disease? Such cases are known to psychiatric science. In that case your initiative with the club is harmful – it does not dissipate the illusion, it merely concentrates it.'

'My God, what has illusion got to do with it? This is something far more terrible!'

The Doge jumped to his feet, but so clumsily that he knocked over the goblet standing on the desk with his broad sleeve – it fell on to the floor and shattered into pieces. This minor incident sent the conversation in a new direction.

Bending down and taking out his handkerchief, the Stammerer complained: 'Your cyanide has splashed my gaiters.' (I don't recall if I told you that he is a serious dandy and dresses according to London fashion.)

'Oh, there's no cyanide,' the Doge muttered absentmindedly, with a shudder. 'Just an ordinary sleeping draft. Anyone who drank the malmsey would have slept the sleep of the righteous on the bench on the boulevard. Then I would have phoned, anonymously, for an ambulance. In the hospital they would have washed out his stomach, and that would have been that. All the aspirants, even you, would have thought it was just a stroke of bad luck, meddling by a jealous fate.'

It seemed to me that the Stammerer had still not entirely abandoned his suspicions, because I heard a note of caution in his voice again: 'Let's assume that you could have got away with it. Once. But what would you have done the next time someone landed on the skull?'

'There wouldn't have been any next time. And even this time I have absolutely no idea how the ball managed to land there. There's a magnet under the next pocket, the number seven. The ball's only covered with a thin layer of gold plate, it's actually made of iron. You saw the way it landed on the skull and then suddenly jerked over on to the seven on Caliban's turn? It's strange the magnet didn't work on your turn.'

'There are only two explanations: either the magnet is too weak, or my luck is too strong . . .' The Stammerer murmured, as if he were talking to himself, but then he turned back to the Doge: 'What you say about an evil force sounds incredible, but I've lived in this world for a long time, and I know that incredible things sometimes happen. Carry on with what you're doing, make the seekers write poems, titillate their nerves with the roulette wheel, only put in a stronger magnet, to make sure that today's mishap is not repeated. And if you have no objections, I shall observe your "evil force".'

The Doge folded his hands together prayerfully: 'Not only do I not object, I implore you to help me. I feel as if I'm going insane!'

'So, we are allies. Tell the others what you were going to say. That I drank the wine and fell asleep on the boulevard, and then some intrusive wellwisher called an ambulance.'

They shook hands, and I hurriedly retreated to the hallway, and from there into the street.

Need I explain the feelings that I am experiencing now? I am sure you will agree, Lieutenant-Colonel, that there is no need to arrest Mr Blagovolsky. On the contrary, he should not be hindered under any circumstances. Let him carry on with his good work. For now the 'lovers' are in good hands, but if they should each go their own way, they might do more than simply take their own lives – they might even start up their own suicide clubs.

As far as the 'evil force' is concerned, that is pure hysteria, Mr Blagovolsky's imagination has become inflamed and his nerves are playing him false.

And I, naturally, will continue to keep an eye on this 'Ward No. 6'. If Prospero is the head doctor, then I (ha-ha) am the inspector.

With assurances of my most sincere respect,

ZZ
Written on the night of 4 September 1900

CHAPTER 3

I. From the Newspapers

This is the Only Way?

In memory of Lorelei Rubinstein (1860–1900)

Hang your heads low, all you lovers of Russian literature. Your hearts will surely be filled not only with grief, but with the even more sombre feelings of bewilderment and despair. For a star that shone brightly in the firmament of Russian poetry in recent years has been tragically extinguished: it has fallen and, in falling, carved a bloody furrow across our hearts.

Suicide always has a terrible effect on those who are left behind. It is as though the person who leaves us spurns and rejects God's world and all of us who dwell in it. We are no longer necessary or interesting to him. And it is a hundred times more unnatural when the person who acts in this way is a writer, whose bonds with the life of the spirit and society ought, one would think, to be especially strong.

Poor Russia! Her Shakespeares and Dantes seem to be marked down for some special deadly fate: those who are not slain by an enemy's bullet, like Pushkin, Lermontov and Marlinsky, contrive to carry out the malevolent verdict of destiny themselves.

And now yet another resounding name has been added to the martyrology of Russian literary suicides. We have only just commemorated a bitter anniversary – a quarter of a century since the death of Count A.K. Tolstoy and the effervescent Vassily Kurochkin. They both poisoned themselves. The noble Garshin threw himself down a stairwell, while in his despair Nikolai Uspensky cut his own throat with a blunt knife. Each of these losses has left an open wound on the body of our literature.

And now a poetess, the woman they called the Russian Sappho.

I knew her. I was one of those who believed in her talent, which blossomed at a mature age but promised so very much.

The reason that prompted Lorelei Rubinstein to take up the pen at an age when the first blush of youth was already behind her is well known: it was the death from consumption of the husband she passionately adored, the late M.N. Rubinstein, whom many recall as the most noble and worthy of men. Deprived of the only being dear to her heart, the childless Lorelei turned to poetry for salvation. She opened that passionate, long-suffering heart to us, her readers – opened it unhesitatingly, even shamelessly, because sincere, genuine feeling knows no shame. It was the first time in Russian poetry that sensu-

ality and passion had spoken so boldly through the lips of a woman – following the death of her beloved husband these natural impulses could find no other outlet except in her poems.

Young provincial ladies and schoolgirls secretly copied these spicy lines into their cherished albums. The poor souls were abused for it, sometimes even punished for this enthusiasm for 'immoral' poetry that could teach them nothing good. But that was only poetry! Now Lorelei has set these romantic maidens languishing in neurotic passion a far more terrible and tempting example. I fear that many will wish to copy not only her poems, but also her own terrible end . . .

I know quite certainly that she was a member of the 'Lovers of Death', where she was known as the 'Lioness of Ecstasy'. In recent weeks I was fortunate enough to become more closely acquainted with this astounding woman and was an involuntary witness of the fiery fall of her brilliant star.

No, I was not with her at that crucial moment when she took the fatal dose of morphine, but I could see that she was sinking, irrevocably sinking. I could see it, but I was powerless. Not long ago she confided to me in secret that the 'Tsarevich Death' was sending her secret signs, and she would not have to suffer the torment of life for much longer. I do not think I was the only one she told about this, but everyone regarded this confession as the fruit of her irrepressible fantasy.

Alas, fantasies can give rise to phantoms: the hard-hearted Tsarevich has come for Lorelei and taken her away from us.

Before she made the transition from this life to the history of literature, the Lioness of Ecstasy left a farewell poem. How little remains in these incoherent, impatient, *final* lines of the heady brilliance that captivated her female admirers!

No more, it's time, the call has
  come.
We shall meet later – do not keep
  me now:
Something, I know, I should
  recall before I go.
But what? But what?
            I cannot think.
My thoughts are in confusion. No
  more, it's time.
I must make haste to learn what
  there will be
Beyond the last horizon
      Forward!
      Tsarevich Death,
Come in your bloody-red apparel,
Give me your hand and lead me
  to the light,
Where I shall stand with arms
  outstretched
Like an angel, like fate, like the
  reflection
Of my own self.
    This is the only way.

What terrible words of farewell! 'This is the only way.' Are you not afraid, ladies and gentlemen? I am, very.

Lavr Zhemailo
Moscow Courier, 7 (20)
September 1900, p.1

122

II. From Columbine's Diary

Puzzles

I really am terribly fortunate to depart this life in the year
that marks the boundary between the old and new centuries. It is as if I have glanced through a door that has
opened a crack and seen nothing deserving enough of my
attention to open the door wider and walk in. I shall halt
on the threshold, flutter my wings and fly away. You can
have your cinematograph, self-propelled carriages and
tunics *à la grecque* (terribly vulgar, in my opinion). Live in
the twentieth century without me. To depart without
looking back – that is beautiful.

And on the matter of beauty. Our members talk about
it a great deal, they even elevate it to the level of a
supreme standard. Essentially, I am of the same opinion,
but a sudden thought: Who is more handsome, Prospero
or Genji! Of course, they are very different, and each
impressive in his own way. Probably nine women out of
ten would say that Genji is more interesting, in addition
to being a lot younger (although he is also very old,
about forty). But without the slightest hesitation, I prefer
Prospero, because he is more . . . significant. When I am
with Genji, I feel calm and lucid, sometimes even light-
hearted, but I am overwhelmed by an 'infinite thrill' only
in the presence of the Doge. There is magic and mystery
in him, and that weighs more heavily than superficial
beauty.

But then, of course, there is quite a lot of mystery about

Genji too. In the last few days he has played Death at roulette three times (if one counts those first two times, with the drum of the revolver) and remained alive! It is truly incredible that the ambulance carriage just happened to be driving along the boulevard at the very moment when Genji lost consciousness after drinking the poisoned wine!

Obviously all this is because there is too much vital energy in this man, and he expends it sparingly, holding it inside himself.

Yesterday he declared: 'I cannot understand, Columbine, why you find the world so disagreeable. You're young, healthy and rosy-cheeked, and p-perfectly cheerful by nature, even though you do try to assume an infernal air.'

I was terribly upset. 'Healthy and rosy-cheeked' – is that all? On the other hand, as they say, you can't blame the mirror. He is right: I lack subtlety and fatality. But even so, it was very tactless of him to say it.

'And what about you?' I retorted. 'As I recall, you were so outraged with the Doge that you even threatened to break up our club, but you keep coming and you even tried to poison yourself.'

He replied with a serious air: 'I adore everything mysterious. There are far too many mysteries here, dear Columbine, and mysteries give me a kind of itch – I shall never calm down until I get to the bottom of everything.' Then suddenly he made a suggestion. 'Do you know what? Why d-don't we solve this puzzle together? As far as I am aware, you have nothing else to do in any case. It will be good for you. You might even come to your senses!'

I did not like his didactic tone, but I thought about Ophelia's inexplicable suicide and remembered Lorelei, without whom our meetings now seemed pale and colourless. And he was right – how long could I just sit at home, waiting for the evening to come?

'Very well,' I said. 'A puzzle to be solved. When shall we begin?'

'Tomorrow, with no d-delay. I shall call for you at eleven, if you would please be so kind as to be ready on time in full marching order.'

There is one thing I do not understand: whether he is in love with me or not. To judge from his manner of restrained mockery – not in the least. But perhaps he is simply trying to appear interesting? Acting in accordance with that idiotic homily: 'The less we love a woman, the more she likes us.' Of course, it is all the same to me, since I love Prospero. But I would still like to know.

Take tomorrow's outing, for instance – what is his real interest in it? Now that is a genuine riddle.

All right. Let Mr Genji try to solve his puzzle, and I shall solve mine.

But they did not set out at eleven the following day – and not at all because the young mistress of the flat had overslept or failed to make her preparations in time. On the contrary, Columbine was waiting for Prince Genji in perfect readiness and fully kitted out. Little Lucifer had been given food and drink and left to rustle about in a large plywood crate full of grass, and Columbine herself had put on an impressive outfit: a Bedouin burnous with little bells (she had spent half the night sewing them on).

His Japanese Majesty politely praised the costume but requested her to change into something a little less eye-catching, citing the particularly delicate nature of their mission. So it was his own fault that they were a little late.

With reluctant loathing, Columbine dressed up in a blue skirt and white blouse from Irkutsk, with a modest grey bolero, and put a beret on her head – the perfect image of a female student, only the spectacles were missing. But the earthbound Genji was pleased.

He did not come alone, but with his Japanese, to whom Columbine was formally introduced on this occasion, with

125

endless bowing and scraping (on Mr Masa's side, that is). In introducing his Man Friday, Genji called him 'observant and sharp-witted' and even 'an invaluable assistant' and the Oriental drew himself erect and puffed out his smooth cheeks so that he looked like a carefully polished samovar.

When the three of them got into the droshky, Columbine was helped in by both elbows, like a queen.

'Where are we going, to Ophelia's place?' she asked.

'No.' Genji replied and gave the driver a familiar address, 'Basmannaya Street, the Giant c-company's apartment building. Let's start with Avaddon. I can't get that Beast out of my head – the one that howled on the night of the suicide.'

The sight of the large, grey five-storey block made the young woman feel rather unwell – she recalled the iron hook and the rope end hanging from it. Genji, however, did not walk into the left entrance, where the flat of the deceased Nikifor Sipyaga was located. He walked into the entrance on the right.

They walked all the way up to the top and rang the bell at a door with a plaque that said 'A.F. Stakhovich, painter'. Columbine remembered that this man, Avaddon's neighbour, had been mentioned by the yard keeper, who had taken Lucifer for an alcoholic hallucination.

The door was opened by a young man with a fiery ginger beard that covered his face almost right up to the eyes. There could be no doubt that this was the artist in person – he was wearing a dressing gown smeared with paint from top to bottom and clutching an extinct pipe in his teeth.

'A thousand apologies, Alexei Fyodorovich,' said Genji, politely doffing his top hat (so he had already found out the man's first name and patronymic, how very meticulous). 'We are friends of your neighbour, the late Mr Sipyaga, who met such an untimely d-death. We would like to reconstruct the woeful sequence of events.'

'Yes, I felt sorry for the student,' Stakhovich sighed, gesturing for them to go in. 'Though of course, I hardly even knew him. A neighbour on the other side of the wall is not like one from the door opposite. Come in, only be careful, it's chaos in here.'

His comment on the chaos was greatly understated. The small flat, an exact mirror image of Avaddon's, was absolutely crammed with frames and canvases and there was all sorts of rubbish underfoot – empty bottles, rags, flattened paint tubes.

The room which Avaddon had made his bedroom served Stakhovich as a studio. Standing by the window was an unfinished painting of a female nude on a red divan (the nude's body had been painted in detail, but the head was still missing), and placed against the opposite wall was the divan itself, covered in a red drape, and there really was a naked damsel reclining on it. She had a snub nose, freckles and loose straw-coloured hair, and she gazed at the visitors with idle curiosity, making no attempt to cover herself up.

'This is Dashka,' the painter said, nodding towards his model. 'Stay there, Dunya, don't move, it cost me a real effort to get you set out properly. They've come to make enquiries about that young fool from next door who hanged himself. They'll be gone in a minute.'

'A-a-ah,' drawled Dashka, alias Dunya, and sniffed. 'The one who hammered on the wall with his fist every time we started arguing a bit too loud?'

'That's the one.'

At this point Prince Genji proved that he was terribly old-fashioned and a total martyr to philistine prejudices. At the sight of the naked model he became embarrassed, turned his head away a full hundred and eighty degrees and started stammering twice as much as usual: in his place Prospero wouldn't have batted an eyelid.

However, the Japanese Masa wasn't even slightly embarrassed. He stared at the recumbent girl, clicked his tongue in approval and declared: 'Beeootifur young rady. Round with fat regs.'

'Masa!' Genji protested, blushing. 'How many times m-must I tell you? Stop staring! This isn't Japan!'

But Dunya was obviously flattered by the comment from the Japanese.

'What exactly are you interested in?' asked the artist, squinting at each of his visitors in turn. 'I really didn't know him at all. I was never in his flat. He gave the impression of being a bit of a cold fish. No socialising, no binges, no women's voices. A real hermit.'

'The poor thing wasn't much to look at either, his face was all covered in furuncles,' Dunya put in, scratching her elbow and looking at Masa. 'But he was interested in the female sex all right. When he ran into me in the entrance, he used to frisk me all over with those eyes of his. If he'd been a bit more perky, he could have been likeable enough. You get furuncles from loneliness. But he had good eyes, sort of sad, and the colour of cornflowers.'

'Shut up, you fool,' Stakhovich shouted at her. 'To hear you talk, you'd think men have nothing on their minds but how to get their hands on your body. But she's right: he was shy, you couldn't get a word out of him. And he really was lonely, a lost soul. He was always muttering something in the evenings. Something rhythmical, like poetry. Sometimes he used to sing a bit out of tune – mostly Little Russian songs. The partition walls here are made of planks, you can hear every sound.'

All the walls of the room were hung with sketches and studies, most of them showing a female torso in various positions and from various angles, and it required no great gift of observation to realise that Dashka-Dunya's body had served as the model for all of them.

'Tell me,' Columbine enquired. 'Why do you always paint the same woman? Is it some kind of style you have? I've read that in Europe there are artists who only paint one thing – a cup, or flowers in a vase, or spots of light on glass – always trying to achieve perfection.'

'What's perfection got to do with it!' Stakhovich exclaimed, turning round to take a look at this curious young lady. 'Where would I get the money for any other models?

Take you, for example. You wouldn't pose for me out of the simple love of art, would you?'

Columbine felt as if the gaze of his narrowed eyes had pierced straight through her bolero, and she cringed slightly.

'You have an interesting profile. The line of the hips is quite captivating. And the breasts must be pear-shaped, slightly asymmetrical, with large areolae. Am I right?'

Masha Mironova would probably have turned numb and blushed bright red at words like that. But Columbine didn't turn a hair and even smiled.

'C-come now sir, how d-dare you say such things?' Genji exclaimed in horror, apparently prepared to intervene there and then for the honour of the lady and tear the insolent fellow into little pieces.

But Columbine saved the artist from the inevitable duel by saying in a perfectly calm voice: 'I don't know what areolae are, but I assure you that my breasts are perfectly symmetrical. However, you are quite right about them being pear-shaped.'

There was a brief pause. The artist examined the intrepid maiden's waist. Genji mopped his forehead with a batiste handkerchief. Masa walked over to the model and offered her a boiled sweet in a green wrapper that he had taken out of his pocket.

'From Landrine?' Dashka-Dunya asked. '*Merci*.'

Columbine imagined Stakhovich, having become world-famous, bringing an exhibition of his work to Irkutsk. The most important canvas was a nude – *Columbine Seduced*. Now that would be a real scandal. It was probably worth thinking about.

But by now the artist was looking at the Japanese instead of her.

'What an incredible face!' Stakhovich exclaimed, rubbing his hands together in his excitement. 'And you don't notice it straight away. The way those eyes sparkle, and those folds! Chingiz Khan! Tamerlaine! Listen, good sir, I absolutely must paint your portrait!'

Columbine was stung. So she only had an interesting silhouette, but he thought this snuffling Oriental was Tamerlaine? Genji also stared at his valet with a certain degree of amazement, but Masa wasn't even slightly surprised – he merely turned sideways so that the artist could appreciate his flattened profile as well.

Genji cautiously took the artist by the sleeve: 'Mr Stakhovich, we have not come here to p-pose for you. The yard keeper told me that on the n-night of the suicide you supposedly heard some unusual sounds on the other side of the wall. Try to describe them in as much detail as possible.'

'That's the sort of thing you don't forget in a hurry. It was a foul night, the wind was howling outside, the trees were cracking, but I could still hear it.' The artist scratched the back of his head as he remembered. 'Well, it was like this. He came home just before midnight – he slammed the front door very loudly, which was something he never used to do.'

'That's right!' Dashka-Dunya put in. 'And I said to you: "He's drunk. Now he'll start bringing whores back." Remember?'

Genji cast an embarrassed sideways glance at Columbine, which she found very amusing. Was he concerned for her morals now? It was already quite clear that Dashka spent the nights here as well as the days.

'Yes, that was exactly what you said,' the artist confirmed. 'We go to bed late. I work and Dunya looks at the pictures in the magazines until I finish. He was dashing around on the other side of the wall, stamping his feet and muttering something. He burst out laughing a couple of times, and then started sobbing – in general, he seemed a bit upset. And then, well after midnight, it suddenly started. This howling – very sinister it was, and it came and went. I've never heard anything like it in my life. At first I thought my neighbour had brought a stray dog home. But it didn't sound like that. Then I imagined he'd gone barmy and started howling himself, but a man couldn't have made sounds like that. It was a sort of deep, hollow sound, but at the same time it was articulate. As if it was chanting something, one word, over and over again. Two, three, four times in a row.'

'O-o-o-oh!' Dashka-Dunya howled in a deep bass voice. 'Right, Sashura? Absolutely terrifying. O-o-o-oh!'

'Yes, it was kind of like that,' the artist said with a nod. 'Only louder, and it was really weird. I'd say it wasn't just "O-o-o-oh", but more like "D-o-o-oh" or "K-o-o-oh". It started with this vague, low sound, and then got louder and louder. Well, we make a bit of noise in here sometimes, so at first we put up with it. But when we went to bed – that was after three in the morning, we couldn't take it any more. I banged on the wall and shouted: 'Hey you, student, what kind of concert is that?' But there was no answer. And it went on right until dawn.'

'Just remembering it gives me goose pimples,' the model complained to Masa, who was standing beside her, and he stroked her bare shoulder reassuringly, then left his hand where it was. Dashka-Dunya didn't object.

'Is that all?' Genji asked pensively.

'Yes,' Stakhovich said with a shrug, observing Masa's manoeuvres with amazement.

'Thank you and g-goodbye. Madam.'

Genji bowed to the model and set off rapidly towards the door. Columbine and Masa went dashing after him.

'Why didn't you ask him about anything else?' she asked him furiously, when they were already on the stairs. 'He'd only just started talking about the most interesting part!'

'He had already told us the most interesting part. That is one,' Genji replied. 'We wouldn't have learned anything else interesting from him. That is two. Another minute and there could have been a scandalous incident, because someone was behaving with extreme impudence. That is three.'

After that he started speaking some kind of gibberish – it must have been Japanese, because Masa understood it very well and started gibbering away in reply. From his tone of voice he seemed to be making excuses.

Outside in the street Columbine suddenly felt as if she had been struck by lightning.

'The voice!' she cried out. 'During the seance Ophelia mentioned some voice! Remember, when she was talking to Avaddon's spirit!'

'I remember, I remember. Don't shout like that, p-people are looking at you,' said Genji, the staid guardian of propriety. 'But did you realise what that voice was singing? What it was calling on Avaddon to do? And in a way that left absolutely no room for doubt?'

She tried howling quietly: 'Do-o-o-oh! Ko-o-o-oh!'

She imagined it was the dead of night, with a storm outside the window, a flickering candle flame, a white sheet of paper with crooked lines of writing. Oh my God!

'Go-o-o!, g-o-o . . . Oi!'

'Yes, "oi!" indeed. Just imagine it, a terrible inhuman voice repeating over and over again "Go, go, go", hour after hour. And just b-before that Avaddon had been openly named as the Chosen One. That's more than enough. Just write your farewell poem and p-put the noose round your neck.'

Columbine stopped and squeezed her eyes tight shut in order to remember this moment for ever. The moment when the miraculous had entered her life with all the incontrovertibility of scientific fact. It was one thing to dream of the Eternal Bridegroom, without being completely sure that he really existed. It was quite another thing to *know*, to know for certain.

'Death is alive, he sees and hears everything, he is here beside us!' Columbine whispered. 'And Prospero is his servant! It's all absolutely true! It's not just a fantasy, it's not a hallucination! Even the neighbours next door heard it!'

The surface of the pavement swayed beneath her feet. The young lady squeezed her eyes shut again in fright and grabbed hold of Genji's arm, knowing that afterwards she would be angry with herself for being so weak and impressionable. Why, of course Death was a thinking, feeling being, how could it be otherwise?

She recovered quite quickly. She even laughed as she said: 'Isn't it wonderful that there are so many strange things all around us?'

It was well-put, impressive, and she glanced at Genji in the right way, throwing her head back slightly and half-lowering her eyelashes.

It was just a pity that he was looking off to one side and not at Columbine.

'Mmm, yes, there are certainly many strange things,' he murmured, not really seeming to have heard what she said. ' "Go, go" is impressive enough. But there is another circumstance even m-more surprising.'

'What's that?'

'It is strange, surely, that the voice carried on howling right until dawn?'

'Why is it?' Columbine asked after thinking for a moment.

'Avaddon hanged himself no later than three o'clock in the morning. There was no answer when Stakhovich started hammering on the wall some time after three. And the results of the autopsy indicate that d-death occurred at about three. If the Beast was sent by Death to summon her lover, then why would it carry on howling until d-dawn, when the guest had already arrived?'

'Perhaps the Beast was mourning him?' Columbine suggested uncertainly.

Genji looked at her reproachfully.

'From the Beast's point of view, it ought to have been rejoicing, not mourning. And then, long after the man had died, the Beast was still wailing "Go, go". Doesn't Death's emissary strike you as being rather stupid?'

Yes, this is a very strange and mysterious story, thought Columbine. And the greatest mystery of all is why you brought me with you, sir.

The look in the prince's blue eyes was warm and friendly, but she could not sense any hidden motive.

In short, it was a puzzle.

She shook the crystal teardrop from her lashes

From Basmannaya Street they drove for a long time past places that looked like hospitals and barracks, then the buildings on the streets gradually shrank and changed from stone to wood, until eventually the landscape became entirely rural. Columbine, however, did not look around much, she was still under the impression of the revelation that had been granted to her. Her companions did not speak either.

But then the carriage halted in the middle of a dusty, unpaved street lined with small, single-storey houses. On one side she could see the steep bank of a small river or a narrow ravine through the gap between two wooden fences.

'Where are we?' Columbine asked.

'On the Yauza,' Genji replied, as he jumped down from the footboard. 'According to the description, th-that house over there is the one we need. This is where Ophelia used to l-live. Or to use her real name, Alexandra Sinichkina.'

Columbine could not help smiling at the funny name. Alexandra Sinichkina was even worse than Maria Mironova. No wonder the girl had preferred to be called Ophelia.

It turned out that the oracle of the 'Lovers of Death' had lived in a tidy little house that had four windows with white shutters, embroidered curtains and flowers on the windowsills: behind the house there was a green, leafy apple orchard, and the branches of the trees were bowed under the weight of gold and red fruit.

The knock at the gate was answered by a neat old woman of about forty-five, dressed in black.

'Her mother,' Genji explained in a low voice as the old woman walked towards them. 'A provincial secretary's widow. She and her daughter lived alone.'

When Ophelia's mother came closer, her eyes proved to be as bright and clear as her daughter's, but the eyelids were red and swollen. That was from crying, Columbine guessed, and she felt a sharp tingling in her nose. How could you explain to the poor woman that what had happened was not a misfortune at all, but the greatest possible blessing? She would never believe it.

'Good afternoon, Serafima Kharitonovna,' Genji said with a bow. 'P-pardon us for disturbing you. We knew Alexandrovna Ivanovna . . .'

He hesitated, evidently uncertain how to introduce himself. After all, he wasn't really a Japanese prince. But he was spared the need.

The widow opened the wicket gate and sobbed.

'So you knew my Sashenka? She did have some friends after all? Thank you for coming to see me, I've been sitting here all on my own, with no one at all to talk to. The samovar's all ready. We don't have any relatives, and the neighbours don't call, they turn their noses up. Of course, a suicide is a disgrace to the entire street.'

Their hostess led them into a small dining room where there were embroidered covers on the chairs, a portrait of some bishop on the wall and an old-fashioned clock ticking in the corner. She obviously really was in desperate need of company, because she started talking immediately and carried on with hardly a pause. She poured tea, but didn't drink any herself, just ran her finger round the rim of the full cup.

'While Sashenka was alive, we had plenty of lady visitors, everyone needed my daughter. They wanted her to read the candle wax, or cure a headache, or turn away the evil eye. Sashenka could do everything. Even tell if someone's betrothed was still alive in a faraway country. And she did it all out of the goodness of her heart, she didn't accept any gifts, she said that was wrong.'

'Was it a talent that she was born with?' Columbine asked sympathetically.

'No, dear young lady, she wasn't born with it. She was a

weak child, always ailing. The Lord didn't grant me children for long. He gave them to me for a year or two, or four at the most, and then took them back again. I buried six of them, and Sashenka was the youngest. I was so happy that she stayed in this world. She was sickly, but she was still alive – at five, and six, and seven. Every extra day was like a holiday for me, I praised God for it. And on Whit Sunday, when Sashenka was just eight, God worked a genuine miracle . . .'

Serafima Kharitonovna stopped talking and wiped away a tear.

'Miracuw? What sort of miracuw?' asked Masa, who was listening closely – he even stopped slurping from his saucer and put down his honeycake with a bite taken out of it.

'Lightning struck the tree where she and two of the neighbours' children were sheltering from the rain. The people who saw it said there was a loud crack and blue smoke, and the little boys dropped down dead, but my Sashenka just stood there without moving, with her fingers stretched out and sparks flying off her fingertips. She was unconscious for three days, and then she suddenly came round. I sat by her bed and all that time I didn't eat or drink a thing, all I did was pray for the Holy Virgin's intervention. Sashenka opened her eyes, and they were as bright and clear as a holy angel's. And she was all right, she got up and started walking. And she wasn't just alive, she was never ill again, never. But even that gift wasn't enough for the Lord. In His mercy he decided to make Sashenka someone really special. At first I was frightened, but then I got used to it. I knew that when my daughter's eyes turned transparent, it meant she was in her special state – she was hearing and seeing things that ordinary people couldn't. At moments like that she could do all sorts of things. The year before last a little three-year-old boy went missing from round here and no one could find him. But Sashenka just sat for a while, then she moved her lips and said: "Look in the old well". And they found him, alive, only he had a broken arm. That's what she was like. And always talking about miracles and mysteries. She has a whole cupboard full of books in her room. Fairytales and fortune-telling and novels about all sorts of fairies and enchantresses.'

Ophelia's mother glanced at Columbine.

'And you were her friend? Such a fine-looking girl. And you dress modestly, not like these modern girls. Don't you cry. I cried a bit myself, but then I stopped. What's the point of crying? Sasha's in heaven now, no matter what Father Innokentii might say about suicides.'

At that Columbine started crying in earnest. She felt so sorry for Ophelia and her wonderful gift that had been lost, she just couldn't stand it.

Never mind, the whimpering worshipper of death told herself, hiding her red eyes from Genji and blowing her nose into a handkerchief. I'll describe everything differently in the diary. So as not to seem like a fool. Like this, for example: 'A crystal teardrop glinted in Columbine's eyes, but the giddy girl shook her head and the teardrop flew off. There is nothing in the world that is worth feeling sad over for more than a minute. Ophelia did what she thought was right. The crystal teardrop was not dedicated to her, but to the poor old woman.' And she could write a poem too. The first line simply wrote itself:

She shook the crystal teardrop from her lashes

'Tell me, what happened that night?' Genji asked, tactfully turning away from Columbine. 'Why d-did she suddenly run off and drown herself?'

'Why, it didn't happen like that at all,' said the widow, holding up her hands. 'She came home late, later than usual. My Sashenka lived as she liked. I knew she wouldn't get up to anything bad. She often came back late, almost every day, but I always waited up for her, and I never pestered her with questions about where she'd been and what she'd been doing. I knew she'd tell if she wanted to. She was special, not like the other girls. I used to sit here, with the samovar all ready. Sashenka didn't eat much, she was like a bird, but she liked her tea, with lime flowers . . . Well, I heard a cab drive up, and then a minute later she came in. Her face was really glowing, I'd never seen her like that before. I couldn't help myself, I just had to find out why: "What's happened to you? Another miracle? Or have you fallen in love?" "Don't ask, mama," she said. But I know her, and I wasn't born yesterday. I could tell she'd been meeting a lover. It made me feel afraid, but happy too.'

Columbine shuddered when she remembered that evening and the way Prospero had told Ophelia to stay after the seance. Oh, tormentor! Oh, tyrant of poor helpless puppets! But what point was there in feeling jealous of a dead woman? And in any case, jealousy was a banal and unworthy feeling. If you had a lot of rivals, it meant you had chosen a worthy object for your love, she told herself, and suddenly wondered who actually was the object of her love – Prospero or Death? It didn't really matter. She tried to picture the Eternal Bridegroom, and he appeared to her, not as a young Tsarevich, but as a wise, hoary-haired old man with a stern face and black eyes.

'She only drank one cup of tea,' the provincial secretary's widow continued. 'Then she stood right here, in front of the mirror, which she'd never done before in her life. She turned round this way and that way, laughed quietly and went to her room. But she came back less than a minute later, she hadn't even changed her shoes. And her face was still the same, special. But her eyes were transparent, like two pieces of ice. I was frightened. "What is it?" I asked. "What's happened?" She said: "Goodbye, mama, I'm leaving now." She wasn't here any more, she was far away, she wasn't looking at me. "I've been given a Sign," she said. I dashed over to her and held her hand, I couldn't make sense of anything. "Where are you going in the middle of the night? And what sort of sign do you mean?" Sashenka smiled and said: "The kind of sign you can't mistake. Like King Balthazar's. It's meant to be. It's fate. I'm used to listening to fate. Let me go. There's nothing to be done." She turned towards me and gave me a sweet look. "It's only goodbye until we meet again. We will definitely meet again." She said it very calmly. And like a fool, I let go of her hand. Sashenka kissed me on the cheek, put on her shawl and walked out of the door. I should have kept her here, stopped her, but I wasn't used to gainsaying her when she was in that special state . . . I didn't follow her outside. Later I followed the tracks of her heels and I saw she'd gone straight into the orchard, down to the river and into the water . . . without even stopping once. As if someone was waiting for her there.'

Genji asked quickly: 'When she went out, d-did you go into her room?'

'No, I sat here until the morning, waiting.'

'And in the morning?'

'No, I didn't go in there for two days. I kept running to the police station, or hanging about by the gate all the time. I never even thought of going down to the river. It was only later, when I came back here from the mortuary after the identification, that I tidied her room. And I don't go in there any more. Let everything stay the way it was when she was here.'

'May we take a look?' Genji asked. 'Just through the d-doorway? We won't go in.'

Ophelia's room was simple, but comfortable. A narrow bed with metal balls on the uprights and a heap of pillows. A dressing table with nothing but a comb and a hand mirror on it. An old bookshelf of dark wood, crammed full of books. A small writing desk with a candlestick under the window.

'Candurs,' said the Japanese.

Columbine raise her eyes to the ceiling, assuming that this simple-minded son of the Orient named every object that he saw – she had read somewhere that primitive peoples had that habit. Now he would say: 'Table. Bed. Window.' But Masa glanced sideways at his master and repeated: 'Candurs.'

'Yes, yes. I see,' Genji said with a nod. 'Well done. Tell

me, Serafima Kharitonovna, did you put new candles in the candelabra?'

'I didn't put them in. They hadn't been touched.'

'So when your daughter came in here she d-didn't light them?'

'I suppose so. I've left everything just as it was, I haven't disturbed anything. That book lying open on the windowsill – let it stay there. Her slippers under the bed. The glass of pear compote – she loved that. Perhaps her soul will look in every now and then to take a rest . . . Sashenka's soul has no place of its own. Father Innokentii wouldn't allow her to be buried in hallowed ground. They buried my daughter outside the fence, like a little dog. And he wouldn't let me put up a cross. Your daughter's sin is unforgivable, he said. But what sort of sinner is she? She was an angel. She stayed on earth for a little while and brought me joy, and then flew away again.'

As they walked back to the carriage and then drove along the streets shrouded in the shadows of early evening, Masa kept muttering angrily in his strange squawking language.

'Why has he suddenly forgotten how to speak Russian?' Columbine asked in a whisper.

Genji said: 'He is being t-tactful. He does not wish to offend your religious sensibilities. He is roundly abusing the Christian Ch-church for its attitude to suicides and their families. And he is absolutely right.'

Black roses

At the entrance to the wing of a building on Povarskaya Street, where Lorelei Rubinstein had still lived only three days earlier, there were three heaps of flowers lying on the pavement. Most of them were black roses, which she had mentioned in a poem written shortly before her death – the one she had read for the first time one evening at Prospero's apartment and then printed shortly afterwards in *The Refuge of the Muse.* There were notes, too – white spots against the background of the flowers. Columbine picked one out, opened it and read the inscription in small girlish hand-writing:

> *Oh Lorelei, you have gone on before,*
> *Pathfinder on the road into the night,*
> *And, following the image I adore,*
> *I too shall walk the dark path into light.*
>
> T.R.

She picked up another: 'Oh, how right you are, dear, dear one! Life is vulgar and unbearable! Olga Z.'

Genji also read it, looking over her shoulder. He knitted his elegant black eyebrows and sighed. Then he resolutely rang the bronze doorbell.

The door was opened by a rather wizened lady with an anxious, tearful face who kept dabbing at her red, wet little nose with a handkerchief. She introduced herself as Rosalia Maximovna, one of 'poor Lyalechka's' relatives, although the subsequent conversation made it clear that she had lived with Lorelei as her housekeeper, or simply as a dependent.

Genji spoke to her quite differently from the way in which he had spoken to Ophelia's mother. He was dry and businesslike. Masa didn't open his mouth at all, he sat down at the table and didn't move, staring straight at Rosalia Maximovna through narrowed eyes.

The pitiful creature gazed at the severe gentleman in the black tails and the taciturn Oriental with a mixture of fright and obsequiousness. She answered Genji's questions at length, with masses of detail, and from time to time he was obliged to bring her back to the point. Every time Rosalia Maximovna became flustered and began batting her eyelids helplessly. The conversation was also seriously impeded by a lapdog – a vicious dwarf bulldog that kept yapping at Masa and snapping at his trouser leg.

'Had you lived with Madam Rubinstein for a l-long time?' was the first question that Genji asked.

It turned out that she had been there for seven years, ever since Lorelei (whom she also referred to as 'Lyalechka' and 'Elena Semyonovna') had been widowed.

When she was asked whether the deceased had ever attempted to take her own life before, the answer was very long and confused.

'Lyalechka never used to be like this. She was cheerful, she used to laugh a lot. She loved her husband Matvei very much. They had an easy, happy life together. They didn't have any children – they were always going to the theatre and at-homes, they often went to resorts and to Paris, and all sorts of places abroad. But when Matvei Natanovich died, it was as if she lost her mind, the poor thing. She even took poison,' Rosalia told him in a whisper, 'only not enough to kill her that time. But after that she was all right, she seemed to have got used to things. Only her character had changed, completely changed. She started writing poems and in general . . . she wasn't quite herself, somehow. If not for me, she wouldn't have eaten properly, she just drank coffee all the time. Do you think it was easy for me keeping house for Elena Semyonovna? She spent all the money that Matvei Natanovich left on the memorial for his grave. She was only paid a pittance for her poems at first, then it was more and more, but that was still no help. Lyalechka used to send ten-rouble wreaths to the cemetery every single day, and sometimes there wasn't a crust of bread in the house. The number of times I told her: "You should put something aside for a rainy day!" But would she listen? So now there isn't anything. She's dead, and what am I supposed to live on? And the flat's only paid up until the first of the month. I have to move out, but where to?' She buried her face in the handkerchief and started sobbing. 'Zhu . . . Zhuzhechka is used to eating well – a bit of liver, marrow bones, cottage cheese . . . But who needs us now? Oh, I'm sorry, just a moment . . .'

And she ran out of the room in floods of tears.

'Masa, how did you manage to m-make the dog shut up?' Genji asked. 'Thank you, it was bothering me rather badly.'

Columbine suddenly realised that the bulldog had not barked once, but only grunted malevolently under the table during the entire monologue, which had been extended to some considerable length by nose-blowing and sobbing.

Masa replied in a steady voice: 'Dog sirent because eating my reg. Masta, have you arready asked everyfin you want? If not I can howd for ronger.'

Columbine glanced under the table and gasped. The mean little beast had grabbed poor Masa by the ankle and was growling viciously and shaking its round head from side to side! No wonder the Japanese looked a bit pale and he was smiling painfully. He was a real hero! Just like the Spartan boy with the fox cub!

'Oh, Lord, Masa,' Genji sighed. 'That's g-going too far.'

He leaned down swiftly and squeezed the dog's nose between his finger and thumb. The little beast snorted and immediately opened its jaws. Then Genji took it by the scruff of the neck and tossed it into the hallway with a remarkably accurate throw. There was a squeal, followed by hysterical barking, but Masa's tormentor didn't dare come back into the room.

And at that point Rosalia Maximovna returned, a little calmer, but Genji had already assumed a relaxed pose, leaning back slightly in his chair, with his fingers clasped across his stomach in a most innocent fashion.

'Where's Zhuzhechka?' Rosalia Maximovna asked in a voice hoarse from sobbing.

'You still have not told us what happened that evening,' Genji reminded her sternly, and Lorelei's aunt started blinking in fright.

'I was sitting in the drawing room, reading the *Home Doctor*, Lyalechka subscribes to it for me. She'd just got back from somewhere or other and gone into her boudoir. Then suddenly she came running into the room with her eyes blazing and her cheeks bright red. "Aunty Rosa!" she cried. I was frightened, I thought it must be a fire or a mouse. But Lyalechka shouted: "The last Sign, the third one! He loves me! He loves me! There is no more doubt. I must go to him, to the Tsarevich! My Matvei has waited too long". Then she put her hand over her eyes and said in a quiet voice: "No more, my torment is over. Now dost Thou release Thy servant, oh Lord. No more playing the jester for me." I didn't understand anything. You can never tell with Elena Semyonovna if something has really happened or she's just fantasising. "Who is it who loves you?" I asked her. "Ferdinand Karlovich, Sergei Poluektovich or that one with the moustache, who arrived with the bouquet yesterday?" She had lots of admirers, you couldn't remember them all. Only she didn't care a brass farthing for any of them, so her raptures seemed strange to me. "Or has someone else turned up?" I asked her, "Someone completely new?" But Lyalechka laughed, and she looked so happy, for the first time in all those years. "Someone else, Aunty Rosa," she said. "Someone quite different. The genuine one and only. I'm going to go to bed now. Don't come into my room until the morning, whatever happens." And she walked out. In the morning I went in, and she was lying on the bed in her white dress, and she was all white too . . .'

The aunt burst into tears again, but this time she didn't go running out of the room.

'How am I going to live now? Lyalechka didn't think about me, she didn't leave a single kopeck. And I can't sell the furniture – it's the landlord's . . .'

'Show me where Elena Semyonovna's b-boudoir is,' said Genji, getting to his feet.

Lorelei's bedroom was startlingly different from Ophelia's simple little room. It had Chinese vases as tall as a man, and painted Japanese screens, and a magnificent dressing table with a myriad bottles, jars and tubes standing in front of a triple mirror, and all sorts of other things too.

There were two portraits hanging above the luxurious

bed. One was a perfectly ordinary photograph of a bearded man in a pince-nez (obviously the deceased husband Matvei himself), but Columbine found the second one intriguing: a swarthy, handsome man dressed in blood-red robes, with immense half-closed eyes, sitting astride a black buffalo and holding a club and a noose in his hands, and there were two terrifying four-eyed dogs huddling against the buffalo's legs.

Genji walked up to the lithograph, but it was not the image that interested him, it was the three black roses on the top of the frame. One had not completely wilted yet, another was badly wrinkled, and the third was absolutely dry.

'My God, who is that?' Columbine asked, looking at the picture.

'The Indian god of death, Yama, also known as the King of the Dead,' Genji replied absentmindedly, staring hard at the gilded frame. 'The dogs with four eyes are searching for p-prey among the living, and Yama uses the noose to pull their souls out.'

'Tsarevich Death, come in your bloody-red apparel, give me your hand, lead me into the light,' said Columbine, reciting two lines from Lorelei's last poem. 'So that was who she meant!'

But Genji failed to appreciate her astuteness.

'What roses are these?' he asked, turning to the aunt. 'From whom?'

'They . . .' she said, and started blinking very, very fast. 'How can I remember, when so many people used to give Lyalechka flowers? Ah yes, I do remember. She brought the bouquet home on that last evening.'

'Are you sure?'

Columbine thought Genji was being too severe with the poor old woman. Rosalia Maximovna pulled her head down into her shoulders and babbled: 'She brought them, she brought them herself.'

There seemed to be something else he wanted to ask her,

but glancing at Columbine, he obviously realised that she disapproved of his manner and, taking pity on the unfortunate woman, left her in peace.

'Thank you madam. You have been a g-great help.'

The Japanese gave a ceremonial bow, from the waist.

Columbine noticed that as Genji walked past the table he inconspicuously placed a banknote on the tablecloth. Was he feeling ashamed then? Yes, that must be it.

The expedition was over. Columbine had still not found out if Genji was in love with her, but that was not what she thought about on the way back. She suddenly felt quite unbearably sad.

She imagined how her mother and father would feel when they found out that she was gone. They would probably cry and feel sorry for their daughter, and then, like Ophelia's mother, they would say: 'She stayed in the world for a short time, and then she flew away.' But it would be easier for them than for Serafima Kharitonovna, they would still have their sons, Seryozha and Misha. They're not like me, Columbine comforted herself. They won't get picked up by the wild east wind and carried away into the sunset to meet their doom.

She felt so moved that the tears started pouring down her cheeks.

'Well, how did you like our excursion?' Genji asked, looking into his companion's wet face. 'Perhaps you will l-live for a little longer after all?'

She rubbed her eyes, turned towards him and laughed in his face.

'Perhaps I will, perhaps I won't,' she said

In front of her house she jumped out of the carriage, gave a careless wave and ran into the entrance with a light clatter of heels.

Sitting down at the table without even taking off her beret, she dipped a pen in the inkwell and wrote a poem that came out in blank verse, like Lorelei's. And for some reason it was in traditional folk style – could that be because of Ophelia's mother, the old provincial secretary's widow?

Not with white linen, but black velvet
Was my wedding couch arrayed,
A narrow bed, and all of wood,
Covered with lilies and chrysanthemums.

Dearest guests, why look you so sad,
Wiping teardrops from your cheeks?
Feast your eyes in joy on the bright glow
Of my slim face below the plaited wreath.

Ah, you poor and wretched, sightless souls,
Look closely now and you will see
That on this bed ringed with candles bright
My own true love lies here along with me.

Oh, how divine the beauty of his face!
Oh, how bright the twinkling of his eye!
How sweetly do his gentle fingers play!
How happy you have made me, bridegroom mine.

She wondered what Prospero would say about the poem.

III. From the 'Agents' Reports' File

To His Honour Lieutenant-Colonel Besikov
(Private and confidential)

Dear Lieutenant-Colonel,

I always knew that helping you was a risky and dangerous business – both for my reputation as a decent individual and, possibly, for my very life. Today my very worst fears have been confirmed. I really do not know what causes me greater torment, the physical suffering or the bitter realisation of how little you value my self-sacrificing efforts.

I indignantly reject your repeated offer to 'pay my expenses generously', although it is unlikely that any of your highly paid 'collaborators' demonstrates as much zeal and devotion to the cause as does your humble servant. However, my unselfish scrupulousness does not change the essence of the matter – you have in any case effectively transformed me from a principled opponent of nihilism and devilry into a vulgar spy!

Have you never entertained the thought, dearest Vissarion Vissarionovich, that perhaps you underestimate me? You regard me as a pawn in your game, whereas perhaps I am a piece of an entirely different calibre!

I am joking, only joking. How can we grains who have fallen between the millstones ever grow up to the heavens above? But even so, you should be more tactful with me, a little more formal. After all, I am a cultured man and also of European stock. Do not take this as an attack on yourself or an out-burst of Lutheran arrogance. I only wish to remind you that the fancy social graces mean more to a 'pepper-and-sausage German' than they do to a 'Russak'. As it happens, you are not a Russak, you are a Caucasian, but that does not change the essence of the matter.

I have re-read what I have written and I feel sick with myself. How amusing you must find my rapid transitions from voluptuous self-abasement to unbending pride.

Ah, but it is not important, really it is not. The important thing is to remember that what is good for the Russian is death for the German.

And apropos of death.

From the latest instructions that I have received from you it is clear to me that you are no longer much concerned about the fate of the poor 'Lovers of Death', who dwell on the very edge of the precipice. You demonstrated far more interest in one of the members of the club, whom in previous reports I have dubbed the Stammerer. I have the feeling that you know far more about this man than I do. Why do you find him so intriguing? Do you really believe in the existence of a secret organisation called 'Lovers of Life'? And who is this 'very highly placed individual' whose personal request you are carrying out? Which of your superiors has taken an interest in this man?

Whatever the answer might be, I have dutifully performed the strange assignment you set me, although you did not even condescend to tell me the reasons for it. I followed the Stammerer, and although I was not able to establish his place of residence, it was not, as you shall see, due to my own fault.

No, this really is absolutely outrageous! Why can you not set your own police agents to follow the Stammerer? You write that he is not a criminal 'in the strict sense of the word', but when has that circumstance ever been an obstacle for you and your kind? Or is your reluctance to attach official agents to the Stammerer explained by the fact that he has, as you informed me rather vaguely, 'too many well-wishers in the most surprising places'? Surely not in the Department of Gendarmes too? Are you concerned that one of your colleagues might inform the Stammerer that he is being followed? Then who is this man after all, if even you are being so cautious? Why must I be left to wander in the dark? I absolutely demand explanations! Especially after the monstrous incident of which I, through your good services, have been the victim.

Nonetheless, I am presenting my report. I do not know if you will extract anything useful from it. I abstain from making any comments of my own, for I do not understand very much myself – I simply present the facts.

Tonight there was another game with the Roulette Wheel of Death, again without any result (we must assume that Blagovolsky has indeed installed a more powerful magnet). We have new members to replace the lost Ophelia and Lioness of Ecstasy. Since Lorelei Rubinstein's suicide, the young maidens of Moscow have gone absolutely insane – the number of them wishing to join the mysterious club has increased several times over, for which we must thank the press's fondness for carrion. The most persistent of these young persons attain their goal. This time Prospero introduced Iphigenia and Gorgon to us. The former is a plump student with bushy golden hair, very pretty and very stupid. She read a poem about a drowned child: 'The little mite could not be saved, they lowered him into his grave', or something of the kind. Why a foolish sheep like that is drawn to the embraces of death is a mystery. The latter is a nervous brunette with sharp features, she writes jerky and extremely indecent poems, although she herself is probably still a virgin. But then, our voluptuous Doge will soon put that right.

Gdlevsky read some new poems. Prospero is right, he is a true genius, the hope of the new Russian poetry. But then, you are not interested in poetry, I believe. Even so, there is something worthy of note here. Recently Gdlevsky has been in a constant state of excitement. I wrote you once that he is literally obsessed with the mystic nature of harmony and rhyme. He read in some spiritualist book that it is only possible to associate with the World Beyond on Friday, and therefore this day of the week is special. Every event that takes place on a Friday has a magical significance, it is a message, a sign, one only needs to know how to decipher it. And Gdlevsky is putting all his energies into deciphering these messages. It started last Friday, when he declared that he would tell his fortune from a rhyme. He took the first book that came to hand down off the shelf, opened it, jabbed his finger at the page and hit upon the word 'breath'. He became indescribably agitated and started repeating 'breath – death, breath – death'. Since today was also a Friday, as soon as he had greeted us, he grabbed a book that was lying on the table, opened it and – can you imagine – it happened to be Shakespeare, and it opened at the first page of *Macbeth*! Now the boy is absolutely certain that Death is sending him messages. He is waiting impatiently for the third Friday in order finally to make certain, and then he will feel perfectly entitled to do away with himself. Well, let him wait, coincidences like that don't happen three times in a row.

We went home early, at half past nine – the entire ceremony lasted no more than twenty minutes. Blagovolsky effectively pushed everyone out of the door, leaving behind only Gdlevsky. He was obviously frightened for his favourite and wanted to distract him from his malign fantasy. It would be a pity if the new sun of Russian poetry were to be extinguished before it has even risen. Although, of course, there would be one more beautiful legend: Venevitinov, Lermontov, Nadson, Gdlevsky. The death of a young talent is always beautiful. But that does not interest you, so I shall proceed to my report proper.

As you requested, I followed the Stammerer, meticulously observing all the recommendations I had been given: proceeding on foot, I always remained on the opposite side of the street and maintained a distance of at least fifty paces; in a cab I increased the distance to two hundred paces; I diligently took notes in a notebook, not forgetting to include the time, and so forth.

And so.

On Rozhdestvensky Boulevard the Stammerer halted a cabby and told him to drive to the corner of Borisoglebskaya Street and Povarskaya Street. In the evening sounds carry a long way, and the cabby repeated the address very loudly, which made my task easier. I got into the next free carriage and told the driver to drive rapidly to the place, without bothering to follow the Stammerer, and therefore arrived there before him. I hid in a gateway, from where I had a good view of the entire crossroads. I only had to wait for two or three minutes.

The Stammerer (or, to follow the usual terminology in your spheres, the 'mark') knocked on a door and entered the wing of house number eighteen. At first I thought that he was lodging there, and the assignment you had set me was completed. But then after a little thought it seemed strange to me that a man would knock at the door of his own home. I decided to check. It was a single-storey wing, so it was not difficult to glance into the lighted windows, since at that late hour the street was already deserted and my manoeuvre would not attract any attention from passers-by. I picked up an empty box from outside a general shop, set it by the wall and peeped in through the gap between the curtains.

The Stammerer was sitting at a table with an elderly lady dressed in black. Since his top hat and gloves were lying there at his elbow, I realised that he was only visiting, and evidently not for very long. I could not hear their conversation. The Stammerer said nothing for most of the time and only nodded occasionally, but the woman almost never closed her mouth – she was telling him about something, glancing beseechingly into his face and constantly dabbing at her tearstained eyes with a handkerchief. He asked her several brief questions and she replied with obvious eagerness, looking as if she felt guilty and was trying to justify herself. Eventually the Stammerer got up and left, leaving a banknote on the table. His hostess greedily grabbed it and hid it behind a picture hanging on the wall.

Afraid of being discovered, I jumped down off the crate, ran off smartly to a short distance and stood behind a tree. I had not let my carriage go, but told the driver to wait round the corner. And I was right to do so, because at that time it would not have been easy to find another cab.

The Stammerer, for instance, stood on the pavement for eight whole minutes before he was able to continue his journey. If it were not for my foresight, the chase would have been broken off at that point.

I told my driver to keep his distance and only urge the horse on when the droshky in front of us turned a corner. We drove out on to Sadovaya Street, where it was possible to increase the distance even more, and drove straight for twenty-six minutes before turning on to Basmannaya Street. The Stammerer got out in front of a five-storey house (5B). I thought that this time he must surely have come home, but it immediately became clear that I was mistaken yet again. This time he did not even let his cab go. I drove on past as far as the next turning and told my driver to wait again.

Both entrances to the house were locked, but the Stammerer did not wake the yard keeper. I saw him go into the courtyard, and I followed him cautiously. Looking round the corner I saw him fiddle briefly with a lock, open the back door and go inside. This seemed most curious to me. Why would such an impressive gentleman, in an English redingote and a top hat, be creeping into back entrances in the middle of the night?

I checked the lock and saw that it was very primitive – it could easily be opened with a tie pin, which was evidently what the Stammerer had done. In the battle between caution and excitement, the latter won the upper hand and I made up my mind to go in. In order not to make a racket I took off my boots and left them outside before slipping through the door.

I could hear the mark's footsteps as he climbed up to the

top floor, the fifth. What he did there, I do not know – I did not venture to clamber up after him. I thought I heard something squeak quietly, then there was total silence. I waited impatiently for fifteen minutes and decided that was enough. I went outside and what do you think? My boots had disappeared! Oh, the fine people of Moscow! An empty yard in the middle of the night, but some villain had still spotted them. And how deftly it had been done – I was only five paces away, but I hadn't heard a thing!

Imagine my position. Cool weather, and it was damp – there had been a shower of rain recently – and there was I in my socks. I was absolutely furious. I wanted to run to my carriage and go home. But then I thought: why don't I take a look up at the fifth floor and see if any of the windows are lit?

No, there weren't any lights on, but I suddenly noticed some kind of white spot run across the glass of one of the windows – the one next to the staircase. On looking closer I could see it was someone with an electric torch. Who else could it be if not the mark?

Now you must appreciate the full extent of my devotion to the cause. Chilled through, with wet feet, I nonetheless decided to see the assignment through to the end.

The Stammerer came out twenty minutes later, and the pursuit continued. There were no carriages about on the streets now, so the clatter of wheels and hooves on cobble-stones carried very far, and I had to drop back a long way, so that I almost lost him twice. I was only hoping that the Stammerer had finally finished his business and was going home for the night, and I could hurry home, soak my feet in hot water and drink raspberry tea. You should know that I have a tendency to catch colds, followed every time by a stubborn cough.

Beyond the Yauza we drove into the suburbs, and I remember how surprised I was that the Stammerer could have chosen such a disreputable area in which to reside. I was finally convinced that his travels were over when I saw him let his driver go. I told mine to wait again, although he complained that the horse was tired and it was time for his tea. I had to give him an extra fifty kopecks for the wait – but it soon emerged that the money had been wasted. By the way, my outgoings today in carrying out your assignment amounted to a substantial sum: three roubles and fifty kopecks. I am not telling you this out of mercenary interest, but so that you will understand how much my altruism costs me in every possible way.

I concealed myself very successfully behind a well, in the thick shade of a spreading tree, whereas the Stammerer was brightly illuminated by the moon, so that I could observe all his movements while remaining completely safe, if, that is, one does not take into account the danger to my health from my frozen feet.

The house that the mark approached seemed quite unremarkable to me. A log building with four dark windows and a planking fence with a gate at the side. This time the Stammerer did not attempt to gain entry. He approached the second window from the left and started making movements that I could not understand. I thought at first that he was drawing a rectangle round the edge of the frame. But then I heard a slight rasping sound, and I realised that the Stammerer was scraping something on the glass. Then he took some item that I could not see out of his pocket, there was a plopping sound, the glass glinted in the moonlight and came out of its frame. I realised that the Stammerer had cut it out with a glasscutter. I do not know for what purpose. He took off his redingote, carefully wrapped his strange booty in it, and set off along the street in the direction from which he had come. Now it was clear why he had let his cab go. The glass could have been broken by jolting over the cobbled surface of the road. I was obliged to part company with my driver too, following which I set off after the mark, taking every possible precaution.

As I have already written, following the evening rain it was a clear, moonlit night, and so the Stammerer's tall figure was visible from a long distance. I followed about a hundred and fifty paces behind, for obvious reasons making no sound, and he could not have noticed me.

We walked for a terribly long time – across a bridge, then down a long street, the name of which I do not know, then past Kolanchovskaya Square and the railway station. I bruised my feet all over against the cobblestones and tore my socks, but I firmly resolved to see the job through to the end. The restless Stammerer had to be on his way home now. It was impossible to imagine that he would engage in yet another escapade while carrying such a fragile load.

However, I was not able to discover his address, which was the main purpose of the assignment that you had set, because something terrible and mysterious happened to me in Ascheulov Lane off Sretenka Street.

I had to increase my speed, because the Stammerer had disappeared round a corner and I was afraid of losing him. As a result I let my guard down somewhat and walked past a gateway without even glancing into it. However as soon as I drew level with the dark aperture, I suddenly found myself grabbed by the collar from behind with monstrous, super-human strength, so that I was almost lifted up off the ground. There was a terrible, bloodcurdling hissing sound and a baleful, whistling voice, the very memory of which freezes the blood in my veins, uttered a word that sounded like a curse: 'TIKUSYO!' I would pay dearly to know what it means. The next moment a blow of terrible force came crashing down on my poor, unfortunate, dumbfounded head and consciousness mercifully abandoned me.

I came to in the gateway. According to my watch, I must have lain there unconscious for at least half an hour. I do not know what disaster befell me, but it was not a robbery – I still had my watch and wallet and all my other things. Trembling in terror, I ran as far as Sretenka Street, stopped a night cab and drove home.

Now, as I write this report to you, my feet are soaking in a basin of hot water and I have a bag of ice tied to the back of my head, where a huge lump has come up. The soles of my feet are battered and bloody, and it is highly likely that I have a severe chill. I hardly need mention my shattered nerves – I sat down to write this letter to you because I am afraid to go to bed. I am sure that as soon as I fall asleep I shall hear that nightmarish, hissing voice. And I am very upset about my stolen boots. They were goatskin and almost brand-new.

And so, highly respected Lieutenant-Colonel, now that you know all the details of what I have suffered, through your good services, I shall make my demand. You may, if you wish, regard it as an ultimatum.

You must give me an absolutely exhaustive explanation of the reasons why your 'very highly placed individual' is interested in the Stammerer, who this mysterious gentleman is and what this devilish business is all about in the first place.

Affronted and perplexed,

ZZ
12 September 1900

CHAPTER 4

I. From the Newspapers

There are More Things in Heaven and Earth . . .

Non-scientific musings concerning the epidemic of suicides in Moscow

Do you believe in science and progress?

And so do I, my reader. I believe with all my heart and I am proud of the achievements of the scientific geniuses who point out to us the way ahead into the twentieth century: electric light bulbs, the cinematograph and 1000-tonne battleships.

But do you believe in wizards, hexes and evil spirits?

Why, naturally, you do not, otherwise you would not be reading our enlightened newspaper, but the spiritualist *Puzzle* or *A Glimpse into the Abyss*. And if I, Lavr Zhemailo, were to tell you that the devil really does exist, you would think that your humble servant, who

has been doggedly tracking one of the most dangerous secret societies of the century, has succumbed to the influence of mystical spells or lost his mind and any day now he will find himself a patient in the Bozheninka psychological clinic or, even worse, will soap up a rope and follow the example of the subjects of his own sombre articles.

There are rumours creeping round Moscow. Sinister, exciting, intoxicating, seductive rumours. In society drawing rooms, in artistic salons, where cultured individuals take tea, there is a great battle taking place between the materialists and mystics. People argue loudly, until their voices grow hoarse. Or, if there are children in the house, they argue in whispers, but no less furiously. The mystics would seem to be gaining the upper hand, and the mysterious word 'Signs' is now heard more and more often.

Even those who have never before taken an interest in poetry declaim the nebulous verse of suicides that speaks of emissaries in white cloaks, howling Beasts and Tsareviches who bring death.

This is frightening, very frightening. But it is even more interesting!

Has Death herself, in full regalia, complete with scythe and shroud, really taken to stalking the streets of our peaceful city, glancing into faces and marking *her own* with some secret sign? Or perhaps these are merely amusing pranks played by the Devil (whose name must not be mentioned after dark)?

I have amused you, you are smiling. And you are right to smile. The key to this box of tricks is far simpler than that.

The wasting disease of obscurantism has infected people's minds and hearts. The brains of those who have contracted this terrible plague eagerly soak in the vapours of darkness and they gaze intently into the gloom, seeking for 'Signs', ready to accept anything strange or inexplicable as an invitation to throw themselves into the icy embrace of Her Majesty Death.

And then, glancing at the clouds at sunset, it is quite possible to see in them the silhouette of a gallows tree, as happened to sixteen-year-old F., who apparently had no connection with the 'Lovers of Death' (see the article 'Death of a Schoolboy' in our issue of 9 September); some listen with bated breath to the howling of the night wind in the chimney or shudder when they see a word that rhymes with death. Never before has the Old Capital known such an orgy of suicides as in recent days. Three yesterday, two the day before yesterday, four the day before that – and that does not include the ones who were saved, who probably number ten times more!

Five foolish young women have already poisoned themselves, following the example of Lorelei Rubinstein, who is unlikely to be lying easy in her grave as she is showered with curses by the unfortunate families of the girls who have died.

Yes, of course, in rational terms I understand very well that this is all a matter of the psychological malaise of modern society. But my God, how greatly I am tempted to repeat after the Prince of Denmark: 'There are more things in heaven and earth than are dreamt of in our philosophy!'

Indeed there probably are. For death, gentlemen, is no chimera or magic trick, but a scientifically established fact. From the point of view of physics it is an inexplicable loss of energy which, as far as I can recall from my grammar-school studies, directly contradicts the law of its conservation. Where does the vital energy really disappear to at the moment of death? Can it not return in some changed or transformed guise? What if there is some natural anomaly involved here? What if there is some invisible but entirely real cloud of death-dealing energy hovering over Moscow?

Has this really never happened before? Have not entire cities perished for reasons unknown, as if they were deprived of the very source of life? Ancient Babylon, Athens and Rome suffered decline and desolation. Historians blame a barbarian invasion, economic decline or spiritual crisis. But what if there is a different explanation for everything? Any ancient and populous city, in which hundreds of thousands and millions of people have left this life over the long centuries, is veritably choking in the tight embrace of graves and burial grounds. Dead bones are everywhere; in the graveyards, on the beds of the rivers, under the foundations of the houses, under the feet of people in the streets. The air is thick and oppressive with the final breaths of those who have died and the bursts of vital energy released. Does not the country dweller feel this asphyxiation when he first finds himself in the ancient capital and breathes in its vapours?

If we take all the inhabitants of Moscow over seven centuries, there will be far more dead than alive. You and I are in the minority, ladies and gentlemen. So is it really surprising that some, indeed, many of us feel drawn to join the majority? The focus of energy is there, not here.

Scientists will say that I am talking nonsense. Very possibly. But a hundred or two hundred years ago, invisible magnetism and electricity seemed like witchcraft to the precursors of our all-wise academics, and the sight of an automobile would have absolutely terrified them, not to mention X-rays or moving pictures. Who can tell, respected doctors and masters of science, perhaps the twentieth century will discover other forms of energy that our sense organs and imperfect instruments are not capable of detecting?

It is for the future to answer.

As for the modest reporter Zhemailo, who can see the future no more clearly than you can, you may rest assured, respected *Courier* readers, that your humble servant will remain on the trail of the 'Lovers of Death', and henceforth you will be the first to learn of all my new observations and discoveries.

Lavr Zhemailo
Moscow Courier, 13 (26)
September 1900, p.2

II. From Columbine's Diary

Unpredictable and capricious

I still do not know what he wants with me. He is certainly not trying to court me, and yet we spend quite a lot of time together. Supposedly I am helping him investigate the circumstances of poor Ophelia's death and at the same time all the other mysterious events connected with our club.

But sometimes I have the feeling that he is simply taking care of me, like some simple-minded, stupid provincial girl who has suddenly found herself in the big city. Perhaps I am a provincial, but I am not stupid and certainly not simple-minded. I am no longer the person I used to be. I have come to understand perfectly well these ordinary, boring people with their ordinary, boring concerns, which means that I myself have ceased to be ordinary and boring.

And yet I am glad of his tutelage. I have nothing to busy myself with during the day, and the evening meetings do not last for very long: three or four volunteers try their luck at the roulette wheel, and that is the end of it. Since that first evening when Genji won, no one else has landed on the skull, although Caliban, for instance, never misses a single evening. I shall describe my own attempt of the day before yesterday. It took me a long time to prepare myself for it, and the six that I was granted was simply insulting, if you really think about it! Measured according to the values of a pack of cards, it means that for Death I am the lowest card of all. But the most monstrous thing (which I did not write about before) is that what I felt when I failed was not disappointment, but intense, keen, absolutely shameful relief. I am clearly not yet ready.

After the departure of the Lioness of Ecstasy, for a short while I was the only woman in the club. I have already described the two new female aspirants briefly, but it turns out that I was too indulgent towards them. They are absolute nonentities! And while Iphigenia is tolerable, because she understands her own limitations, the second one, Gorgon, is always acting like a queen, straining to be the centre of attention. She is often successful, but in a less flattering sense than she would wish.

Goat-hoofed Kriton, naturally, started paying his attentions to both of them immediately – I heard him pontificating to Iphigenia about the naturalness of nudity. But of course, it was Prospero who gathered the pollen from these young blossoms: three days ago he told Gorgon to stay, and yesterday the rosy-cheeked fool. What is really strange is that I did not feel even slightly jealous. I have come to the conclusion that matters of carnal sensuality are not really of interest to me. A further proof of this came the day before yesterday, when Prospero suddenly took me by the hand after the game and led me after him.

I went. Why not? Alas, the magic was not repeated. In general, the whole business turned out rather stupidly. He lay me down on the bearskin again, blindfolded me and spent a long time running a cold, wet brush over my body (it turned out later that he was drawing magical signs in Chinese ink – I barely managed to wash them off). It tickled, and several times I gave way and giggled. The physiological part of the ritual was completed very quickly.

In general, I feel more and more persuaded that the 'raptures of sensuality' which Russian writers mention in such vague terms and *'les plaisirs de la chair'*[1] which are described in much greater detail in modern French literature, are just one more piece of make-believe, invented by humanity to romanticise the onerous obligation to continue the race. It's just like cognac. I recall, when I was little, I used to dream that when I grew up I would drink cognac too – Papa took such great pleasure in taking a glass before dinner in the evening. One day I plucked up my courage, moved a chair over to the sideboard, climbed up on it, picked up the carafe and took a sip out of it . . . I think that was the moment when I realised how much pretence there is in people. To this day I find the very sight of cognac revolting. How can anyone voluntarily drink that acrid muck? It would seem to be exactly the same with physiological love. I am sure that what gave Papa pleasure was not the cognac itself, but the ritual: Sunday, a grand dinner, the crystal carafe glinting, the anticipation of a leisurely, relaxed evening. The same applies to the act of love: everything that precedes it is so captivating that one can forgive the meaningless and shameful nature of the act itself, which fortunately does not last for long.

(I shall have to cross this paragraph out later – not because of the boldness of the ideas, that is really rather good – but it has turned out much too childish somehow. I shall dwell on the physiology in some other place, in greater detail and with less naivety.)

I think that Prospero noticed my disappointment – when we parted he had a thoughtful, perhaps even bewildered look. But his parting words were beautiful: 'Go and dissolve into the night.' I immediately felt like some creature of fantasy, a true phantom of the night. As I walked along the boulevard my steps were light and ethereal.

Even so, I am no longer a helpless puppet in his hands.

1. Pleasures of the flesh

Prospero's power over me is no longer absolute, his enchantment has weakened.

But why am I trying to be cunning with myself? It is not that the enchantment has weakened, it is just that Prospero no longer occupies my mind as much as he did before. It is not simply because I do not know how to keep myself occupied that I spend so much time with Genji. He intrigues me. Sometimes we say nothing for a long while, like yesterday in the coffee shop. But at other times we make conversation on the most surprising topics. Although he is taciturn, Genji is an engaging conversation partner. And a useful one, too, there are many things to be learned from him.

But what I really cannot stand about him is his vain male gallantry. Today I tried once again to make him accept the obvious: 'How can you be so blind, with your stupid materialism and your attempts to find a rational explanation for everything? Our world is a little spot of light, surrounded on all sides by darkness. And a myriad eyes watch us keenly from out of that darkness. Mighty hands guide our actions, pulling on invisible strings. We will never manage to understand this mechanism. Your attempts to anatomise the Signs from the Beyond are simply laughable!'

Instead of replying, he said: 'That is a very p-pretty dress, Mademoiselle Columbine, it suits you very well.'

The dress I was wearing really was rather good: light-blue silk with Brussels lace – at first glance entirely conventional, but with little bells sewn to the cuffs and bottom flounce, so that every movement is accompanied by a faint, gentle ringing sound – it is my own invention. However, this compliment paid so out of place made me angry.

'Don't you dare talk to me like some empty-headed idiot!' I exclaimed. 'What an appalling masculine manner!'

He smiled: 'Those could be the words of a suffragette.

But I thought you were giddy Columbine, a plaything in the hands of the wicked Harlequin.'

I blushed. I believe I did tell him something of the sort early in our acquaintance. How provincial! I would never utter such simpering banalities now. And yet only two weeks have gone by. Why have I changed so quickly?

Evidently the reason is that there is always someone dying close by, very close by. Death himself is circling round me smoothly and gracefully, and with every day the circles grow narrower. And Genji still talks about an investigation!

He is terribly secretive and tells me almost nothing. I don't know his real name or what he does for a living. I think he's an engineer – in any case he's very interested in technical novelties and he becomes very lively when the subject of self-propelled carriages and motorbicycles comes up.

What do I really know about him? He has lived abroad for ten years, moving from one country to another. He makes only short visits to Russia – for some reason he is not on good terms with the Moscow authorities. He told me he had to change his flat because Masa spotted some-one following them almost right in front of their very building. The Japanese dealt with the police agent rather roughly, because he cannot stand their kind ever since he was a bandit in his youth. They had to move out of Ascheulov Lane, which is only five minutes' walk from Prospero's house, to the Spassky Barracks on the other side of Sukharevka Street, where one of the officer's flats happened to be free.

If I try to get any details out of him, he replies evasively, and I can never tell if he is talking seriously or making fun of me.

Columbine raised her eyes from her diary to look at the window and chewed thoughtfully on her pen. What would be the best way to describe today's meeting in the café Rivoli?

She had arrived very late. That is, she had actually arrived before the agreed time and then strolled up and down on the opposite side of the street. She had seen Genji go into the café, and then spent another half-hour inspecting the shop windows. Arriving for an engagement on time was *mauvais ton*, a provincial habit that had to be extirpated. Just to be on the safe side, she had kept her eyes on the door. If he got bored of waiting and decided to leave, she would have to walk up and pretend that she had only just arrived.

I suppose I must look rather strange, thought Columbine: an extravagantly dressed young woman just standing here with nothing to do, like Lot's wife transformed into a pillar of salt. She looked around and noticed that she was indeed being stared at by a youth wearing a check jacket and a ridiculous straw boater with a silk ribbon. He licked his lips impertinently (a gold tooth glinted in his mouth). At least he didn't wink. He had obviously taken her for a cocotte. Well, let him. If not for the persistent attention of the young pup, she would have kept Genji languishing for longer.

He didn't appear to be languishing, though. He was sitting there quite calmly, reading the newspapers. He didn't utter a single word of reproach to Columbine for being late and he ordered her a cup of hot chocolate and cakes. He himself was drinking white wine.

'What interesting things have you read?' she asked in a perfunctory tone of voice. 'I really don't understand people who read the newspapers. All the really important things don't happen to other people, they happen to you and inside you. They won't write about that in any newspapers.'

He was dismayed by this judgement.

'Oh c-come now! Lots of interesting things happen to other people.'

'Oh yes?' Columbine said with a derisive smile. 'Well then, try to interest me in your news. What is going on in the world?'

'By all means.' He rustled the pages of his paper. 'Right. News from the theatre of military operations in the Transvaal. That is not likely to interest you . . . Let us try the sports section.' Genji turned the page. ' "Yesterday on Krestovsky Island in St Petersburg a match was held between the German and Petersburg f-football clubs. The Petersburg team was the attacking side and won a convincing victory over its opponents, putting the ball between the German posts for eighteen goals, while conceding only seven." How about that?'

She winced eloquently.

'What about the North Pole? A very curious article indeed. "Prince Ludwig d'Abruzzo has had to cut short his attempt to reach the North Pole using Siberian dogs and return to Spitsbergen. Three members of the expedition lost their lives amidst the hummocks of ice, while His Highness himself suffered severe frostbite and lost two fingers on his left hand. The failure of yet another attempt to reach the most northerly point on the planet has inspired Captain Johannesen to undertake a new project. The experienced arctic explorer intends to tame polar bears to replace the weak huskies. The captain claims that training young bears will take about three years, after which they will be ready to pull sleighs across the ice or a boat across the water with exceptional ease. Johannesen said that the preparations for his unusual expedition enjoy the p-patronage of Princess Xenia, wife of the heir to the throne, Prince Olaf." '

At that point Genji sighed for some reason and Columbine put her hand over her mouth as if she were yawning.

'All right then,' he conceded, realising that he would not succeed in interesting the lady in sport. 'Let's try the "Miscellaneous" section, there's always something curious in there. Take this for instance. "Swindlers' Original Trick. On 14 September the peasant Semyon Dutikov, newly arrived in Moscow, was walking along Sadovaya Street from the Kursk railway station and, not knowing how to get to Cherkassky Lane, he asked a man whom he did not know to show him the way. The man agreed and as they were walking along one of the more out-of-the-way lanes, the stranger pointed out a wallet lying in the middle of the pavement. It proved to contain seventy-five roubles. Dutikov agreed to split the money two ways, but just then a b-broad-shouldered gentleman came running out of a gateway, shouting that he had dropped the wallet, and there had been two hundred roubles in it . . ." Ah, the rogues! Poor peasant Dutikov!'

Taking the opportunity offered by Genji's breaking off from reading, she said: 'Why don't you read out something from the "Art" section? Who cares about your swindlers anyway? It's clear enough that your peasant was completely fleeced. Serves him right for hankering after someone else's property.'

'I hear and obey, Mademoiselle. "A New Play. The young writer Maxim Gorky has arrived in Moscow, bringing with him a new play that he has just written, which has not yet been submitted to the censor. He proposes to give the play the title *Philistines*. Gorky's first attempt at d-drama attracted lively interest from the directors of the Accessible Arts Theatre."'

'Phoo, phi-li-stines,' Columbine drawled. 'He might as well write a play about tramps or a flophouse. Our Russian writers are absolutely incorrigible. There's little enough beauty in life already, without all this, but they just carry on scrabbling in the dirt. Read about something more glamorous.'

'Here's something glamorous. "Multi-Millionaires' New Amusement. Newport, the most fashionable bathing resort of the American rich, has recently developed a genuine mania for automobile riding. The offspring of the most prominent American families can be seen hurtling along the highway and the seafront at dizzying speeds of up to thirty versts an hour. The police are recording a constant increase in the number of accidents caused by races between self-propelled carriages. The young Harold Vanderbilt was almost seriously injured recently when he crashed his Panhard-Levassor into a wagon of hay." And thirty versts an hour is not the limit!' Genji exclaimed enthusiastically. 'And anyway, it's not just a matter of speed! I'm certain that the auto-mobile is m-more than just an amusement, you can t-travel immense distances in it. And I shall prove that I'm right just as soon as I have concluded my business in Moscow!'

Columbine had never seen the imperturbable Genji so excited. The late Lorelei had been right: men were absolute children.

But then the Japanese prince's eye fell on the newspaper page again and his face darkened.

'What is it?' she asked cautiously.

'Another article about the Khitrovka Blinder,' he replied reluctantly, running his glance over the lines. 'They just don't seem able to catch him. It's nothing new, just idle j-journalistic speculation.'

'The Khitrovka Blinder?' Columbine queried, wrinkling up her pretty nose. 'Ah, that's the criminal who gouges out his victim's eyes? Yes, yes, I've heard about him. What a vulgar name for him! Why do crimes have to be so beastly boring? Where have the genuine artists of villainy gone? I would execute murderers, not because they kill, but because they make such a mediocre, vulgar job of their bloody deed!' This thought had only just occurred to Columbine. She felt the sudden inspiration was quite brilliant and provocative, but her uninspired companion failed to respond and gloomily closed his newspaper.

After the café they went for a stroll along Kuznetsky Most Street and Theatre Passage, where they met a demonstration of shopkeepers from Hunter's Row coming towards them, led by heralds from the municipal duma – they were march-ing in honour of another Russian military victory in China: General Rennenkampf had taken some place called Goujang and also Tsian-Gouan. They were carrying portraits of the tsar, icons and religious banners, and shouting in chorus: 'Hoorah for Russia!'

The marchers were hot and sweaty, red in the face and happy, but at the same time angry, as if someone had offended them.

'Look,' said Columbine, 'they are coarse, half-drunk and malicious, but they are patriots and they love their homeland. See how happy they all are, but what could Tsian-Gouan really mean to these shopkeepers? But you and I are educated, polite, dressed in clean clothes, and quite unconcerned about Russia.'

'What kind of patriots are they?' Genji said with a shrug. 'Just loudmouths, nothing more. For them it's just a legitimate excuse for b-bawling and shouting. True patriotism, like true love, never shouts itself out loud.'

She couldn't immediately find anything to say to that, it set her thinking. Ah, but no! True love did shout itself out loud, most certainly it did. Imagine that she'd fallen in love with someone, and he'd been taken away from her, wouldn't she shout out loud? She'd howl loud enough to deafen the entire world. But then, perhaps that's a matter of temperament, Columbine thought with a sigh. The tight-buttoned Genji probably wouldn't shout out even if you cut him to pieces – he'd consider it beneath his dignity.

She suddenly felt the urge to stir him into action, grab him by the shoulders and give him a really good shaking that would disturb that perfect parting in his hair.

'Why are you always so calm?' she asked.

Instead of shrugging the question off or changing the subject to something trivial in the way he usually did, he replied simply and seriously: 'I was not always like this, Mademoiselle Columbine. In my young days any trivial n-nonsense was enough to excite me. However, life has tested my sensibilities so frequently and so cruelly that now it is very hard to get through my defences. And, in addition, Confucius wrote: "The reserved man commits fewer blunders".'

She had no idea who Confucius was. Probably some ancient know-it-all, but she didn't like the maxim.

'Are you afraid of blunders?' she laughed disdainfully. 'Why, I want to build my whole life on blunders. I think nothing could be more beautiful.'

He shook his head: 'Are you familiar with the Eastern

doctrine of the reincarnation of souls? No? The Hindus, the Chinese and the Japanese believe that our soul lives not just once, but many times, repeatedly changing its corporeal integument. Depending on your actions, in the next life you may be promoted or, on the contrary, demoted to being a caterpillar or, say, a thistle. In this regard blunders are extremely dangerous, each one distances you further from a state of harmonious b-balance, thereby reducing your chances of being reborn as something more dignified.'

Columbine thought this final remark rather offensive, but she found this Eastern theory so astounding that she made no attempt to protest.

'In the next life I would like to turn into a dragonfly with transparent wings. No, a swallow! Is it possible to decide in advance who you will be born as next time around?'

'It is not possible to decide, but it is probably possible to guess – at least when life has almost been lived to the end. One of the Buddhist teachers asserts that with age the features of a man's face change to suggest who or what he will be when he is reborn into the world again. Do you not find that our D-Doge, for instance, is remarkably like an eagle-owl? If, during your next birth, you are flitting above a dark forest on light swallow's wings and you hear a hooting sound, then beware! It might well be the reincarnated Mr Prospero luring you into his snares again.'

She laughed. With his round, piercing eyes, hooked nose and disproportionately large cheeks, Prospero really did look like an eagle-owl.

All right, there was no need to write about the conversation with Genji, Columbine decided, but what she had to write about Prospero was important. She dipped her steel nib into the inkwell and carried on.

I have written here that, strangely enough, I am not at all jealous of the Doge's relations with Iphigenia and Gorgon. But I think he is jealous of me! I can feel it, I know it for certain. Women are never mistaken about such things. He is annoyed that I no longer gaze at him with melancholy, sheepish eyes as I used to do. This evening he paid no attention to either of them, he looked only at me. Both of the little fools were absolutely furious, and I must confess I enjoyed that, but it did not set my heart beating any faster. He lauded my new poem to the heavens. Oh, what bliss that praise would have been for me only a short while ago! But today it brought no joy at all, because I know perfectly well that the poem is mediocre.

Playing roulette is beginning to pall. The main sign is the abundance of volunteers. Today, in addition to our perennial player, Caliban, whose howls of disappointment are simply comical, even Petya and Kriton found the courage to spin the wheel (the former deep-red in the face, the latter deadly pale; a curious psychological detail, that – following a safe outcome, Petya turned as white as a sheet and Kriton blushed). The industrious anatomist Horatio suppressed a yawn as he spun the ball – I saw it quite distinctly. Cyrano even indulged in a little amusing mischief: while the roulette wheel was spinning, he sang the chansonette 'Spin, my darling girl'. The Doge observed this bravado in silence, with his forehead wrinkled into a frown. He must realise that the idea of the Wheel of Fortune has been a failure. Death clearly does not wish to abase herself by taking part in this cheap circus performance.

Only the German twins are still as diligent and serious as ever. Every time he throws the ball, Rosencrantz casts an expressive glance in my direction, but his attentions do not go any further than that. I notice that he and Guildenstern often exchange glances, as if they were talking to each other with their eyes. It seems to me that they understand each other perfectly well without words. I read somewhere that this happens with twins. One of them simply glances at the other, who hands him a cigarette case. And another thing: when the ball is skipping round the cells, the twin who has thrown it doesn't look at the wheel, but only at his brother, trying to guess the result from the expression on the face that is so much like his own. Gdlevsky observes our games with ironical con-descension. He is waiting for the great day – tomorrow is Friday. We all tease him, but he maintains a haughty silence and smiles with an air of confident superiority. It is easy to see that in his opinion all the other aspirants are nonentities and he is the only one worthy to become Death's beloved. Caliban, infuriated by yet another failure on the wheel, called the schoolboy 'an insolent pup' and things almost went as far as a duel.

And at the end of the evening, Columbine played a trick that surprised even her. When the 'lovers' began going home, the Doge came over to her, his light-haired Bac-chante, and took her chin between his thumb and forefinger.

'Stay,' he ordered her.

She responded with a long, intriguing glance. Then she gave his hand a glancing kiss with her pink lips and whispered: 'Not today. I am going, dissolving into the night.'

She swung round lightly and walked away, and he was left standing there, perplexed, gazing beseechingly after the slim figure of the unpredictable and capricious enchantress.

And serve him right.

Friday is a special day

That Friday Columbine left her flat earlier than usual to go to the meeting of the club – it was that kind of evening; with a subtle, tremulous thrill, it held the promise of something either very good or, on the contrary, very terrible, or perhaps very good and very terrible at the same time.

She had already sensed the exciting savour of tragedy in the morning, when she saw the deceptively clear September sky covering the city like a semi-transparent porcelain chalice.

Before breakfast she performed her usual morning exercise to teach her soul not to be afraid of death. She went out on to the balcony, opened the cast-iron gate that led into emptiness and stood right on the very edge, listening to the rapid beating of her heart. The sounds coming up from the street had an eloquently hollow echo, the windows opposite her shimmered with tremulous patches of light, and below her the angel captured by Möbius and Sons stood with its wings spread wide.

Then came the day, empty and meaningless – a pause, a drawing-in of breath, the silence before the velvet curtains of the night parted. But in the early evening Columbine's keen hearing caught the distant sounds of a mystical orchestra, discordant as yet, but already magical, and she simply could not stay at home any longer.

As she walked along the purple streets with her heels clattering, the sweetly alarming sounds of the overture came drifting towards her and with every step the thunderous melody became clearer and clearer.

Columbine was prepared for anything, and as a sign of her resolution she had dressed herself in the colours of mourning. The meek schoolgirl, seeking to comprehend the secrets of death, had put on a modest black dress with a narrow white collar and a lilac apron with a mourning border, she had woven her hair into two vestal plaits and drawn them together with a crimson ribbon.

She walked unhurriedly, thinking about beautiful things. About how Friday was a special day, forever soaked in the blood of the dreamy and starry-eyed Pierrot, whom the cruel Harlequins had nailed to planks of wood nineteen centuries before. Because the scarlet drops would not dry up, but kept oozing out and dribbling down the cross, shimmering and glittering in the sun, the fifth day of the week was filled with a deceptive, flickering gleam of calamity.

From the boulevard Columbine turned into a sidestreet,

and there the overture came to an end, and she heard the first solo aria of this ominous opera – an aria so absurdly comical that the dreamer very nearly laughed out loud. For a moment she imagined that the night had played a joke on her by inviting her to a tragedy and instead staging a farce.

Standing there on the pavement under a streetlamp, about ten steps away from Prospero's house, was a shabby old organ grinder wearing a red fez and spectacles with blue lenses. He was furiously turning the handle of his squeaky instrument and bawling out a stupid little song at the top of his tuneless voice – it must have been his own composition.

> *Oh, barrel-barrel organ,*
> *The road leads ever on.*
> *Who can tell this poor boy*
> *Where his happiness has gone?*

There were many couplets, but most of the song consisted of a repeated refrain, uncouth doggerel, like all the other verses. The tin-plated throat repeated it over and over again:

> *Spin the lacquered handle*
> *But it won't bring happiness.*
> *No amount of twirling will give me back my Beth!*
> *No amount of twirling will give me back my Beth!*
> *No amount of twirling will give me back my Beth!*

Columbine stood and listened for a minute or two, then burst into loud laughter, tossed the amusing old man a coin and thought: a pessimist like that – and a poet too – really ought to join us 'lovers'.

'Today we shall spin the Wheel of Death for the last time,' the Doge announced to the assembled company. 'And if a Chosen One is not named yet again, I shall invent a new ritual.'

First Caliban and then Rosencrantz threw the little gold ball, and both were rejected by Death.

'I know what the trouble is,' said Cyrano, wrinkling up his monumental nose. 'The ambulance carriage that brought Prince Genji back to life is to blame for everything. It stole Death's betrothed from under the very wedding wreath, so to speak. And now the Great Lady has taken offence at our roulette wheel. So help me, Genji, you ought to drink poison again. You're the reason the roulette wheel is being stubborn.'

Someone laughed at this audacious joke. Genji smiled politely, but Prospero looked so unhappy that Columbine felt sorry for him.

'No, no!' she exclaimed. 'Let me try my luck! If Death is offended with men, then perhaps a woman will be lucky? After all, the Tsarevich summoned the Lioness of Ecstasy!'

Once she said it, she felt frightened. What if she did land on the skull? Her presentiment, and her funeral garb both pointed to the same thing.

She strode up to the table very quickly, to give herself no time to imagine the possible consequences, grabbed the little ball and prepared to throw it.

At that very moment the last of the 'lovers', Gdlevsky, who was late, walked, or rather, came rushing into the room like a tornado. His ruddy face with the first timid fluff of a moustache was glowing with happiness and delight.

'I have it!' he shouted from the doorway. 'I have the third Sign! And precisely on a Friday! The third Friday in a row! Do you hear, do you hear what he is singing?' Gdlevksy pointed triumphantly at the window, through which only a minute earlier they could hear the wheezing of the barrel organ and the hoarse howling of the old man. 'Did you hear what he was singing? "No amount of twirling will give me back my Beth"! And over and over again!'

But now, as if to spite him, the organ grinder had fallen silent. And apart from Columbine, none of the aspirants seemed to have bothered to listen to the refrain of the idiotic little song, so Gdlevsky's announcement caused general bewilderment.

'What Beth? What is she spinning?' Kriton asked in amazement. 'What are you talking about, young man?'

'The barrel organ,' Gdlevsky explained agitatedly. 'But that's not important at all. The important thing is the rhyme: Beth – death. It's the Sign! No doubt about it! The third Sign! I've been chosen, chosen!'

'Wait, wait!' the Doge asked with a frown. 'You're imagining things! Where is this organ grinder?'

Everyone dashed to the window, but the street was deserted, with not a soul to be seen. The old man had dissolved into the thickening darkness.

Without saying a word, Genji turned and walked quickly out into the hallway.

Everyone turned to look at the schoolboy again. Rosencrantz, who did not understand Russian very well, asked his brother: *'Was bedeutet twirling?'*[2]

There was obvious envy in the glance that he cast at Gdlevsky.

'Why him? Why this young pup?' Caliban groaned. 'What makes him any better than me? How can you call this fair! Doge, you promised!'

The Doge flung up one hand angrily.

'Quiet everyone! Boy, Death does not tolerate cheating. You are not playing fair! Yes, there was a barrel organ here for a long time, but naturally I did not listen to the song. Perhaps he did sing a word that rhymes with "death", but there are many words in a song, not just one. Why did you decide to pick out "Beth". You're as bad as Rosencrantz with his fruit drink.'

Rosencrantz flushed. A few days earlier he had also come running in beaming with pride and said he was now Death's Chosen One, because he had been sent a clear and unmistakable Sign. When he was eating supper in Alyabev's

2. What does twirling mean?

restaurant on Petrovka Street, just before he finished his meal, he had been given a carafe of something bloody red 'on the house'. When he asked what it was, the waiter had 'smiled mysteriously' and said: 'You know, it's Mors.'[3] Rosencrantz had darted out of the room without finishing his supper and run all the way to Prospero's house.

The mention of the Mors was greeted with laughter, but Gdlevsky was not even slightly disconcerted.

'No cheating. It's a Friday again, gentlemen, the third in a row. I didn't sleep all night, I knew it would happen! I didn't go to my lessons. I've been walking the streets since this morning, waiting for the Sign. Listening to conversations that I came across by chance, reading posters and signboards. I have played entirely fair, been absolutely honest! On the Arbat I saw a signboard that said "Aron Speth, Hardware and Ironmongery". I've walked past there a hundred times and never noticed that shop before. It simply took my breath away. That's it, I thought! What sort of absurd name is that? Names like that don't even exist. Speth – death, it's so obvious! But I wanted to make certain, so that there couldn't possibly be any doubt. If it had ended on Speth, that would have been it, but the last word was "ironmongery". Ironmongery – what on earth rhymes with that? So it was no good, and I walked on by. And I had such a desolate feeling. No, I thought, I'm not a Chosen One, I'm the same as all the rest. On my way here I was almost crying. Then suddenly I turn the corner and I hear "give me back my Beth, give me back my Beth, give me back my Beth". Three times, gentlemen, three times on the third Friday. First I hit on the word "breath" by sheer chance, and then I opened a book at *Macbeth*, and now this name, "Beth". What could possibly be any clearer? And even if it is a proper name, what does that matter! What are you all staring at?' the schoolboy asked with a sardonic laugh. 'Do you envy me? I'm the Chosen

3. A drink made from berries, but also 'Death' in Latin

179

One, not you! It's me, the very youngest! So what if I am young? I'm a genius, I could have been a new Lermontov. Death chooses the best, not the worst. First Lorelei, and then me. And anyway, I couldn't give a damn for Lermontov! Or for the whole world, or for all of you! Spin your roulette wheel, titillate your wretched nerves. The only thing I have to say to you is "adieu". The Princess has chosen me! Me, not you!'

He looked round defiantly at everyone with his inflamed eyes and walked out, still laughing triumphantly.

'Stop! Come back immediately!' Prospero shouted after him.

In vain.

'What this Lermontov deserves is a good box on the ear,' Horatio declared pensively, stroking his Van Dyke beard.

White with fury, Caliban brandished his clenched fist.

'Impudent, cocky, puffed-up little polack! How dare he compare himself with Lermontov! The impostor!'

'Lermontov was impudent and cocky too,' Cyrano remarked. 'It will be a pity if the boy does anything stupid. He really is exceptionally talented. Lermontov was killed by someone else, but this one wants to climb into the grave himself.'

They left feeling subdued, in fact almost crushed.

Columbine had an uneasy, wretched feeling now, not at all like the one she had had before the meeting as she walked slowly through the evening streets. The stupid, arrogant boy, she thought. Prospero is absolutely right. How can the ludicrous croakings of a hoarse tramp be taken for a Sign from the Eternal Bride? And he's sure to kill himself, he won't back down, if only out of pride. And what a loss that would be for Russian literature, which had already lost its most gifted poetess only a few days earlier!

Columbine stopped on the boulevard, feeling that she couldn't simply walk home and go to bed as if nothing had happened

Gdlevsky had to be stopped. By any means, at any price!

But how? What could she do?

She knew his address. One day shortly after she became a member, Gdlevsky had told her that his parents lived in Kolomna, but he had transferred to a Moscow grammar school for the final year of study, and he rented a room in Kleinfeld's apartments on Maslovka Street. The boy had been terribly proud of the fact that he lived on his own, like a grown-up.

Well what if she did go to his place, then what? Why would he listen to Columbine if Prospero himself had been unable to stop him? Now even the Doge carried no authority for him. Why, of course not, Gdlevsky was a 'Chosen One', a 'genius'!

What should she do?

The answer came to mind quickly.

Among the 'lovers' there was only one man capable of stopping the crazed poet doing something foolhardy. Even by force, if necessary. Genji! Of course, he always knew what to do. How unfortunate that he had gone out and not heard the schoolboy's monologue right to the end!

She had to go to see Genji immediately, without wasting a moment. She just hoped he would be at home. Gdlevsky would not kill himself until he had written his farewell poem, so she might be in time.

She knew the Japanese prince's approximate address. Hadn't Genji told her he had moved from Ascheulov Lane to the officers' building at the Spassky Barracks?

The cabdriver delivered the agitated young lady to Spasskaya-Sadovaya Street and pointed to a long building painted official pale yellow. 'That's it, the officers' block.'

But it proved difficult to find the right room, because she did not know the tenant's name. Columbine described Genji in detail to the doorkeeper, not forgetting to mention the stammer and the grey temples. She said she'd put his card somewhere and couldn't find it, that she had a terrible memory for names – she could remember addresses, but names eluded her. She needed to see the gentleman she had described on a matter of the utmost urgency. The black-bearded doorkeeper heard her out without saying a word and, of course, he didn't believe her. He looked the agitated girl over from head to toe, chewed on his lips and declared.

'How do we know, perhaps His Excellency will give us the rough side of his tongue for a visit like this. This is a barracks, young lady, strangers aren't allowed.'

'His Excellency!' So there was no mistake, Genji hadn't deceived her and he did live here. Columbine was so delighted that she wasn't even offended by the insulting remark. Let Blackbeard think that she was some kind of impertinent admirer or *demi-mondaine* – what difference did that make?

Columbine had mastered very well the lesson in dealing with the tribe of yard keepers and doorkeepers that she had once learned from Genji.

'No, he won't,' she said confidently. 'He'll reward you for it. And meanwhile, take this.'

And she handed the attendant a rouble.

Cerberus immediately stopped growling and started wagging his tail. He put the banknote away in his peaked cap and told her: 'All sorts come to see His Excellency. Even Khitrovka bandit types – not up to Your Grace's standard. His Excellency is staying in the apartment of his friend Lieutenant-Colonel Smolyaninov. On a temporary basis. His Honour Mr Lieutenant-Colonel is in China at present, but we have orders always to let his friend stay for as long as he likes. And his name is Mr Neimless. Erast Petrovich. That's him.'

'Erast Petrovich Neimless?' Columbine repeated the strange name and then could not resist asking: 'But why do you call him "His Excellency"?'

'We have a well-practised eye for a real gentlemen, even if he calls himself Ragamuffinov. Only you've wasted your time in coming, young lady, Mr Neimless is out, he hasn't come back home yet. His valet is home though.'

'The Japanese?' Columbine asked, to make sure. 'Masa?'

'Masail Mitsuevich,' the attendant corrected her sternly. 'A most particular gentleman. Would you like to see him?'

'I would, Since Erast . . . e-e-er . . . Petrovich is not here.'

'By all means. My wife will show you how to get there. Fenya! Fenya! Show this young lady the way!' the doorman shouted, turning towards the open door of the porter's lodge. There was no answer.

'She must have gone out. And I didn't even notice,' Blackbeard said in surprise. 'Well, never mind, you won't go astray. Walk along the wall, and when you turn the corner, the steps and porch are right there.'

The porch was quickly found, but when she knocked no one answered. Eventually Columbine's patience ran out – after all, every minute was vital – and she angrily smashed her open palm against the door, which opened with a creak; it hadn't been locked after all. A moment later the visitor was already in the small, spartan hallway, where the coat stand was hung with military greatcoats and civilian coats, as well as various belts, whips, bridles and other assorted horse tackle.

'Masa, where are you?' Columbine called. 'I've come on urgent business. Will Mr Neimless be back soon?'

She heard rustling sounds and whispering behind a door decorated with a poster of French cancan dancers. Angry now, Columbine moved resolutely towards the sound, jerked the door open and froze.

The Japanese was standing there in his shirt front and cuffs, but with no trousers, helping a lady of ample dimensions who was much taller than him squeeze into a calico skirt. The effect produced by the unexpected visitor's appearance was dramatic. The well-endowed lady squealed and squatted down, covering her impressive breasts with her hands, but Mr Neimless's amazing valet set his plump hands against his thighs and bowed in ceremonial fashion.

'What business, Corumbine-san?' he asked on straightening up. 'Urgen'-urgen' or simpry urgen'?'

'Urgent-urgent,' she replied, trying not to look at the fat

woman with no clothes on or the hairless legs of the Japanese, although this was not the moment for conventional propriety. 'We need to go and rescue someone immediately, or something dreadful will happen. Where is your master?'

Masa knitted his sparse eyebrows, thought for a moment and declared decisively: 'Masta not here. And terephone not ring. I rescue zis someone.' He bowed to his lady love, who had not yet recovered from her state of shock, and pushed her towards the door. 'Vewy gratefuw, Fenya-san, prease remember us kindry.'

Fenya (evidently the same woman who had not responded to the doorman's call) grabbed her shoes, blouse and stockings and shot out of the door. Columbine turned away so that the Oriental could finish getting dressed.

A minute later they were already hurrying towards the gates, with Masa working his short legs so briskly that his companion could hardly keep up with him.

They rode in a cab for a long time, then they had to search for the Kleinfeld apartments in the dark, until eventually they found the grey, three-storey house opposite the Petrovsky Park. As befitted a poet, Gdlevsky rented a room on the attic floor.

As they walked up the stairs (the Japanese leading and Columbine following) she kept repeating: 'If only we're in time, if only we're in time.'

The door was locked and no one opened it when they knocked.

'Shall I go down to get the yard keeper?' Columbine asked in a trembling voice.

'No need. Stand aside a rittur, Corumbine-san.'

She stepped back. The Japanese uttered a peculiar abdominal sound, leapt up in the air and struck the door a terrifyingly powerful blow with his foot, sending it flying off its hinges with a crash.

They dashed to the room, their shoulders colliding in the narrow corridor.

The first thing that Columbine noticed in the twilight was

the rectangle of the wide-open window. And she caught a pungent, strangely familiar smell. It was the smell the butchers' stalls had when she was still a child and the cook Frosya used to take her to the market to buy offal and intestines for the home-made sausage.

'Yes, was very urgen', absorutery urgen',' Masa sighed. He struck a match and lit a kerosene lamp.

Columbine cried out.

The poet was lying on his front, with his face in a large, gleaming puddle. She saw the light-brown hair on the back of his head, soaked in blood, the arms flung out impotently.

They were too late!

What a terrible hurry he was in, Columbine thought.

She turned away with a shudder and saw a sheet of paper on the table, beside the lamp. Walking across to it on leaden legs, she read the lines of regular, even writing, without a single slip of the pen.

The curtains swayed to and fro,
Brocade whispering my name.
The candle on the bureau
Choked out its own dim flame.

The fingers of some dark shades
Have plucked some invisible string.
Could she really have espied
My icon lamp's flickering?

Will this morbid dream of strife
Surrender in joy to Death?
Will the candle flame of life
Be snuffed by her virginal breath?

Not the death of whom we write,
In the daily prose of our time,
But the Other, in whom we delight
As the Mistress of our rhyme.

'Oh God,' she groaned. 'Why was he in such a great hurry?'

'To get away quickry, before he noticed,' Masa replied, with his face almost touching the dead man. Then he stuck his head out of the window. 'He did job and wen back ou'.'

'Who went?' Columbine sobbed. 'Where did he go? What are you talking about?'

Masa's answer came as a shock.

'Ze kirrer. Came in by fire radder, broke his skull and crimb back ou'.'

'What killer? Gdlevsky killed himself! Ah yes, you don't know anything about it!'

'Himself?' Masa picked up the piece of iron pipe. 'Rike zat?' He took off his bowler hat and pretended to hit himself on the back of the head. 'Rike zat very difficur', Columbine-san. No, young man was sitting at tabur. Someone crimbed in window. Young man frightened, ran towards door. Kirrer catch him and hit him on back of head with pipe.'

He squatted down beside the body and poked about in the bloody mess with his fingers. Columbine grabbed hold of the edge of the table as the room suddenly swam before her eyes.

'Skurr smashed to smi-the-reens,' said the Japanese, clearly savouring the impressive word. 'Very, very strong kirrer. No many so strong. That good. Wirr be easier for masta to find him.'

Columbine was still struggling to recover from this new shock. Gdlevsky hadn't committed suicide? Someone had killed him? But who? What for? It was ludicrous, insane!

'We have to send for the police!' she muttered.

The only thing she wanted was to get out of that room with its fresh smell of slaughter as soon as possible.

'I'll do it. I'll go down to the yard keeper!'

Masa shook his head.

'No, Corumbine-san. First ze masta. Ret him rook. Porice rater. Wait here. I go rook for terephone.'

He was gone for about twenty minutes, and those were the worst twenty minutes of Columbine's life. That was what she thought as she stood at the window, looking out at the lights shining beyond the black bulk of the Petrovsky Park. She was afraid to turn round.

When she heard a light rustling sound behind her, she squeezed her eyes shut and cringed, pulling her head down into her shoulders. She imagined Gdlevsky's corpse getting up off the floor, turning its shattered head and walking towards the window with its hands reaching out. There is nothing worse than standing with your back to an unknown danger. Columbine squealed and swung round.

It would have been better if she hadn't.

Gdlevsky had not got up off the floor, he was still lying there, face down, but his hair was moving in a strange manner. Columbine looked closer and saw two mice crawling about in the wound and sniffing at it.

Choking on her own scream, she dashed to the door, flew out on to the stairs and ran into Masa on his way back up.

'I rang from night chemist's,' he reported. 'Masta at home. He come now. He very gratefuw to you, Corumbine-san. You can go home. I must be here, cannot see you to cab. Zis is unforgivabur.' And the Japanese bowed guiltily.

God, how she ran to get away from those cursed Kleinfeld apartments! She ran all the way to Triumphal Square before she found a night cab.

When she had caught her breath and gathered her thoughts a little, she started pondering on the meaning of what had happened. The meaning proved to be simple, clear and frightening.

Since Gdlevsky had not killed himself but *been* killed (Masa had proved that irrefutably), there was only one creature that could have done it – if, of course, you could call this force a creature. No one had climbed into the attic window from the fire ladder. It was not someone, but Something that had entered the room. That was the explanation for a blow of such monstrous, *superhuman* power.

'Death is alive,' Columbine repeated to herself, gazing with wide-open eyes at the cabdriver's stooped back.

187

The creature that went by the name of Death could walk round the city, look into windows, strike blows of fearsome power. It could love and hate, it could feel insulted.

How Gdlevsky had insulted Death was clear. The arrogant boy had declared himself her Chosen One, when he had no right to that title, he had arbitrarily invented Signs that did not really exist. He was a genuine impostor, and for that he had suffered the fate of impostors.

The sheer grandeur of what had happened set her trembling.

Columbine meekly handed the driver the extortionate sum of two roubles, although the journey should have cost seventy-five kopecks at the most.

She didn't remember walking upstairs to the fifth floor, but as she was taking off her lilac mourning apron, a small rectangle of thick white paper fell out of the pocket. She picked it up absentmindedly and read the single word written on it in beautiful Gothic letters: 'Liebste'[4].

At first she smiled, imagining that shy Rosencrantz had finally plucked up the courage to take decisive action. But then she remembered that the German had not come near her even once during the whole evening, so he couldn't possibly have slipped the note into her pocket.

But who had written it? And why in German?

In German, Death was a male noun – der Tod.

'So now my turn has come,' Columbine said to her reflection in the mirror.

The reflection's lips smiled, its eyes staring in wild fright.

Columbine opened her diary and tried to describe her feelings. With a trembling hand she traced out the words: 'Have I really been chosen? How jolly and how frightening!'

4. Most beloved

III. From the 'Agents' Reports' File

To His Honour Lieutenant-Colonel Besikov
(Private and confidential)

Dear Lieutenant-Colonel,

I must confess that your note, delivered this morning by courier, came as a great shock to me. I already knew about the murder of Gdlevsky, because even before your messenger arrived I had a visit from one of the 'lovers' who was absolutely shattered by the incredible news. My initial response to your request to provide the detective police with every possible assistance was intense indignation. I decided that you had lost all sense of proportion and wished to reduce me to the status of a petty informer from Khitrovka.

However, after I had calmed down a little, I took a slightly different point of view of the matter. A genuine tragedy had occurred. A young man with an immense talent that promised great things – perhaps as great as Lermontov or Pushkin – had been killed at the age of eighteen, before he could make any substantial contribution to Russian literature. A few brilliant poems will find their way into anthologies and collections, but that will be the poor youth's entire legacy. What a bitter, senseless loss! If Gdlevsky had laid hands on himself, as he was planning to do, that would have been a tragedy, but his murder is worse than tragic. It is a national disgrace. It is the duty of every patriot who holds dear the honour of Russia to do everything in his power to assist in clarifying this shameful affair. Yes, yes, I regard myself as a true Russian patriot, it is well known that the most sincere and passionate patriots are always drawn from the national minorities (to which you and I belong).

And so I have decided to do everything in my power to assist your colleagues from the police. Having analysed the information that you provided about the circumstances of the crime, I was struck by the following.

It is not clear why anyone would wish to murder a person who intended in any case to kill himself only a minute or an hour later.

And if someone did resort to murder for some purpose or other, then why did they not disguise the crime as a voluntary death? Nobody would ever have thought of suspecting foul play when the farewell poem had already been written.

The first explanation that comes to mind is coincidence – just as Gdlevsky was preparing to commit suicide (you wrote that he had a loaded pistol ready in the drawer of his desk), a robber who knew nothing about the young man's fatal intentions climbed in through his window and hit him over the head with a length of metal pipe. A cruel joke played by fate. You write that the police regard this account of events as the most likely and ask my opinion.

I do not know what answer to give.

I think it might well interest you to know how the members of the club regard what has happened. Naturally, the story has made a very grave impression on everyone. The predominant feeling is fear, and fear of a mystical nature. Everyone is terribly frightened. No one mentions the idea of a robber who happened to climb in through the window. The general opinion is that Gdlevsky angered the Goddess with his boundless presumption, and she smashed his arrogant head to pieces. 'No one should dare try to lure the Eternal Bride to the altar by deceit,' is how our chairman expressed his own response.

As you know, I am a materialist and refuse to believe in the work of the Devil or evil spirits. I would sooner believe in the coincidental burglar. Only, if it was a burglar, why was he carrying a piece of metal pipe? And furthermore, you write that nothing was taken from the flat. Of course, it is possible to find an explanation for everything. We could assume that he took the weapon with him just in case, simply for use as a threat. And he didn't steal anything because he took fright at what he had done and fled. Well, that is certainly possible.

In any case, I am well aware that you asked for my opinion largely out of politeness, remembering my rebuke about airs and graces, and what you actually require are observations, not hypotheses. Well then, by all means.

I observed the behaviour of all the aspirants very carefully today, looking for anything suspicious or strange. Let me say straight away that I saw nothing suspicious, but I did make one astonishing discovery, which you will no doubt find interesting.

We did not play roulette today. Nobody did anything but discuss Gdlevsky's death and what it might mean. Naturally, the general mood was alarm and agitation, everyone tried to talk louder than everyone else, and our Doge was like a captain struggling at the helm of ship that is out of control. I also made a few comments for the sake of appearances, but most of the time I observed the others' faces keenly. Suddenly I saw Cyrano (the one whom I have referred to in previous reports as Big Nose) casually walk over to the bookshelves and run his eye over them – he seemed to do it quite absentmindedly, and yet I had the impression that he was looking for something very specific. He glanced round to make sure that no one was watching (which immediately made me even more curious), took out one of the volumes and started leafing through the pages. For some reason he looked up at the light, licked his finger and ran it over the edges of the pages. And then he even touched them with his tongue. I do not know the significance of these manipulations, but I was intrigued.

What happened next was remarkable. Cyrano put the book back in its place and turned round. I was astounded by the expression on his face – it was completely red, and his eyes were gleaming. He strolled slowly round the room, pretending to be bored, and when he reached the door, he slipped out into the hallway.

I cautiously left the room after him, expecting that now he would go out into the street and I would follow him – he really was behaving very strangely. However, Cyrano walked down the dark corridor leading into the apartment and darted into the study. I went after him without making a sound and put my ear to the door. The study can be reached by a different route – from the sitting room through the dining room, but that could have attracted attention, which Cyrano clearly wished to avoid, and I soon realised why. The reason for the entire manoeuvre was the telephone in Prospero's study.

Cyrano twirled the handle, gave a number in a low voice – I remembered it, in case it was important: 3845. Then he put his hand across the opening of the mouthpiece and said: 'Romuald Semyonovich? It's me, Lavr Zhemailo. Have you put the edition to bed? Excellent! Hold it. Leave a column on the first page. About sixty lines. No, better make it ninety. I assure you, this will be a bombshell. Wait for me, I'm leaving straight away.' His voice was trembling with excitement.

So much for Cyrano! A fine aspirant he is! And our smart alecks kept wondering how the reporter from the *Courier* could be so well-informed about the internal life of the club. But what a newspaperman! He has known for ages where the future suicides gather, but he carries on duping the public, pretending that he is searching incessantly, and meanwhile he has made a name for himself and also, no doubt, earned himself a tidy sum. Who had ever heard of Lavr Zhemailo even a month ago? But now he is the star of Russian journalism.

The reporter darted back out of the study so quickly that I barely managed to press myself against the wall in time. He did not notice me, because he hurried off towards the front door. The door into the study was left slightly ajar. And then something else strange happened. The opposite door – the one leading into the dining room, was also slightly ajar, but it suddenly squeaked and closed of its own accord! I swear to you that I am not making this up. There was no draught. That ominous creaking sound made me feel quiet unwell. My knees started trembling, my heart started pounding so rapidly that I was even obliged to swallow two tablets of cordinium. When I finally pulled myself together and ran out into the street after the journalist, he had already disappeared.

But then what point would there have been in following him, when it was already clear that he was going to his newspaper's office?

I wonder what 'bombshell' he had in store for his readers.

Never mind, we shall find that out from the morning edition of the *Moscow Courier*.

With every assurance of my heartfelt respect,

ZZ

17 September 1900

CHAPTER 5

I. From the Newspapers

Lavr Zhemailo is Dead

Active opponent of suicide takes his own life

The world of Moscow's newspapers has been shaken by woeful news.

Our trade has lost one of its most brilliant pens. A bright star that only recently made its appearance in the journalistic firmament has been extinguished.

The police are conducting an investigation and following every possible line of enquiry, including the possibility of a ritual execution carried out by the 'Lovers of Death', although it is quite clear to all those who have read Lavr Zhemailo's brilliant articles in the *Moscow Courier* that the members of that secret club are in the habit of ending their own lives, not those of others. No, what happened was not a murder, but a tragedy that is in some ways even more lamentable. Our colleague took too heavy a burden upon his own shoulders, a burden that was perhaps too onerous for any mortal to bear, and that burden broke him. Now he is on the far side of that fatal dividing line, he has joined the 'majority' of which he wrote in his visionary article that caused such a stir, 'There are more things in heaven and earth . . .'

We knew Lavr Zhemailo as a tireless opponent of the terrible phenomenon which many of us call 'the plague of the twentieth century' – the epidemic of apparently motiveless suicides that is mowing down the ranks of our educated youth. The deceased was a genuine crusader, who threw down the gauntlet to this insatiable, bloodthirsty dragon. How long is it since he came to conquer Moscow, this self-effacing reporter from Kovno who won his reputation at the provincial level and then, like many before him, moved to Russia's Old Capital? He had to start again here, from the very bottom of the journalistic hierarchy – as a journeyman reporter, recording the petty chronicle of everyday life, describing house fires and other insignificant events. But talent always breaks through, and very soon the whole of Moscow was following with bated breath as the indefatigable journalist tracked the sinister 'Lovers of Death'. In recent weeks Lavr Zhemailo appeared only rarely in the offices of the *Courier*. Our colleagues told us that his enthusiasm for the investigation was so great that he had virtually turned his entire life into a secret operation and submitted his reports only via the municipal post – no doubt he was afraid of being exposed by the 'Lovers of Death', or of attracting too much attention

from the gentlemen of the police force. An outstanding example of a man's genuine dedication to his profession!

Alas, the medic who seeks to treat epidemic illnesses runs the risk of contracting the plague himself. But perhaps a different comparison is appropriate here, with those devotees of the public health who quite deliberately inoculate themselves with the bacillus of some deadly ailment in order to study its infectious mechanism more closely, so that they can save others.

God only knows what turmoil ravaged our colleague's soul on the final evening of his life. We know only one thing – he remained a journalist right up to the very last minute. The day before yesterday he phoned the maker-up at the *Moscow Courier*, Mr Bozhovsky, and told him to hold the morning edition because he had 'a bombshell' for the front page.

Now we know what 'bombshell' the deceased had in mind – his own suicide. Well, the conclusion of Lavr Zhemailo's career was certainly dramatic. It is only a pity that the horrific news failed to make the morning edition of the *Moscow Courier*. Fate played a final trick on the journalist – his body was only discovered at dawn, after the newspaper had already been printed, even though the spot he chose for his suicide was very visible – Rozhdestvensky Boulevard, which is only a stone's throw from Trubnaya Square. The body hanging on an aspen tree really ought to have been noticed by some late passerby or the local constable, or a night cabby, especially since it was lit up by a nearby gas lamp, but it hung there until after five in the morning, when it was spotted by a street sweeper who came out to start clearing away the leaves.

Sleep well, passionate soul. We shall finish the job that you began. Our paper solemnly vows to raise the fallen banner anew and carry it forward. The demon of suicide will be banished from the streets of our Christian city. The *Moscow Gazette* will continue the journalistic investigation begun by our colleagues from the *Courier*. Watch out for our forthcoming articles.

The Editors
Moscow Gazette, 19
September (2 October) 1900,
front page

II. From Columbine's Diary

Chosen!

After I discovered in my handbag a second card with the single word *'Bald'*[1] written in the familiar Gothic letters, absolutely no doubt remained: I have been chosen, chosen!

Yesterday's effusive outpourings on the subject of this realisation were laughable – the cluckings of a frightened hen. I have not simply crossed them out. I have torn out the two pages. I shall insert something more appropriate later.

Later? When later, if I have been told *'Bald'*?

The short word echoes inside my head, setting it ringing. When I go out I am not myself, I stumble into people on the pavement, I feel terrified and delighted by turns. But the main feeling I have is one of pride.

Columbine has changed completely. Perhaps she is no longer Columbine at all, but the alluring Distant Princess, far beyond the reach of any simple mortal.

All other interests and contingencies have been set aside, lost all meaning. Now I have a new ritual that sets my heart trembling: in the evening, when I get back from Prospero's house, I take out the two small white rectangles, look at them, kiss them reverently and put them away in a drawer. I am loved!

The change that has taken place in me is so great that I

1. Soon

feel no need to conceal it. Everyone in the club knows that
Death is writing notes to me, but when I am asked to
show these messages I always refuse. Genji is particularly
persistent. As a man of intelligence, he realises that I am
not fantasising, and he is very concerned – but I do not
know if his concern is really for me or for the threat to his
materialist views.

I cherish these messages and will not show them to
anyone, they are mine and mine alone, addressed to me
and meant for my eyes only.

I behave like a real queen at our meetings now. Or if
not a queen, then at least the favourite or bride of the
king. I am betrothed to the Royal Bridgroom. Iphigenia
and Gorgon are green with envy, Caliban hisses in spite
and the Doge looks at me with the melancholy eyes of a
beaten dog. He is no Prospero, no master of the spirits of
the earth and the air. He is not even Harlequin. He is the
same kind of Pierrot as the mummy's boy Petya, who
once turned the head of a little fool in Irkutsk with his
curly locks and bombastic versicles.

The evenings at the Doge's apartment are my triumph,
my benefit performance. But there are other times when I
feel weakness creeping up on me. And then I am almost
overcome by doubts.

No, no, I do not doubt the authenticity of the Signs. It is
a different question that torments me: am I ready? Will I
not feel regret, be unwilling to leave the light for the
darkness?

The outcome is always the same. Perhaps I do feel
regret, but the choice will be made with no hesitation. To
fall into the abyss, into the dark embrace of my mysterious, ardently desired Beloved.

After all, it is now absolutely clear that death does not
exist – at least, not the kind of death that I used to
imagine: non-existence, absolute blackness, nothingness.
There is no death, but there is Death. His kingdom is a

magical land, great, mighty and beautiful, where such great bliss and wonderful new insights await me that the mere anticipation of it sets my heart aching sweetly. Ordinary people crawl into this magical land howling in terror, whimpering and afraid, broken by fatal disease or the ravages of age, with their physical and spiritual powers exhausted. But I shall enter the halls of Death, not as some pitiful dependent, but as a precious favourite, a long-awaited guest.

Fear hinders me. But what is fear? The sharp nails with which the foolish, pitiful, treacherous flesh clutches at life in order to wheedle a respite out of fate – for a year, a week, even a minute.

Yes, I am afraid. I am very afraid. Especially of pain at the final moment. And even more afraid of the pictures painted by my cowardly brain: a hole dug in the ground, the thud of dry lumps of earth against the lid of a coffin, death-worms in eye-sockets. And there is something from my childhood, from Gogol's *Horrific Revenge*: 'In the bottomless pit the dead gnaw on the dead man, and the dead man lying under the earth grows, gnawing on his own bones in terrible torment and shaking the ground horrifyingly.'

Rubbish, rubbish, rubbish.

'It's time for me to go'

They argued heatedly, trying to shout each other down.

'The place where the meetings are held is an open secret,' the anatomist Horatio declared. 'Cyrano must have given the address to his editors! I wouldn't be surprised if we were being observed by newspaper hacks from the windows of nearby houses. And one day we'll go out after a meeting and be met by flashing magnesium. We should stop the meetings temporarily.'

'Shtupid nonsense!' retorted Rosencrantz. 'You haf no faith! Ve must trust in *Schicksal!*'

'Destiny,' his brother explained.

'Yes, yes, destiny! Let things be as zey vill.'

'It is not very likely that Cyrano gave the secret away,' said Kriton, supporting the young man. 'Why would he kill the chicken that was laying his golden eggs?'

Simple-minded Iphigenia fluttered her eyelids and said what was on everybody's mind: 'Gentlemen, we're better off together, aren't we? You can see, Death plays by his own rules. He takes whoever he wants. It's frightening to sit at home alone with no one to talk to, but here we can all keep each other company . . .'

The 'lovers' looked at each other and there was a pause. We are like accomplices in a crime or condemned prisoners awaiting execution, thought Columbine.

'But where's Prospero?' Petya asked plaintively, glancing round at the door. 'What does he think?'

Genji moved to a seat in the corner, to smoke a cigar. He calmly released thin streams of bluish smoke into the air, taking no part in the conversation. Caliban also remained silent, listening to the arguers with a condescending smile.

The bookkeeper had been behaving strangely in general this evening. What had happened to the habitual brash impatience with which he had always waited for the spiritualist seance or the 'Wheel of Death'?

Caliban only spoke when the Doge entered the salon, dressed in a black judge's robe. The most fanatical of Death's champions walked out into the centre of the room and shouted: 'Stop talking rubbish! Listen to me instead! It's my turn to celebrate now! I've been chosen! I've been sent a message too!' He waved a piece of paper in the air. 'See, you can check for yourselves. I'm not hiding anything. It's a fact, not some foolish fantasy.'

The last remark was accompanied by a contemptuous glance, directed at Columbine.

Everyone crowded round the bookkeeper. The small

rectangle, one eighth of a standard sheet of writing paper, was passed from hand to hand. It bore three words written in block capitals: 'TESTED, APPROVED, DRAFTED'.

'And I certainly have been tested!' Caliban explained excitedly. 'For patience and fidelity. Now it's clear why she made me suffer for so long. She was testing my constancy. And I passed the test. You see – "approved"! And "drafted"! I came to say goodbye and wish you all the same good fortune, and to apologise for being so gruff sometimes. Try to remember Savely Papushin, the most detestable of all sinners on this earth, with kind thoughts. That's my real name, there's no point in hiding it any more – they'll write it in the newspapers in any case. Amnestied with a free pardon! Congratulate me, ladies and gentlemen! And I'd like to thank you, dear Teacher.' He grabbed Prospero's hand with heartfelt feeling, 'If not for you, I'd never have got out of the asylum, I'd still be rolling around on the floor and howling like a dog. You gave me hope and you made it real! Thank you!'

Caliban wiped away a tear with his huge red hand and blew his nose.

'Let me see that please.' Prospero took the piece of paper with a sceptical air and turned it over in his hands.

'Well, let us test this,' he said thoughtfully and suddenly held the paper over a candle. The message immediately caught fire, turning into a curl of black ash. The bookkeeper howled wildly: 'What have you done? That's a message from the Eternal Bride!'

'You've been tricked, poor Caliban,' said the Doge, shaking his head. 'Why would any of you play such a cruel joke, ladies and gentlemen?'

Caliban's eyes started out of his head in horror.

'How . . . how could you, Teacher?'

'Calm down,' Prospero told him sternly. 'This message was sent by a human being, not Death. The ancient books state quite definitely that a letter from the Beyond will not burn in fire.'

Then the Doge suddenly turned to Columbine: 'You say

that Death has already written to you twice. Tell me, have you tested the notes to see if they will burn?'

'Of course I have,' Columbine replied quickly, but inwardly she cringed.

A trick! A shabby trick! One of the aspirants had slipped these notes to her and Caliban so that he or she could mock and sneer! The trickster must think they were the two most stupid members of the club!

The scorching realisation came to her immediately. The victim of deceit cast a withering glance at Gorgon to see if she was laughing. Gorgon responded with a gaze charged with even greater hostility. Aha, she had given herself away!

Never mind, the rotten bitch wouldn't dare own up – Prospero would throw her out of the club in disgrace if she did.

Columbine looked Gorgon straight in the eye and said defiantly: 'I tried with a match and a candle – they don't burn. And my cobra' – she took hold of Lucifer by the neck, just as he was about to dive into her décolleté to find a warm spot, and showed everyone his small rhomboid head – 'sank his fangs into the paper and recoiled in terror.'

If she was going to lie, she might as well do it properly.

'I asked you not to bring that vile creature here,' said Prospero, gazing at the snake in disgust. He had taken a dislike to the poor snake ever since that first night when it had snapped at his finger.

Columbine was about to defend her pet, but Caliban interrupted her.

'Hers didn't burn, but mine went up in flames?' he groaned, heartbroken, and shouted so loudly that the candle flames flickered. 'That's not fair! It's unjust!'

The brawny bookkeeper burst into tears, just like a little child.

While everyone was comforting him, Columbine quietly slipped out and set off in the direction of the boulevard. She felt like crying herself. What a vile, blasphemous joke! What a bitter taste was left now after the mystical rapture of the last few days, that special, sweet thrill of being chosen!

Revenge, her soul was thirsting for revenge! The best thing would be to whisper to Caliban which member of the club had been having fun writing notes. Caliban was no gentleman, he wouldn't go easy on Gorgon. He'd flatten her foxy little face for her. And it would be good if he broke her nose or knocked a tooth out, Columbine thought hardheartedly.

'Mademoiselle C-Columbine!' a familiar voice called out behind her. 'Will you permit me to accompany you?'

Apparently Prince Genji, with his preternatural astuteness, had discerned the storm raging in her soul. When he caught up with Columbine, he glanced with apparent unconcern into the false Chosen One's red face, then started talking to her, not about the notes or Caliban's fit of hysterics, but something quite different, and his voice didn't have its usual slightly mocking humour, it was very serious.

'Our sessions remind me more and more of a f-farce, but I do not feel like laughing. There are too many dead bodies. I have been coming to this absurd club for three weeks now, with no result whatsoever. No, what am I saying! There has been a result, b-but a negative one. Ophelia, Lorelei, Gdlevsky and Cyrano have died under my very nose. I failed to save them. And now I can see this black whirlpool sucking you in!'

Ah, if only you knew, Columbine thought, but she didn't give herself away – on the contrary, she knitted her brows mournfully. Let him worry a bit, let him try to persuade her.

Genji really did seem to be worried – he kept talking faster and faster, and gesturing with one gloved hand when he couldn't find the right word straight away: 'Why, why urge death on, why make her task any easier? Life is such a fragile, defenceless jewel, it is already threatened by a myriad dangers every minute of the day. You will have to die anyway, that cup will not pass you by. Why leave the theatre without watching the play to the end? Perhaps this play – in which, by the way, everyone p-plays the leading role – will yet astonish you with some surprising twist of the plot?

Indeed, it is sure to astonish you more than once, and perhaps in the most delightful fashion!'

'Listen, Japanese Prince Erast Petrovich, what do you want from me?' Columbine retorted furiously to this sermon. 'What delightful surprises can your play promise me? I know the finale in advance. The curtain will fall in 1952, or thereabouts, when I am getting out of an electric tram (or whatever people will use for travelling in a half century from now) and I fall, break the neck of my femur, then spend a fortnight or a month lying in a hospital bed until pneumonia eventually finishes me off. And of course, it will be a paupers' hospital, because by that time I shall have spent all my money, and there'll be no way I can get any more. And in 1952 I shall be an ugly, wrinkled old woman of seventy-three with a *papirosa* always stuck in my mouth, no one will need me and the new generation won't understand me. In the morning I shall turn away from the mirror in order not to see what my face has turned into. With my character I shall never have a family. And even if I do – that only makes the loneliness all the more desperate. Thank you for such a wonderful destiny. Who do you think would want me to live to see that, and why? God? But I think you do not believe in God, do you?'

Genji winced painfully as he listened to her. He replied passionately, with profound conviction: 'No, no and no again! My dear Columbine, you must have trust in life. You have to entrust yourself to its flow, b-because life is infinitely wiser than we are! It will deal with you as it wishes in any case, sometimes rather cruelly, but in the final analysis you will come to realise that it was right. It is always right! In addition to the gloomy prospects that you picture so vividly, life also possesses many magical qualities!'

'And what are they?' Columbine laughed.

'If nothing else, the ability, which you have mocked, of presenting surprising and precious gifts – whatever your age or physical condition.'

'Such as?' she asked and laughed again.

'They are countless. The blue sky, the green grass, the morning air, the sky at night. Love in all its manifold shades and hues. And in the t-twilight of life, if you have deserved it – tranquillity and wisdom . . .'

Sensing that his words were beginning to have an effect, Genji redoubled his efforts: 'Yes, and on the subject of old age, what makes you think that your year of 1952 will be so very terrible? I, for instance, am certain that it will be a wonderful time! Fifty years from now Russia will have universal literacy, which means that people will learn to be more tolerant with each other and distinguish the beautiful from the ugly. The electric tram that you mentioned will become merely the most ordinary means of transport. Flying machines will glide smoothly across the skies. Many more remarkable miracles of technology that we cannot even imagine today will appear! You are so young. The year of 1952, a time inconceivably far away, is well within your reach. And why have we drawn the line at 1952! By that time medicine will have developed so far that life expectancy will have greatly increased, and the very concept of old age will be pushed back to a later stage of life. You are sure to live to be ninety – and see the year 1969! Or perhaps to a hundred, and then you will even catch a glimpse of 1979! Just imagine it! Don't those n-numbers take your breath away? Sheer curiosity should be enough to compensate for all the ordeals that the start of the new century apparently has in store for us. We must negotiate the narrows and rapids of history in order later to enjoy its smooth, even flow.'

How beautifully he spoke! Despite herself, Columbine listened admiringly. He's right, she thought, a thousand times right. And she also wondered why he had mentioned love. Was it simply a figure of speech, or was there a special meaning in his words, one intended specially for her?

From that point her thoughts started off in a different direction, far removed from philosophising and attempts to guess the future.

What is Mr Erast Petrovich Neimless's personal life like,

Columbine wondered, squinting sideways at her companion. All the signs indicated that he was an inveterate bachelor, one of those who, as her nanny used to say, would rather strangle himself than get married. Was he really content to live year after year with only his Japanese for company? Oh, hardly, he was far too handsome.

She suddenly felt it was a terrible pity that she had not met him earlier, before Prospero. Perhaps then everything would have turned out quite differently.

They parted at the corner of Staropansky Lane. Genji removed his top hat and kissed the thoughtful young lady's hand. Before walking into the entrance, she glanced round. He was standing in the same place, under a streetlamp, holding the top hat in his hand while the wind ruffled his black hair.

As Columbine climbed the stairs, she imagined how everything would have been if she had met Genji earlier. And as she unlocked her door she was humming a song to herself.

But five minutes later she had shaken off all this maudlin folly and knew that none of the things Genji had spoken about had ever existed – life was not good and wise, there was no love. There was only one thing – a great magnet that was drawing her to itself like a little iron filing. It had already caught her, and it would never let her go.

What happened during those five minutes?

She sat down at the desk as usual, to write down all the events of the day in her diary, and then, suddenly remembering Gorgon's mean joke, she angrily jerked open the drawer, grabbed the two little rectangles of cardboard and held a lighted match to them, in order to destroy the evidence of her shameful gullibility.

Less than a minute later, Columbine was convinced that the messages would not burn. She had used up several matches and singed the tips of her fingers. But the paper had not even darkened at all!

She grabbed her handbag in order to take out her cigarette case. She needed to smoke a *papirosa* and gather her thoughts. The handbag fell from her trembling hands, its contents scattered across the floor and Columbine's eye was caught by a small piece of white card, exactly like the two previous ones. She picked it up and read the single word that was written on it: '*Komm*'.[2]

So there it was. Irrefutable.

Columbine sat there for a few minutes without moving, and thought. Not about the One who had sent her this summons, but about the Japanese prince. 'Thank you, dear Genji,' she thought, taking leave of him. 'You are clever and handsome. You wished me well. I would certainly have fallen in love with you – everything was leading to that, but an even more impressive admirer than you has put in an appearance. Everything has finally been decided. It's time for me to go.'

Enough of that.

All she still had to do was write the concluding chapter in her diary. The title simply wrote itself.

How tenderly Columbine departs from the City of Dreams

Tenderly, because tenderness is precisely the feeling that now suffuses the traveller's entire being as her voyage approaches its brilliant conclusion. And this feeling is both sweet and sad.

Columbine sat at the desk for a long time as the three white candles on it slowly burned down. She thought about various ways in which she could make her departure, as if she were searching through the dresses in her wardrobe for one to wear at a ball, measuring them against herself, looking in the mirror, sighing and tossing each rejected outfit on to a chair. No good, no good. Somehow she did not really feel afraid. The three white

2. Come

cards, neatly laid out on the desk, radiated a calm strength that supported her. Columbine knew for certain that it would hurt a little bit at first, but after that everything would be very, very good: the vain girl was more concerned with something that was not really so important – how she would look when she was dead. But then, perhaps this was the most important problem that she still had to decide in her short life that was now rushing rapidly to its finale. After her departure she wanted to look like a beautiful doll laid out in an elegant box, so the quick means like a rope or a jump from the balcony were not suitable. The best way, of course, would be to take a sleeping draft – to swallow an entire crystal phial of opium, then wash it down with sweet tea and blackcurrant jam. Columbine had tea, and she had blackcurrant jam. But she did not have any soporific substances in her apartment, because she had never suffered from insomnia: as soon as she put her head on the pillow and parted her golden tresses to both sides, she immediately fell into a sound sleep.

Finally the difficult choice was made.

Fill the bath with warm water. Add a few drops of lavender oil. Anoint her face and neck with miraculous Lanoline cream – 'the ideal way to preserve attractive skin' – from the little tin tube (she only needed to preserve it for two or three days, until the funeral, after that she wouldn't need attractive skin). Put on her white lace dress, which was a bit like a wedding dress. Tie back her hair with a scarlet ribbon that would match the colour of the water. Lie down in the bath, run a sharp knife across her veins (under the water, so that it wouldn't hurt too much), and slowly go to sleep. Whoever found Columbine would say: She was like a white chrysanthemum floating in a glass of *vin rosé*.

Now there was one last thing she had to do: write a poem. And that would conclude the story of Columbine, who flew into the City of Dreams from the magical distance, spread her ethereal wings there for a short while and then darted from the light into the shadow.

> *From light into shadow she flitted,*
> *Then the little fairy was gone.*
> *There was nothing she regretted,*
> *We shall miss her rapturous song.*

No, that's no good at all. The first line is from a poem by someone else, and God only knows what that last line means.

> *I have no faith in any God or Devil*
> *I know to die is no more than to sleep.*
> *A letter has informed me I must travel,*
> *Now I have an appointment I must keep.*

That's no better. I simply can't stand that third line, it makes me feel sick. 'Travel' – what sort of word is that for a poem? This is really hard. And the water's getting cold. I'll have to let it out and fill the bath again.
Come on now!

> *How vain the Prince of Denmark's hesitations,*
> *His ponderings 'To be or not to be?'*

No. It has to be less heavy, without any irony. Light and airy.

> *Death is not sleep and not oblivion*
> *I shall be greeted on awakening*
> *By a delightful flowering garden*
> *Where falling water sweetly sings.*
>
> *Pinch yourself hard until it hurts*
> *And waken in an open forest glade.*
> *Leave all your dreams of prison in the past*
> *Die into freedom and be not afraid.*

Will they realise that the falling water is the sound of the tap filling the bath? Ah, never mind if it's not clear! I've wasted enough paper already. Whoever said that a farewell poem has to be long? Columbine's will be short, absurd and break off when it has hardly begun, just like her short and absurd (but nonetheless beautiful, very beautiful) li . . .

Before Columbine could finish writing the word, the silence of the night was broken by the ringing of her doorbell.

Who could it be at this hour, after two in the morning?

At any other time she would have been afraid. Everyone knew that a doorbell rung in the middle of the night boded no good. But what should she be afraid of, when she had already settled her final account with life?

Maybe she shouldn't answer? Let them ring away.

Lucifer was warming himself on her bosom: she settled his little head more comfortably in the hollow over her collarbone and tried to concentrate on her diary, but the continuous ringing would not let her.

All right, she would have to go and see what surprise life had in store for her just before it came to an end.

Columbine didn't bother to turn on the gas lamp in the hallway. She had already guessed who had come to visit her so late – Genji, it couldn't be anyone else. He had sensed something. Now he would start remonstrating with her again, trying to convince her. She would have to pretend that she agreed with everything, wait for him to go and then . . .

She opened the door.

It was dark on the stairway too. Someone had turned off the light. She could make out a vague silhouette. Tall and massive – no, it wasn't Genji.

Her visitor didn't say anything, all she could hear was loud, fitful breathing.

'Did you want to see me?' Columbine asked, peering into the darkness.

'Yes, you!' a hoarse voice rasped – it sounded so savage and malevolent that she took a sharp step back.

'Who are you?' she cried out.

'Your death! With a small letter.'

Columbine heard gruff, throaty laughter. She thought she recognised the voice, but she was so frightened that she couldn't understand a thing, and before she could gather her wits the shadow stepped into the hallway and seized her round the neck with fingers of iron.

The voice hissed: 'You'll be black and blue, with your tongue hanging out. A fine Chosen One!'

The terrible visitor laughed again, wheezing like a decrepit old dog barking.

The reply to his laughter was an angry hiss from Lucifer, who had woken up. The bold little snake had grown a lot in the last few weeks of feeding on milk and minced meat. He sank his fangs into the attacker's hand.

The attacker growled, grabbed the grass snake by the tail and smashed it against the wall. It only took a second, but that was enough for Columbine to dart away. She didn't make a decision or choose her moment, she simply went away, following her instinct like an animal.

She ran down the corridor with her mouth wide open, but not uttering a sound. She ran blindly, with no idea of where she was going or why, urged on by the most effective goad of all – the fear of death, vile and loathsome. It was not Death lumbering along after her, but death – filthy, foul-smelling and terrifying. The death from her childhood. With the rich, thick soil of the graveyard. The white death-worms. The grinning skull with holes instead of eyes.

A sudden thought occurred to her: she should run into the bathroom, bolt the door and then shout and hammer on the steel pipe so that the neighbours would hear. The bathroom door opened outwards, the handle was flimsy, if he tugged hard, it would break off, and the door would stay locked.

It was a wonderful idea, good enough to save her. But it would take three seconds, or at least two, for her to do it, and she didn't have them.

In the doorway of the room a hand grabbed her sleeve from behind. Columbine jerked away as hard as she could, sending buttons flying. But she recovered her voice.

'Help!' she shouted at the top of her lungs. And then she carried on shouting. As loud as she could manage.

She darted out of the room to the left, into the kitchen. There was the door of the bathroom, she could hear the water splashing out of the tap. No, not enough time.

Left again out of the kitchen, into the corridor. The circle was completed. Where to now? Back into the room or out on to the stairs? The front door was still open.

Better on to the stairs. Maybe someone would look out of their door?

She flew out on to the dark landing with a scream and went dashing down the steps. If only she didn't stumble!

Columbine's long skirt hampered her. She tugged it up above her knees with a jerk.

'Stop, thief! Stop!' the hoarse voice roared behind her.

Why 'thief'? Columbine wondered, and at that very moment, just before the final flight of steps, the heel of her shoe slipped sideways with a crunch.

The fugitive screeched and fell, landing with her chest and stomach on the steps, and slid downwards. She hit her elbows against the stairs, but she didn't feel any pain, she was just very afraid.

Realising she wouldn't have time to get up, she pressed her forehead against the floor. It was cold and smelled of dust. She squeezed her eyes shut.

The door of the entranceway banged loudly and someone shouted out: 'Don't move! I'll fire!'

The hoarse voice answered: 'Here, take this!'

There was a deafening crash and Columbine's ears were suddenly blocked. She hadn't been able to see anything in the dark, and now she couldn't hear anything either.

As well as the dust, there was another smell now. An acrid smell, vaguely familiar. She remembered what it was – gunpowder. When her brother Misha used to shoot crows in the garden it had smelled like that.

She heard a faint voice in the distance.

'Columbine! Are you alive?'

Genji's voice.

Hands that were strong but gentle, not rough like those others, turned her over on to her back. She opened her eyes and then squeezed them shut again.

There was an electric torch shining straight into them.

'That's blinding,' Columbine said.

Then Genji put the torch down on a step and she could see that he was leaning against the banisters with a smoking revolver in his hand; his top hat had slipped to one side and his coat was unbuttoned.

Columbine asked in a whisper: 'What was all that?'

He picked up the torch again and pointed the beam to one side. Caliban was sitting by the wall, with his dead eyes staring down at the floor. There was a trickle of something dark running from his half-open mouth and another trickle, absolutely black, running from the round hole in his forehead.

He's dead, Columbine guessed. The bookkeeper was still clutching a knife in his hand, holding it by the blade instead of the handle.

'He was about to throw it,' Genji explained. 'He must have learned that from his shipmates while he was still sailing the seas. But I fired first.'

Even though her teeth were chattering and she had hiccups, Columbine asked: 'W-why? What f-for? I was g-going to do it anyway, myself . . .'

How strange, she thought, now I'm stammering, but he isn't.

'Later, later,' Genji said to her.

He carefully picked the young lady up in his arms and carried her up the stairs. Columbine pressed her head against his chest. She felt very content just then. He was holding her so comfortably, just right. As if he had made a special study of how to carry enervated and exhausted young women.

She whispered: 'I'm a doll, I'm a doll.'

Genji leaned his head down and asked: 'What?'

'You're carrying me like a broken doll,' she explained.

A quarter of an hour later Columbine was alone in her flat, sitting with her feet pulled up on to the armchair, wrapped in a rug and crying.

Alone because, after wrapping her in the rug, Genji had gone to get a doctor and the police.

With her feet pulled up because the entire floor was wet – the bath had overflowed.

But she was not crying because she was afraid (Genji had told her there would be nothing more to be afraid of). She was crying in grief: brave Lucifer was lying on her knees still and lifeless, like a patterned ribbon.

Columbine sobbed and sniffed as she stroked the rough scales on her rescuer's back.

But she stopped crying when she turned to look in the mirror and saw the crimson graze on her forehead, her swollen nose and red eyes and the blue stripes on her neck.

She ought to tidy herself up a bit before Genji got back.

III. From the 'Agents' Reports' File

To His Honour Lieutenant-Colonel Besikov
(Private and confidential)

Dear Lieutenant-Colonel,

You may consider the epic story of the 'Lovers of Death' at an end. I shall try to set forth for you the events of this evening without omitting anything of significance.

When we all gathered at the usual time at Prospero's apartment, I immediately realised that something quite exceptional had happened. The meeting was not chaired by Blagovolsky, but the Stammerer, and it soon became clear that our Doge had been overthrown and the reins of power had been taken up by the strong hands of a new dictator, although not for long and only in order to declare the society disbanded.

It was from the Stammerer that we learned of the quite incredible events of the previous night. I will not retell them here, because you have undoubtedly been informed about everything by your own sources. I presume that the Moscow police and your people are searching for the Stammerer in order to question him about what happened, however, I cannot help you with that. It is absolutely obvious to me that the man acted correctly, and if he does not wish to meet representatives of the law (and his words certainly gave me that impression), that is his right.

The necessity for the killing, which was committed in self-defence, was also confirmed by Columbine, who almost met her end at the hands of the insane Caliban (the aspirant to whom I have referred in previous reports as the Bookkeeper

– his real name is no doubt already known to you). The poor girl's neck, which still bore the signs of the violence done to her, was covered with a scarf, a bruise was clearly visible under a thick layer of powder on her forehead, and her voice, usually so clear, was quite hoarse from crying desperately for help.

The Stammerer began his lengthy speech by denouncing the idea of suicide, a matter in which I am entirely in agreement with him. However, with your permission, I shall not reproduce this inspired monologue, since it is of no interest to your department. I will only note that the speaker was remarkably eloquent, although he stammered more than usual.

However, the information that the Stammerer provided will probably be of some use to you. This part of his speech I shall relate at length and even in the first person, without reproducing the stammer, in order to be able to interpose my own comments from time to time.

The Stammerer began as follows, or pretty much so.

'I live abroad for most of the time and only rarely visit Moscow, since for some time now the climate of my native city (I thought he was a Muscovite, from his accent) has not been very good for my health. But I follow events here carefully: I receive letters from friends and read the major Moscow newspapers. Reports of an epidemic of suicides and the "Lovers of Death" could not fail to attract my attention, since not too long ago I happened to deal with the case of the "Nemesis" club in London – a criminal organisation which had mastered the rare criminal speciality of driving people to commit suicide in order to profit from their deaths. It is hardly surprising that the news from Moscow made me prick up my ears. I suspected that there might be a perfectly natural and practical reason for the unusually high frequency of motiveless suicides. Was the story of the "Nemesis" club being repeated, I wondered. What if certain malevolent individuals were deliberately pushing gullible or easily influenced people to take the fatal final step?

'Two days after I arrived in Moscow yet another versifier,

Nikifor Sipyaga, took his own life. I went to examine his flat and became convinced that he had indeed been a member of the "Lovers of Death". The police did not even bother to enquire who paid for this poor student's quite decent accommodation. I, however, ascertained that the deceased's flat was rented for him by a certain Sergei Irinarkhovich Blagovolsky, a man who had led an unusual and rather eccentric life. My conjecture was confirmed by observation of Mr Blagovolsky's home: it was the place where the secret meetings were being held.

'Having managed to become one of you without any great difficulty, I was able to continue my investigations from within the club. At first all the evidence definitely pointed to one particular individual. (The Stammerer cast an eloquent glance at Prospero, who was sitting there hunched over pitifully.) However, more thorough investigation of the string of suicides and, in particular, the most recent events – the murders of Gdlevsky and Lavr Zhemailo (yes, yes, Mr Zhemailo was also murdered), as well as the attempt on Mademoiselle Columbine's life – have thrown a completely different light on this whole story. It is a strange story, so tangled and confused that there are many details I have still not untangled completely, but yesterday's events served me as the sword with which to slice through this Gordian knot. The details have ceased to be important, and it will in any case not be very difficult to establish them now.

'Lorelei Rubinstein poisoned herself with morphine after three black roses appeared in her bedroom in some mysterious fashion, one after another, and this woman obsessed with the idea of suicide took them as a summons from Death. I was able rather easily to establish that the black roses had been put in Lorelei's room by the aunt who lived with her, an avaricious and stupid individual. She had no idea that she was doing anything wrong. She thought she was helping the latest admirer of the poetess's talent. For performing this rather strange but, at first glance, innocent errand, the stranger paid her five roubles on each occasion, making it a condition of payment that she keep the matter secret. During my first conversation with this woman, I could see that she was frightened – she already knew what her simple assistance had led to. And when she told me that the dead roses were a single bouquet, I knew immediately that she was lying – the three flowers were at different stages of withering.

'I went back to the woman again, with no witnesses, and made her tell me the truth. She confessed everything and gave me a very rough description of the mysterious admirer, saying that he was tall, uncouth and clean-shaven with a coarse voice. I was unable to get any more out of her – she is unintelligent, unobservant and has weak eyesight. It is clear now that it was Caliban who visited her, but at the time I still suspected Mr Blagovolsky and only realised later that my theory was wrong. If I had demonstrated a little more astuteness, the schoolboy and the reporter and, probably, Caliban himself would still be alive.'

He paused in order to rein in his feelings. One of us took advantage of the silence to ask: 'But why did Caliban want to drive some to suicide and kill others, and in such a cruel manner?'

The Stammerer nodded, as if acknowledging the reasonableness of the question.

'You are all aware that he was not an entirely normal individual. (I thought this remark amusing. As if all the other 'lovers' were normal!) However, there were circumstances in his life of which I have become aware only now, after his death. Caliban, or Savely Akimovich Papushin (that is his real name), worked as a bookkeeper on board a merchant vessel in the Volunteer Fleet. His ship was travelling on the route from Odessa to Shanghai when it was caught in a typhoon. Only three members of the crew survived and managed to reach a small deserted island in a life boat. To be precise, it was not so much an island as a series of rocky cliffs protruding from the surface of the ocean. A month and a half later a British tea clipper that happened to be in those waters discovered a single survivor – Papushin. He had not died of thirst because it was the rainy season. He did not explain how he had managed to survive for so long without food, but the remains of his two comrades were discovered on the sand: skeletons that had been gnawed absolutely clean. Papushin said that crabs had devoured the corpses. The English did not believe him and held him under lock and key until they arrived at their first port of call and then handed him over to the police authorities. (I myself have absolutely no doubt that our bookkeeper killed his two comrades and gobbled them up – it is enough to remember the bloodcurdling verse that he composed, which always included cliffs, waves and skeletons searching for their own flesh.) Papushin was held in a psychiatric clinic for more than a year. I spoke with his psychiatrist, Dr Bazhenov, today. The patient was plagued by constant nightmares and hallucinations, all connected with the subject of cannibalism. During the first week of treatment he swallowed a spoon and a shard of a broken plate, but he did not die. He did not make any further attempts at suicide, having decided that he was unworthy of death. Eventually Papushin was released on condition that he report for regular examinations and interviews with his doctor. At first he came, but then he stopped. During his final interview he seemed calmer and said that he had found people whom would help him "solve his problem".

'We all remember that Caliban was the most zealous advocate of voluntary death. He waited impatiently for his own turn to come and was bitterly jealous of others' "luck". Every time the choice fell on someone else, he fell into black despair: Death still considered him unworthy to join the comrades whom he had killed and eaten. But had he not changed, purged himself through contrition, did he not serve Death faithfully, love and desire her passionately?

'I became a member of the club too late, and it is hard for me now to tell how or why Papushin reached his decision to push certain of the aspirants into suicide. In Ophelia's case, he probably simply wanted to get rid of her, to put an end to the spiritualist seances – he no longer believed that the angry spirits of the "lovers" would ever summon him. Here, as in Avaddon's case, Caliban displayed an uncommon ingenuity, of which I would never have suspected him capable. It is, however, well known that individuals of a maniacal bent can be exceptionally cunning. I will not go into the technical details here, since they have no bearing on our immediate business.

'Why did he decide to push the Lioness of Ecstasy over the edge? Possibly she irritated him with her excessively rapturous manner. The cruel joke that Papushin played on poor Lorelei probably seemed very witty to his sick, perverted mind. I cannot suggest any other motive.

'In Gdlevsky's case, however, everything is quite clear. The boy boasted too much about how greatly Death favoured him. The story of the Friday rhymes is genuinely astonishing – there are too many coincidences. I suspected foul play and tried to pursue the organ grinder whose song Gdlevsky had taken as his final Sign. But the tramp seemed to have disappeared into thin air. That evening I walked round all the streets in the vicinity, but failed to find him . . .

'Caliban's love for Death was genuine insanity. He loved her passionately, in the way that men love *femmes fatales*. In the way that José must have loved Carmen and Rogozhin loved Nastasya Filippovna – constantly tormented by desire and consumed by desperate envy of his more fortunate rivals. And the schoolboy actually boasted about his imaginary triumph! In killing Gdlevsky, Caliban eliminated a rival. He deliberately arranged things so that you others would realise it was no suicide and the boy was a usurper, Death did not walk to the altar with him. To use the language of the newspapers, it was a genuine crime of passion.'

The mention of newspapers reminded me of Lavr Zhemailo.

'But what happened to Cyrano?' I asked. 'You said it was a murder. Papushin again?'

'Certainly, Zhemailo's death was no suicide,' the Stammerer replied. 'Caliban somehow discovered who Cyrano was. A few minutes before his death the journalist phoned his newspaper's offices (it must have been from here, it couldn't have been anywhere else) and promised to deliver an incredible news story. I don't know what he had in mind, but I remember the events of that evening very clearly. Cyrano went across to the bookshelves, looked at the spines of the books, and took out one volume. Then he went out and didn't come back again. That was at about ten o'clock in the evening. The autopsy established that he died no later than eleven.'

(So that was the meaning of the mysterious movement of the door that I observed in the study that evening! While I was eavesdropping on Cyrano from the corridor, at the same time Caliban was hiding on the other side, in the dining room. That was when he had seen through the correspondent's mask!)

'The police surgeon,' continued the Stammerer, 'determined that Zhemailo died of asphyxiation, even though, in addition to the furrow left by the rope, his neck bore the clear imprints of fingers. Papushin obviously followed the journalist, overtook him on the boulevard, which was completely deserted at that late hour, and strangled him, which would not be difficult, since nature had endowed the killer with such great strength. Short, flabby Cyrano could not possibly have offered any serious resistance to the enraged bookkeeper. Afterwards Caliban hung the body on a tree, using the victim's trouser belt. This was no crime of passion but an act of revenge. Caliban regarded membership of the club as a sacred ministry, Cyrano was a villainous traitor. That was why he hung him on a Judas tree, an aspen.'

(At this point, to be quite honest, I broke into a cold sweat. I imagined what the madman would have done to me if he had found out about my correspondence with you. Do you at least understand the monstrous risk to which I exposed myself in carrying out your assignment?

My heart started pounding, my fingers started trembling and after that I listened less attentively, and so I will convey the conclusion of the speech in somewhat abbreviated form.)

'The fact that he had got away with the two previous murders and his ever-increasing resentment drove Papushin into attempting yet another crime. He decided to kill Columbine, Death's new favourite. The madman must have found it particularly hard to bear the humiliation he had suffered when his cherished message from the Eternal Bride was publicly declared a forgery. And Columbine had already stated that fire did not touch *her* Signs.

'At this point I should really explain that it was Papushin's profound conviction – a conviction that the Doge did everything possible to support and encourage – that suicide is the noblest manner in which to leave this life or, as Sterne put it, the aristocrat of deaths. By preventing Columbine from dying of her own free will, Caliban would have exposed her as a usurper – in exactly the same way as he had already done with Gdlevsky.

'And that is exactly what would have happened yesterday if I had not felt concerned about Mademoiselle Columbine's state of mind and decided to see her home. We said good-night outside the house, but I decided to keep an eye on her windows so that I could intervene immediately if I noticed anything suspicious. Naturally, the idea of a murder never even entered my head – what I was afraid of was that the young woman intended to take her own life.

'One of her windows was lit and every now and then I saw a shadow move across the curtain. It was already very late, but Mademoiselle Columbine had still not gone to bed. I wondered if I should go upstairs? But how would it look, a man visiting a solitary young woman at that time of night? No, it was absolutely unthinkable.

'I didn't see Caliban make his way into the entrance, he entered from the yard, through the back door. At a quarter past two I thought I heard muffled screams from somewhere above me, but I could quite well have been mistaken. I listened closely and a few seconds later I quite distinctly heard someone shout: "No! No! Skulls! Worms!" The shouts were coming from the entrance. I didn't understand what the words meant, and I still do not understand why Mademoiselle Columbine uttered them, but I immediately dashed towards the front door. Just in time, as it turned out. A few moments later it would have been too late.'

(At this point Columbine had a fit of hysterics. She started sobbing, threw herself on the Stammerer's chest, babbled incoherently and kissed him several times on the forehead and cheeks, inflicting some damage to the dandy's coiffure and collar. After the distressed maiden had been given a drink of water and seated in an armchair, the Stammerer concluded his address.)

'That is all, ladies and gentlemen. I hereby declare the club of "Lovers of Death" disbanded. There is no Death with a capital letter. That is one. The death that does exist has no need of lovers, male or female. That is two. Your turn to meet this boring lady will inevitably come, but all in good time. It is one meeting that you cannot avoid. That is three. Goodbye.'

We left in silence, and the commonest expressions on people's faces were bewilderment or indignation. No one said goodbye to Prospero, not even his odalisques. He just sat there, completely crushed. And I should think so! How could this adored clairvoyant and self-appointed saviour of souls have been so fatally mistaken? He himself had introduced a dangerous maniac into the club and given him every patronage and favour – in effect, he had encouraged a murderer! I would not like to be in his skin.

Or would I? So help me, I believe the position of a deposed idol, who yesterday was exalted to the heavens and today is cast down, humiliated and trodden in the dirt, offers a gratification no less acute than is to be found in the most triumphant success. We Germans know about such things, because we have absolutely no sense of measure. The subtle sweetness of disgrace that is known only to the proud was felt very keenly by Fyodor Mikhailovich Dostoevsky, the most German of all Russian writers. It is such a pity that we have not had a chance to talk about literature. And now we never shall.

And so I conclude my final report, for I have fulfilled the terms to which I agreed. You can in turn report to your superiors that the epidemic of suicides in Moscow is now over. Attribute this achievement to your own efforts – I do not mind. I am not ambitious, it is not honours and a career that I require from life, but something quite different, something that I am afraid you cannot appreciate or understand.

Goodbye, Lieutenant-Colonel, remember me kindly. And I shall try to remember you kindly too.

Your ZZ
20 September 1900

CHAPTER 6

I. From the Newspapers

By Motor to Paris

At noon tomorrow a Russian sportsman will set out from Moscow to Paris on a three-wheeled motor vehicle. E.P. Neimless has set himself the goal of establishing a new distance and speed record for self-propelled carriages.

In his bold challenge Mr Neimless intends to cover the 2800 versts separating the capitals of the two friendly nations in twelve days, not including day-time or night-time halts or any halts that may be required for repairs or due to the poor condition of the roads. This latter circumstance, that is, the appalling state of the roads, especially in the Wisla region, is the greatest obstacle to the success of this hazardous venture. We all recall last year's incident in which Baron von Liebnitz's auto was shaken to pieces by the potholes near Pinsk.

The starting point of Mr Neimless's journey will be Moscow's Triumphal Arch. He will be escorted by his valet in a britzka, which will carry his luggage and spare parts for the three-wheeler. We shall be following the daredevil's progress and printing telegrams received from points along his arduous route.

The Moscow Gazette, 22 September (5 October) 1900 p.4

II. From Columbine's Diary

I wake in order to fall asleep

It turns out that I know nothing. Who I am, why I am alive or what life really is. Genji once quoted some ancient Japanese sage who said: 'Life is a dream seen in a dream.'

The ancient Japanese was absolutely right. Only half an hour ago I thought that I was awake. That I had been asleep for many days and only woken when the light of the electric torch shone into my eyes and a worried voice asked: 'Columbine, are you alive?' And at that moment I dreamed that I awoke from a dream. I seemed to hear the sounds of the real world again, to see its living colours, and the glass bell jar separating me from reality was shattered. There was no Eternal Bridegroom called Death, no mysterious and alluring World Beyond, no mystical Signs, no spirits, no summons from out of the blackness.

For three days after I was almost snatched away by 'death with a small letter', I revelled in my imaginary freedom – I laughed a lot and cried a lot, I marvelled at the most common everyday nonsense, ate cakes and sewed a quite incredible dress. I pricked all my fingers very badly, I was working with such awkward material. Every time I cried out I felt even happier, because the pain confirmed the reality of existence. As if pain could not be dreamed!

Today I put on my stunning new outfit and was absolutely delighted with it. No one else has a dress like it. It is made of 'devil's leather', it glitters and shimmers and crackles. Genji bought a driving suit of the same material for his motor journey, and I immediately fell in love with it.

The dress is absolutely unendurable. I always feel either hot or cold in it, but how it sparkles! Everyone in the street kept turning to look at me.

I was absolutely certain that the sun, the sky, the crackling dress, and the handsome man with the dark hair and the calm voice really did exist, that this was real life and I didn't want anything else.

The gaudy fairground sideshow erected by that old liar Prospero had collapsed like a house of cards at the first breath of a fresh, *real* wind.

Genji escorted me to my door again, as he had done for the previous two days. He thought that after what had happened I was afraid to climb the stairs alone. I wasn't afraid at all, but I wanted him to escort me.

He treats me like a porcelain vase. Before he leaves he kisses my hand. I am sure that he has feelings for me. But he is a gentleman and no doubt he feels bound by the fact that he saved my life: what if I do not spurn him simply out of a feeling of gratitude? How funny he is! As if gratitude had anything at all to do with love. But I like him even more for it.

Never mind, I thought. What's the hurry? Let him go on his stupid motor trip. If something starts between us now, he won't be able to test his oil-stove on wheels, and he wants to do it so much. All men really are still boys, no matter what their age.

After Paris I'll really take him in hand. God willing, the oil-stove will break down a hundred versts from Moscow, and then he will be back soon, I fantasised. But I am prepared to wait three weeks, let him set his record. Life is long and there is so much time for happiness.

I was wrong. Life is short. And Genji was only a dream, like everything else – the sun, the sky, the new dress.

I have just woken up.

I came home, drank some tea, twirled in front of the mirror for a moment to admire the way the devil's leather sparkled in the bluish light of the lamp. And then my eyes fell on a small volume in leather binding with gold-edged pages. I sat down, opened the book where it was marked and started to read.

It was a farewell gift from Prospero. A medieval German tract with a long title: *The Secret Meditations of an Anonymous Author on the Experiences of his Life and What he has Heard from People Worthy to be Trusted*. Two days earlier, when everyone walked out into the street in silence, leaving the Doge alone, and no one even said goodbye, I was touched by his imploring glance and I went back from the door, shook his hand and kissed him on the cheek – in memory of all that there had been between us.

He understood what my kiss meant, and he didn't try to kiss me in return or take me in his arms.

'Goodbye, my child,' he said in a sad, formal voice which acknowledged that everything that used to be was over for ever. 'You were the belated festival of my life, and no festival can last for long. Thank you for warming my weary heart with the glow of your sweet warmth. I have prepared a small gift for you – as a token of my gratitude.'

He picked a small volume up off the table and took a sheet of paper out of his pocket.

'Do not read this treatise from cover to cover, it contains many things that are dark and obscure. At your age you should not burden your mind with such doleful wisdom. But you must read the chapter entitled "Cases in which love is more powerful than death". Look, I'm marking it with this sheet of paper. And note the sheet of paper too, it is more than three hundred years old. Extremely precious paper from the sixteenth century, with the watermarks of the French king François I. Perhaps when you've read the chapter I've marked, you might feel like writing me a short letter. Use this sheet of paper – adorned with your writing, it will become one of the most precious relics of my empty and worthless life . . . And do not think badly of me.'

I examined the sheet of paper curiously. Against the light I could see a rounded lily and the letter 'F'. Prospero understands beautiful things. I thought his gift was touching and old-fashioned, enchanting in fact.

I didn't open the book for two days – I was not in the mood for reading treatises. But today, after saying good-bye to Genji for three whole weeks, I decided to see whether the medieval author could tell me anything new about love.

I took out the bookmark, set it aside and started reading. Some learned canon, whose name was indicated on the cover only by the letter 'W', asserted that in the eternal opposition between love and death, the latter usually won the upper hand, but there were some cases, very rare, when the devoted love of two hearts soared beyond the limits set for a mortal being and established passion in eternity, so that with the passing of time love did not wane but, on the contrary, shone ever brighter and brighter. The strange canon believed that the guarantee of passion's immortalisation was a dual suicide, committed by the lovers so that life could not part them. The author believed that in this way they subordinated death to their feelings of love, making it love's faithful slave for ever.

When I was tired of the medieval freethinker's long sentences and the gothic script, I looked up from the yellow pages and started wondering what all this meant. Not the text, the meaning of which was quite clear, despite its florid style, but the gift. Was Prospero trying to tell me that he loved me and that his love was stronger than death? That he was not really death's servant, but had always served only love? And what should I write to him?

I decided that I would start like this: 'Dear Doge, I shall always be grateful to you, because you taught me the rudiments of those two most important disciplines of all – love and death. But these are subjects that everyone must master independently, and everyone must take the examinations on the basis of their own research.'

I opened the inkwell, picked up the sheet of paper and . . .

And I immediately forgot about the treatise, the Doge and the letter. Familiar angular letters had appeared, faintly, but perfectly clearly, through the marbling of the old paper, forming two words: *Ich warte*.[1]

I didn't realise straight away what the words meant. I was simply surprised that they could have appeared like that out of nowhere. After all, two days earlier I had examined the sheet of paper very closely, and it was absolutely blank! The letters were not written with a pen, they had literally bled through, as if they had percolated out of the dense paper. I shook my head to drive away the apparition, but it didn't disappear. Then I pinched myself on the arm to wake myself up.

And I did wake up. The veil fell from my eyes, the hourglass was reversed and the world was turned back from its head on to its feet.

Tsarevich Death is waiting for me. He is no chimera and no fiction. He exists. He loves me, he is calling me, and I must answer his call.

The last time, when Caliban interrupted me, I was still not ready for this meeting – I was concerned with all sorts of nonsense, I was struggling to drag the farewell poem out of myself by force. That was why he gave me a period of grace. But now the time has come. My betrothed is weary of waiting for me, and I am going.

I don't have to invent anything, it's all very simple. How I shall look after I am gone is not important. The dream that is called life will be scattered like mist, and in

1. I'm waiting

its place I shall see a new dream, indescribably more beautiful.

Go out on to the balcony, into the darkness. Open the cast-iron gate. The sheet-metal roof of the building opposite gleams dully in the light of the moon and the stars. It is close, but too far away to jump on to. But anyway, walk back into the room, take a good run and go soaring out into empty space. It will be a breathtaking flight – straight into the embrace of the Eternal Beloved. I feel sorry for my mother and father. But they are far away. I see the little town – log-walled houses amid the white snowdrifts. I see the river – black water, with huge rafts of ice creeping along it. Masha Mironova is standing on one ice-floe and there is a tight bunch of people on another. The black crack between them grows wider and wider. The Angara is like a length of white cloth that has been cut crookedly along its length.

And here is the poem. No need to rack my brains – I just have to write it down.

> *My life has been sheared in half*
> *Like a length of woven cloth.*
> *The two halves have been torn apart*
> *Now I cannot keep them both.*
>
> *Skewed the line that severed them*
> *Though the knife was keen and sharp.*
> *They can never be joined again.*
> *The rent is too wide, the gap too far.*
>
> *Once the cloth was white as snow,*
> *Now its weave is solid black.*
> *Even if I should wish to go,*
> *How can I ever jump back?*
>
> *Overhead the Milky Way,*
> *Below the dreadful dark abyss;*

If I run hard and really try
Perhaps something will come of this?

But my foot will never reach
Across the yawning gap below.
I shall fall straight down from the sky,
Down into the homespun snow.

That's all. Now just run and jump.

To the publisher

I have no time to edit and transcribe this confused but honest story. I have only one request, please discard the lines that have been crossed out. Let the reader see me, not as I was, but as I wish to be seen.

M.M.

III. From the 'Agents' Reports' File

To His Honour Lieutenant-Colonel Besikov
(Private and confidential)

Dear Lieutenant-Colonel,

You must be surprised that I am writing to you again after our meeting yesterday, which took place at your insistence and concluded with my curses, cries and shameful tears. Or perhaps you are not surprised, since you despise me and are convinced of my weakness. But let that be as you wish. Probably you are right about me, and I would never have escaped from your tenacious grasp if not for the events of the night just past.

Consider this letter an official document or, if you prefer, my formal testimony. But if this letter is not sufficient, I am willing to confirm my evidence to any agency of law-enforcement, even under oath.

I could not get to sleep last night, my nerves were strained after our discussion and – why should I pretend otherwise? – I was frightened. I am a man of an impressionable and hypochondriacal disposition, and your threat to have me exiled to Yakutsk, and also to inform the political exiles there that I had collaborated with the gendarmes, had unsettled my nerves completely.

And so I rushed about the room, tousling my hair and wringing my hands – in short, I was in a desperate, cowardly state. I even started sobbing once, I felt so terribly sorry for myself. If I did not detest suicide so fiercely as a result of my poor beloved brother's death last year (he was so like the two young twins in our club!) I would certainly have seriously considered laying hands on myself.

However, you do not need to know about my nocturnal sufferings, and they are unlikely to be of any interest to you. Let me simply say that I had still not got to sleep at one in the morning.

Suddenly my attention was attracted by a terrible popping and rattling noise rapidly approaching the building. I glanced out of the window in fright and saw an outlandish three-wheeled carriage approaching the gates, moving without any horse to pull it. I could make out two figures on the high seat: one was wearing a suit of gleaming leather, a helmet and huge goggles that covered almost all his face; the other looked even stranger – he was a young Jew in a skull cap with side-locks, but also wearing immense goggles.

The man in leather climbed out of his ugly apparatus, walked up the steps on to the porch and rang the bell.

It was the Stammerer, looking very intense, pale and sombre.

'Has something happened?' I asked, surprised and alarmed by this nocturnal visit. This gentleman had never previously shown any interest in my person. I thought he had never even noticed that I existed. And how could he have found out where I live?

I could only assume that somehow the Stammerer had discovered that I had tried to follow him and had come to demand an explanation.

But when he spoke, it was about something completely different.

'Maria Mironova, whom you knew under the name of Columbine, has jumped out of her window,' the Stammerer informed me, without any greeting or apology for the late intrusion. I don't know why I continue to call him by the nickname that I myself invented. There is no longer any point to this ludicrous trick, and in any case you know more about this man than I do. I do not know what he is really

234

called, but in our club he was known by the strange name of Genji.

Not knowing what to say to this dismal news, I simply muttered: 'How terrible. I hope at least she didn't suffer before she died.'

'Fortunately, she is still alive,' Genji declared impassively. 'A fantastic piece of luck. Columbine did not simply throw herself out of the window, for some reason she t-took a run and jumped – a very long way. That is what saved her. Of course, even though the side street is narrow, she could not possibly have jumped to the other side, but luckily for her, directly opposite her balcony there is an advertising sign – a tin angel. Columbine's hem caught on the angel's hand and she was l-left hanging there. Her dress was made of incredibly strong material – the same as my driving suit. It didn't tear. The poor girl was stuck ten sazhens above the ground, unconscious and dangling head down, like a doll. And she was there for a long time, because no one noticed her in the dark. It was very difficult to get her down, they had to call the fire brigade to help. The young lady was taken to hospital, and when she recovered consciousness and was asked for the address of a relative, she gave them my telephone number. They phoned me and asked: "Does Mr Genji live here?".'

I realised that he was not really speaking impassively, but making an immense effort to control his powerful agitation. The longer I listened to my late visitor, the more I wondered why he had come to me. What did he want? Genji is not the kind of man who needs someone to talk to after he has suffered some kind of shock. And in any case, I was not suited to playing the role of his confidant.

'Have you come to me as a doctor?' I enquired cautiously. 'Do you want me to visit her in the hospital? But the young lady must have been examined already. And then, I am not a general practitioner, I'm an anatomist. My patients have no need of medical assistance.'

'Miss Mironova has already been released from hospital,

there is not a single scratch on her. My valet took her to my apartment, gave her hot Japanese vodka and put her to bed. Columbine will be p-perfectly all right now,' said Genji, removing his gigantic goggles, and the gaze of his steely eyes made me feel uneasy. 'I need you, Mr Horatio, not as a doctor, but in a different capacity. Your capacity as a collaborator.'

I raised my eyebrows in puzzlement, trying to pretend that I did not understand the term, but I turned cold inside.

'Don't waste your time, I saw through your cover a long time ago. You were eavesdropping on my conversation with Blagovolsky when I d-declared my purpose in joining the club. The door was slightly open and I saw a glint of light on glass through the crack. You are the only aspirant who wears spectacles. At the time, I admit, I thought *you* were the ubiquitous reporter Lavr Zhemailo. But the death of the journalist made it clear that I was mistaken. Then I asked my servant, with whom you are slightly acquainted, to take a look at you, and he confirmed my second hypothesis – you were the person who tried to t-trail me. On my instructions, Masa then proceeded to trail you. The gentleman in the check jacket whom you met yesterday on First Tverskaya-Yamskaya Street serves in the Gendarmes Department, does he not?'

I shuddered and asked: 'What do you want with me? I've done you no harm, I swear it! The story of the "Lovers of Death" is over and done with, and the club has been disbanded.'

'The club has been disbanded, but the story is not yet over. From the hospital I went to Columbine's flat, and there I found this.' Genji took a sheet of odd-looking marbled paper out of his pocket. Through the marbling I could see the words *Ich warte*. 'This is the reason why Columbine jumped out of the window!'

I gazed at the paper in confusion and asked: 'What does this mean?'

'It means that my conclusions were erroneous because I accepted answers that were too facile and closed my eyes to a number of details and circumstances that didn't fit the overall picture,' Genji replied. 'And that very nearly led to the death of a young woman whose life matters to me. You, Horatio, are going to come with me. You will be an official witness, and afterwards you will report what you have seen and heard to your gendarme b-bosses. For certain reasons that it is not necessary for you to know, I myself prefer not to meet the Moscow police. And I shall not be staying in the city for long. It would delay my record attempt.'

I did not understand the comment about a record attempt, but I decided not to ask. Still looking me in the eye, Genji added: 'I know you are not an irredeemable scoundrel. You are simply a weak man, a victim of circumstances. Your case is not entirely hopeless. As it says in the scriptures: "Out of the weak shall come forth the strong." Let's go.'

His tone was peremptory and I could not resist. And, indeed, I did not wish to.

We drove to Rozhdestvensky Boulevard in the motor. I sat between Genji and his strange companion, clutching the handrail with both hands. The nightmarish device was driven by the young Jew, and on the corners, he cried out: 'Pull, my beauties!' We were moving so fast and jolting so hard that the only thought in my mind was how to avoid being thrown out of my seat.

Genji told the driver to stop at the corner. 'We'll go on from here on foot,' he said. 'The engine makes too much noise.'

The youth stayed to watch the auto and the two of us walked up the side street.

Despite the late hour, there was light in the windows of the familiar house.

'The spider,' Genji muttered, pulling off his gauntlets with immense cuffs. 'Sitting there rubbing his feet together. Waiting for a moth to get caught in his web . . . When I have finished, you will summon the police by t-telephone. Give me your word that you will not try to detain me.'

'I give you my word,' I muttered obediently, although I still did not understand a thing.

The Doge opened the door to us without bothering to ask who had come to see him in the middle of the night. He was wearing a velvet dressing gown that looked like an old-fashioned caftan, with a white shirt and tie visible between the lapels. Prospero looked at us for a moment without speaking, laughed and said: 'An interesting pair. I didn't know that you were friends.'

I was astounded to see that he looked quite different from the way he had been at our last meeting – not pitiful and bewildered, but confident, even triumphant. Just like in the old days.

'To what do I owe the honour of this late visit from such sullen guests?' the Doge asked in the same derisive tone of voice, as he showed us through into the drawing room. 'No, don't tell me, let me guess. The suicides are continuing? The dissolution of the pernicious club has had no effect? And what did I tell you!' He shook his head and sighed.

'No, Mr Blagovolsky,' Genji said in a quiet voice, 'the c-club is no longer active. But there is just one final formality to be settled.'

Before he could say another word, the Doge leapt backwards spryly and pulled his Bulldog revolver out of his pocket. I gasped in surprise and dodged to one side.

Genji, however, was not perturbed in the slightest. He flung a heavy gauntlet into Blagovolsky's face, at the same moment raising one foot in a brown shoe and gaiter and kicking the revolver with incredible agility.

The weapon was sent flying before it could be fired. I quickly picked it up and handed it to my companion.

'May I consider this a confession?' Genji asked in cold fury. His usual stammer had completely disappeared. 'I could shoot you, Blagovolsky, this very moment, and it would be legitimate self-defence. But let us do everything according to the law.'

Prospero had turned pale and his recent scornful manner had disappeared without trace.

'What confession?' he muttered. 'What law are you talking about? I don't understand any of this. I thought you had gone insane, like Caliban, and come here to kill me. Who are you really? What do you want from me?'

'I can see this is going to be a long conversation. Sit down,' said Genji, pointing to a chair, 'I knew you would try to deny everything.'

The Doge squinted warily at the revolver.

'All right, all right. I'll do whatever you say. But let's go to the study. There's a draught here and I'm feeling chilly.'

We walked through the dark dining room and sat down in the study: our host at the writing desk, Genji facing him in a huge armchair for visitors, and I at one side. The wide desk was in a state of great disorder, covered with a jumble of books with bookmarks and sheets of paper covered with writing. At the very centre there was an impressive inkstand of gleaming bronze in the form of several heroes from Russian folktales, and at one edge there was the familiar roulette wheel, which had been exiled from the drawing room and found sanctuary at the very heart of the house. No doubt the Wheel of Fortune was meant to remind our host of his days of former glory.

'Listen carefully and remember everything,' Genji told me, 'so that you can present everything as clearly as possible in your report afterwards.'

Allow me to say that I took my obligations as a witness seriously. I had brought from home the pencil and notebook previously acquired on your advice. If I had not been so prudent, it would not be easy for me now to reconstruct so precisely everything that was said.

At first Blagovolsky ran his fingers nervously across the green baize of the desk, but then he made an effort to control himself, put his left hand under the desk and his right hand on the helmet of the Russian folk-hero inkwell and remained in that position.

'Please be so good as to explain to me what all this is

about, gentlemen,' he said with dignity. 'You would appear to be accusing me of something.'

Genji tried to turn his chair, but it proved to be too massive, and the ends of its thick legs were buried in the deep pile of a square rug that evidently must have been made to order – it was an exact fit for the chair. The Stammerer was obliged to sit in a half-turned position.

'Yes, I accuse you of the most ignoble form of murder – driving people to commit suicide. But I also blame myself, because on two occasions I have made unforgivable mistakes. The first time was here in this very study when you artfully wove truth and falsehood together in the performance that you put on for me, pretending to be a well-intentioned innocent. The second time I allowed myself to be deceived when I mistook the devil's tail for the devil himself.' Genji set the Bulldog on the edge of the desk. 'You are aware of what you are doing, your reason is sound, your actions are thoroughly planned for many moves ahead, but you are insane nonetheless. You are obsessed with power. You admitted this yourself during our previous discussion, with such convincing sincerity and such an innocent expression on your face that I allowed myself to be taken in. Ah, if only I had thought of taking a little of that liquid for analysis on the evening when you broke the goblet! I am sure it was no sleeping draught, but absolutely genuine poison. Otherwise why would you have needed to destroy the evidence? Alas, I have made too many mistakes and the price paid for them has been far too high . . .

'I understand the mechanism of your insanity,' Genji continued. 'You made three attempts to die three times in your life and each time you took fright. You established the suicide club in order to redeem the guilt that you felt for having cheated Death. You threw others instead of yourself into its ravenous jaws, ransomed yourself from Death with the lives of others. How you loved to imagine yourself as the mighty magician Prospero, exalted far above ordinary mortals! I shall never forgive myself for believing your fairytale about saving lost souls. You were not trying to save anyone. On the contrary, you took a romantic passion engendered by our age of crisis – a passion that in ninety-nine cases out of a hundred would have passed of its own accord – and skilfully nurtured the young shoot of a love of death. Oh, you are a very skilful gardener and there was no subterfuge that you disdained. You were very inventive in arranging the so-called "Signs", sometimes exploiting fortuitous circumstances but usually creating them for yourself. You, Blagovolsky, are an excellent psychologist, you unerringly divined the weak spot of every one of your victims. And in addition, I have noticed that you possess considerable skill in the techniques of hypnosis.'

Oh, this was absolutely true! On numerous occasions, I myself had noted the magnetic power possessed by Prospero's gaze, especially in the gentle illumination of the brazier or candles. I always had the feeling that those black eyes could pierce to the very deepest recesses of my soul! Hypnosis – why, naturally, hypnosis explained everything!

'I became a member of your flock too late,' Genji continued, 'I do not know how you drove the photographer Sviridov and the teacher Soimonov to suicide. No doubt each of them received certain "Signs" for which you were responsible, but it is too late now to reconstruct the chain of events. Those who were to die were named by Ophelia during a spiritualist seance. You apparently had nothing to do with it. But I am no novice in such matters, and it was immediately obvious to me that there was a hypnotic connection between you and the medium – you could communicate with her without words. As the spiritualists say, she was tuned to your emanations – a single look, gesture or hint was enough for Ophelia to guess what you wanted. You could implant any thought that you wanted in her mind, the girl was no more than your mouthpiece.'

'All very lyrical,' said Blagovolsky, interrupting the address for the prosecution for the first time. 'And very significant. In my opinion, Mr Genji, it is you who is insane, not I. Do you really think that the authorities will pay any attention to your fantasies?'

He had already recovered from his initial shock. He clasped his fingers together in front of him and stared intently at Genji. A strong man, I thought. It looks as if the Stammerer has met his match.

'Write, Horatio, write,' Genji told me. 'Note down as much detail as possible. Every link in the chain is important here. And the evidence will follow.

'The double suicide of Moretta and Lycanthrope went very smoothly, and once again there was no apparent criminal involvement. Acting under your hypnotic suggestion or, perhaps, on your direct instructions, Ophelia declared at the seance that a messenger in a white cloak would appear to the Chosen One that night, bringing the word. Your calculations were precisely right: the members of the club were impressionable people, mostly of a hysterical disposition. It is strange, therefore, that only two of them dreamed of a messenger in a white cloak who appeared to them that night. And then, according to the farewell verse, the stranger who appeared to the youth was severe, with black eyes, and he arrived in the usual manner, through the door, while the girl dreamed of someone with bright eyes, who preferred the window, but then who would cavil over the petty details of a mystical vision?'

'Nonsense,' Prospero snorted. 'Irresponsible conjecture. Keep writing, Horatio, keep writing. If I am destined to die at the hands of this madman, let the crime not go unpunished.'

I looked at Genji in confusion, and he smiled reassuringly.

'Don't be concerned. We are coming to the evidence now. The first evidence was provided to me by Avaddon, who died the day before I began my investigation. The clues were still perfectly fresh and the murderer had not had time to cover his tracks.'

'Murderer?' I exclaimed. 'So the student was murdered?'

'As surely as if he had been hanged on a gallows. It began,

like the previous cases, with a sentence pronounced by Ophelia under hypnosis. And the business was brought to its conclusion by Signs: the howling of a Beast or, rather, a terrifying, inhuman voice repeating something that sounded like "go, go". The voice was heard by the neighbours next door, so it could not possibly have been a hallucination. I examined the flat very carefully and discovered something rather curious. The hinges and keyhole of the door leading to the back staircase had been oiled very thoroughly, and very recently too. I inspected the lock with a magnifying glass and discovered fresh scratches showing that it had been opened with a key several times, and always from the outside, but no key had ever been inserted in the keyhole from the inside. I could not possibly imagine that the occupant of the flat had lived with the door on to the back staircase unlocked all the time. Therefore, someone must have unlocked it, entered the flat, done something there and quickly withdrawn.

'The next time I visited the flat I went under cover of night and conducted a more exhaustive search, hoping to discover traces of some technical device capable of producing sound. Under the upper cornice of the kitchen window I found two lead pipes like those that are used in pneumatic alarms. They were both artfully concealed under the plaster and had openings that were stopped with corks. I removed the corks, but nothing happened. I had almost decided that they be must some innovative kind of ventilation system, when a gust of wind shook the window pane, and I distinctly heard a low, hollow wail: "G-o-o-o, g-o-o-o". In the dark gloom of the flat it was genuinely terrifying. There was no doubt at all that the sound was produced by the concealed pipes. I replaced the corks, and the wailing immediately stopped. The ancient Egyptians used to employ something rather similar in the pyramids to prevent robbers from desecrating the sarcophagi. Combinations of pipes of different forms, installed where there was a draught, could produce entire words and even phrases. You used to be an engineer, Mr Blagovolsky, and rather a talented one, I believe. It would have been easy for you to design an essentially very simple structure like this. And that explained the mystery of the back entrance. In order to drive the occupant of the flat into suicide, the intruder entered the kitchen on a wild, windy night, removed the corks from the pipes and then calmly left, quite confident of the result of his actions. I knew that you had rented and furnished the flat for the poor student. That is one. The neighbours testified that the Beast did not fall quiet until morning, although Nikifor Sipyaga hanged himself some time before dawn. That is two. Why, one wonders, would the Beast continue calling on him to leave this world when he was already in the next one? I recalled you having told me that you felt concerned about Avaddon and you set out to visit him at the crack of dawn. That was when you closed the openings in the pipes. And that is three.'

'Well now, the pipes are genuine evidence,' Blagovolsky admitted. 'But the question is, against whom? Yes, I helped the poor student with his lodgings. And I was the first to find the body. Is that suspicious? Possibly. But no more than that. No, no, Mr Prince, you have not proven my guilt. Poor Avaddon was one of the incurable cases. No one could have saved him from suicide. He only needed a pretext to lay hands on himself.'

Even so, I could see that Genji's arguments had had an effect on the Doge – he started fidgeting again and reached out to touch the bronze inkwell, as if it could help him.

Genji got up out of his chair and started walking round the room.

'But what about Ophelia? Do you also classify her as an "incurable case"? The young girl had absolutely no desire to die, she was simply fascinated by everything mysterious and inexplicable. She really did possess abilities that modern science is unable to define and analyse. And you exploited her gift to the full. When I led the seance instead of you and summoned the spirit of Avaddon, Ophelia's incredible sensitivity allowed her to sense or guess what I wanted. In the

East they believe that powerful feelings can be preserved for a long time. A strong outpouring of positive or negative energy always leaves its mark. That is the reason why certain places are "cursed" or "blessed". They possess a specific aura. And people like Ophelia possess the rare ability to sense this aura. As she went into her trance, the girl sensed the fear, horror and hopelessness that Avaddon felt during the final minutes of his life. Perhaps the mention of "howling" and a "beast" was simply prompted by Avaddon's farewell poem and there was nothing mystical involved, but you were frightened. What if Ophelia, with her exceptional gifts, should happen to sense foul play? For after all, Blagovolsky, despite your cynical manipulation of human superstition, in your heart you yourself are a mystic and you believe in all sorts of dark supernatural nonsense.'

I thought I saw Prospero shudder at that point, but I cannot vouch for it. Genji sat back down in his chair.

'Bravo,' he said. 'You are cautious. I deliberately left the revolver on the desk, then stood up and moved away a little, hoping that you would try to kill me. I have my trusty Herstahl in my pocket, and I would have put a hole in your head with a perfectly clear conscience, and then our pointless conversation would have been at an end.'

'Why is it pointless?' I asked. 'You wish Mr Blagovolsky to be put on trial, do you not?'

'I am afraid that trying him will do more harm than good,' Genji sighed. 'A sensational trial with glib speeches from eloquent advocates, an imposing defendant, a horde of reporters. What wonderful publicity for other would-be fishers of souls! The judgement of the court is hardly likely to frighten them.'

'From what I have heard so far, only one judgement could be passed – innocent,' Blagovolsky said with a shrug. 'And your trap with the revolver is simply farcical. Do I look like a total dunce? You'd better get on with your story. You tell it rather well.'

Genji nodded imperturbably.

'Indeed, let us go on. After the spiritualist seance that I led, you decided Ophelia was becoming too dangerous. What if she told someone about the hypnotic commands that you sent to her? It is not such a rare thing for a subject to break free of a hypnotist's control. So far the girl was still only under your influence, but during the seance you saw that she submitted to the will of another controller with equal ease . . . What I could not understand was how it was possible to drive someone who had no intention at all of killing herself to commit suicide? I found the answer to this question in Ophelia's implicit faith in supernatural phenomena, her irrational, unconditional submission to the Miraculous and, in general, the undoubtedly anomalous workings of her psyche – these were factors that the criminal could have exploited. And he only needed a few moments to put his plan into action. The girl returned home, happy and full of the joy of life, and went into her room, only to come back out almost immediately, transformed beyond all recognition. She said goodbye to her mother, walked to the bank of the river and threw herself into the water . . . There was one thing Ophelia had said that I could not get out of my mind – that she had been given a sign like the one sent to King Balthazar. And then I had an idea. I went to her house at night and cut the outer pane out of the window of her bedroom. The poor widow must have been surprised in the morning when she discovered that it had mysteriously disappeared. When I shone ultraviolet light through the glass I discovered a blurred, but perfectly legible inscription made with phosphorescent ink. This is a copy that I made of it.'

I recalled the Stammerer's mysterious manipulations at the small house beside the Yauza. So that was what the self-appointed investigator had been doing that night!

Genji took a large sheet of paper, folded in four, out of his pocket and spread it out on the table. The inscription looked like this:

ϛⱵirⱵ

'What's that?' I asked, examining the incomprehensible symbols.

He took the sheet of paper, turned it round and held it in front of the table lamp. Now I could read the letters, illuminated from behind:

Stirb[2]

'When she entered her room, Ophelia saw a word written in glowing letters of fire that seemed to be floating in the air. It told her quite unambiguously to die. The Prince of Death had expressed his will quite clearly, and the poor girl did not dare oppose it. Ever since she was a child she had believed implicitly in the secret signs of destiny. Meantime . . .' – Genji crumpled up the sheet of paper and tossed it on the desk in front of the Doge – '. . . you were certainly still outside, observing events. The most revolting thing about the entire story is not the murder, but the fact that when you had already condemned the girl to death, you decided to enjoy her almost childish body beforehand. You knew perfectly well that she secretly adored you, even worshipped you. You told her to stay when the other aspirants left and I presume that you demonstrated the exceptional ardour of your love – in any case, when Ophelia came home she looked absolutely happy. The nearness of death inflames your lust, does it not? You had thought everything through carefully. After sating your passion, you gallantly drove your victim home, said good night to her at the gate and then quickly wrote your fateful instruction on the bedroom window. You waited to make sure that the trick had worked, quickly wiped the window clean and then went back home. But there was one thing you failed to take into account, Sergei Irinarkhovich. The pane of glass is evidence, incontrovertible evidence.'

'Incontrovertible evidence?' Blagovolsky repeated with a

2. Die (German)

shrug. 'But how can you prove that I was the one who scribbled that word on the glass?'

I also thought that Genji seemed overconfident. Yes, I remembered that Prospero had told Ophelia to stay that evening and, knowing his habits, could easily imagine what had happened after that. However, that was not sufficient for a formal charge in law.

'You are an engineer,' Genji said to the Doge, 'and you probably follow the progress of science. Has the discovery announced by the London police in June this year really escaped your notice?'

Blagovolsky and I both looked at the speaker in puzzlement.

'I am referring to the Galton-Henry dactyloscopic method which makes it possible for the first time to identify a criminal from the prints left by his fingers. The finest minds in criminal investigation have been struggling for years with the problem of creating a system for classifying the papillary patterns on the tips of the fingers. The clearest prints of all are left on glass. You may have wiped off the phosphorescent letters with your handkerchief, but you did not wipe away all the prints of your fingers. I have photographs of the criminal's dactylograms here with me. Would you compare them with your own?'

So saying, Genji took a small metal box out of the immense pocket of his leather jacket and opened it to reveal a small cushion impregnated with dark paint or ink, like those that are used for official stamps.

'I would not,' Prospero replied rapidly, jerking his hands away and putting them under the table. 'You are quite right, scientific progress is constantly surprising us, and the surprises are not always pleasant ones.'

The comment was as a good as a confession!

'When it came to the Lioness of Ecstasy, you dispensed with complicated tricks,' said Genji, going on to the next victim. 'This woman whose spirit was broken by grief really did long for death and she unhesitatingly accepted the appearance of three black roses on her bed as a Sign. This, as we know, was not a difficult trick to arrange.'

'But last time you said the flowers were delivered by Caliban.' I reminded him.

'Yes, and that was the circumstance that led me astray. Since you have mentioned Caliban, Horatio, let us consider the real part played by this singular individual in our story. The bookkeeper confused the case very badly, he threw me off the track and diverted all suspicion from the main criminal. My mistake almost cost gullible Columbine her life.

'You, Prospero, had good reason for favouring this madman, who had been driven insane by extreme suffering and a tormented conscience. He really was your obedient Caliban, the servant of the all-powerful wizard – a servant who was blindly and irrationally devoted to you. You praised his abominable verse, you showed him all sorts of favours and – most importantly of all – he dreamed that you would intercede for him and win the goodwill of Death, so that his "term of imprisonment" would be reduced. At first he dutifully carried out your instructions, obviously without much idea of their real significance. I assume that the concealed pipes in Avaddon's flat were installed by Caliban – you would hardly have been able to manage such a difficult job, requiring a high level of manual skill and uncommon physical strength, and you would not have risked giving such an unusual commission to a stranger. Give three black roses to Lorelei's domestic companion? Why not? You obviously told Papushin that you wanted to play a joke on the Lioness, whose extravagant mannerisms Caliban had always found so irritating.

'How could I ever have believed that this burly halfwit was the evil genius of the "Lovers of Death"? How could he ever have invented the tricks with the letters of fire and the wailing beast? How right the Chinese sage was when he said "The obvious is rarely true" . . .' Genji shook his head angrily. 'But your faithful genie did not stay in his bottle, he escaped and started acting on his own initiative. The searing pain of his desperate desire for death became ever more excruciating. When he took his revenge on Gdlevsky, the bookkeeper ruined your entire artful plan, which was so near to realisation. Why did you need to destroy that proud, talented boy? Merely in order to flatter your own vanity? First the Russian Sappho, then the Russian Rimbaud – and both of them would take their own lives in obedience to your will. You would deprive modern Russian poetry of two of its most brilliant names, while remaining in the shadows, and you had every chance of getting away scot-free. How pitiful, compared to you, were those trivial destroyers of genius, Dantes and Martynov!

'Or did it all happen far more simply and intuitively? A romantic youth, enthralled with his mystical theory of rhyme, happened by chance to open a book at the word "breath", which rhymes with "death" and haughtily informed you about this miraculous Sign. The next Friday you had already made thorough preparations by leaving a book on the table, knowing that Gdlevsky would immediately grab it to tell his own fortune. I remembered the book and I took the first possible opportunity to examine it carefully.' Genji turned towards me. 'Horatio, if it's not too much trouble, would you mind going to the drawing room and bringing back the collected plays of Shakespeare from the third shelf?'

I immediately did as he asked and found the book without any difficulty. When I took it down off the shelf, I gasped: it was the same volume that Cyrano had examined on the last evening of his life!

As I walked back I turned the book this way and that, but I failed to observe anything suspicious about it. Nature, alas, did not endow me with exceptional powers of observation, as Genji confirmed when he took the volume from my hands.

'Look at the top of the book. Do you see the yellow colour extending to the middle of the pages? That is ordinary office glue. Try opening the book at random, at any page.'

I tried opening the book between my finger and thumb and could scarcely believe my eyes – it opened at the title page of *Macbeth*.

'Now do you understand?' Genji asked me. 'The result of Gdlevsky's divination on the second Friday had been determined beforehand.'

Yes, the trick had been precisely calculated for psychological effect. And I suddenly realised that this was the 'bombshell' that Cyrano had intended to print in the morning edition of his paper. Like Genji, he had discovered the trick with the glue and immediately realised that he could season his investigation with a spicy sauce. The entire business had suddenly acquired a criminal flavour. Poor Cyrano had not suspected that *he* would be blown up by his own bombshell . . .

'On the third Friday you decided to make absolutely sure of things and leave Gdlevsky no chance. After his "good luck" on the first two Fridays, the youth's nerves were naturally so wrought up that he was seeing Signs in everything going on around him. It would not have been at all surprising if he had discovered his fateful rhyme without any assistance from you, but to guarantee the outcome you arranged for him to find what he was seeking right outside your house. You paid a wandering organ grinder to sing a song with a particular refrain – but only until a certain young man whose appearance you described in detail would enter the house. I don't think you explained your plans to the organ grinder, but you did impress on him that once he had completed his assignment he should clear out as quickly as possible, and the old man did precisely that, with all the speed that he could muster. When I dashed out into the street two minutes later, I couldn't find him anywhere.

'And so Gdlevsky had been condemned to death by you and would certainly have carried out the sentence himself, if not for Caliban, who had been jealous of your young favourite for a long time. Now it seemed that Gdlevsky was favoured not only by you, but also by Death, and the insane bookkeeper decided to do away with his fortunate rival . . .

'The killing of the reporter Lavr Zhemailo was the only death in which you were not directly involved. That is, if we do not take into account that you once called the newspaper informer a Judas, who would betray you as Christ was betrayed. To Caliban you really were his Saviour, and so when he discovered Cyrano's true occupation, he killed him and hung him on an aspen tree.'

At that moment I must confess that I experienced a certain inner satisfaction. Not a very worthy feeling, but understandable. Apparently you do not know everything and do not notice everything, clever Mr Investigator, I thought to myself. You do not know that Caliban eavesdropped on Cyrano's telephone conversation with his newspaper office.

Genji moved on to the final point of his prosecution speech.

'Your preparations for Columbine's suicide were the most thorough and cunning of all. First you slipped her the three pieces of card with inscriptions in German. The day before yesterday the young lady gave them to me and told me that they did not burn in fire. I subjected the paper to chemical analysis and discovered it had been impregnated with a solution of alums, which had rendered it non-flammable. An old trick that was once used by the Count of St Germain. In order to prompt Columbine to check whether the notes would burn, you deliberately slipped Papushin a note from Death as well, only *it* was written on ordinary paper. The scheme worked perfectly, but there was one thing you failed to anticipate – Caliban felt slighted and decided to take his revenge on Death's Chosen One, just as he had done with Gdlevsky. Fortunately I happened to be at the scene.'

I noticed that Blagovolsky's behaviour had changed now. The Doge was no longer objecting or trying to dispute any of his accuser's assertions. He sat there hunched up, with his face completely drained of blood and his eyes – I could see that they were filled with fear and alarm – trained steadily on the speaker. Prospero must have felt that the end was approaching. His nervous state was also evident from the movements of his hands: the fingers of his right hand were stroking the bronze hero's helmet again, while the fingers of his left clenched and unclenched spasmodically.

'Fate gave you a generous gift in the person of Caliban. You had a very good chance of getting away with everything by shifting the blame for all your crimes on to the dead maniac's shoulders. But you were unable to control yourself, you could not stop. Why did you decide to finish the girl off after all? That is the greatest riddle for me. Could you not forgive Columbine because she had grown indifferent to your charms? Or, as happens so often with hardened killers, did you really, somewhere deep in your heart, want someone to expose you and stop you?'

'No, Mr Psychologist,' said Prospero, suddenly breaking his silence. 'It was neither of those. I simply do not like to abandon a job halfway through when it is going well.'

I immediately took down what he had said word for word: another indirect admission of guilt.

Genji's face darkened slightly; he was evidently taken aback by this audacious reply.

'Your attempt to finish your "job" was certainly most inventive. Columbine told me about the magical words "Ich warte" that appeared out of nowhere on a blank sheet of paper. Most impressive! It is hardly surprising that the girl immediately believed implicitly that it was a miracle. I visited Columbine's flat and inspected both the sheet of paper and the book very closely. Another cunning chemical trick. Several pages before the bookmark you had glued into the book a piece of paper with the two fateful words written on it in lead acetate. And the marbled paper used as a bookmark had been soaked in a solution of sulphurated potash. When the book was closed, the lead acetate started seeping through the pages and about a day later the letters appeared on the marbled paper. This method of secret writing was developed by the Jesuits in the seventeenth century, so it is not original to you. You merely found a new use for the old recipe.'

Genji turned towards me and leaned on the armrest of his chair.

'That is all, Horatio, the facts have been set forth. As for the material evidence, the window pane with the dactylograms is under guard in the porter's lodge of the Spassky Barracks, the pipes in Avaddon's flat are still in place, and I left the book from Blagovolsky's library and the sheet of marbled paper in Columbine's flat. No doubt the sheet of paper glued into the book and the sheet that was soaked in potash also bear the criminal's fingerprints. The investigation should not encounter any difficulties. There is the telephone – make the call. As soon as the police arrive I shall withdraw, and you remember that you gave me your word.'

I stood up to walk across to the telephone hanging on the wall, but Blagovolsky gestured for me to wait.

'Don't be in such a hurry, Horatio. The gentleman detective has demonstrated his eloquence and perspicacity. It is only fair that I should have the right of reply.'

I glanced enquiringly at Genji. He nodded, with a wary glance at Prospero, and I sat down again.

Blagovolsky chuckled, opened the helmet lid of the inkwell and closed it again, then drummed his fingers on it.

'You have unfolded an entire psychological theory that presents me as a cowardly halfwit. According to you, everything I have done can be explained by panic induced by fear of death; an attempt to wheedle a respite out of death by offering up human sacrifices. Nonsense, Mr Genji. Why underestimate and belittle your opponent? At the very least that is imprudent. Perhaps I was once afraid to die, but that was a very, very long time ago, before the stone walls of a prison cell exterminated all strong feelings and passions in me. Apart from one that is, the most exalted of all – the desire to be God. A long period of solitary confinement brings home very clearly the simple truth that you are alone in the world and the entire universe is in you, and so you are

God. If you so wish, the universe will live. If you do not, it will die, with everything that it contains. That is what will happen if I, God, commit suicide. In comparison with this catastrophe, all other deaths are mere trifles. But if I am God, then I must rule, must I not? That is only logical, it is my right. My rule must be real and undivided. And do you know what God's real power over people is? It is not a general's epaulettes, a minister's portfolio, or even a king's throne. In our times dominion of that kind is becoming an anachronism. It will not be enough for the rulers of the new century that is beginning. There must be power, not over bodies, but over souls. Say to someone else's soul, "Die!" – and it dies. As it was with the Old Believers, when hundreds threw themselves into the fire if the elder willed it, and mothers cast their infants into the flames. But the elder left the burning community and went to save another flock. You, Mr Genji, are a limited man and you will never understand this supreme pleasure . . . Ah, why am I wasting time on you? To hell with you, you bore me.'

After pronouncing the last two phrases in a rapid flurry of speech, Prospero suddenly cut his speech short. He turned the bronze inkwell figure clockwise, there was a loud metallic clang and a hatch opened under the chair on which Genji was sitting, creating a hole the precise size of the square rug. The rug, the chair and the man sitting in it disappeared into the black hole.

I shouted out in horror, with my eyes fixed on that opening in the floor.

'Another of my engineering designs!' Prospero exclaimed, choking on fitful laughter. 'The most ingenious one of all!' he waved his hand in the air, unable to cope with his paroxysm of merriment. 'There sits the pompous fellow, the master of life. And then a turn of a lever, releasing a spring and bang! Please be so good as to fall down my well-shaft.'

Wiping away his tears, he told me: 'You know, my friend Horatio, last year I got the idea of deepening the basement. When the workers started digging they discovered an old brick-lined well. Very deep, almost thirty sazhens. I told them to build the shaft upwards with bricks so that it reached the floor at this point. And then I built the hatch on the top myself. I like to do a bit of work with my hands in my spare time, it helps me to relax. The late Mr Genji was mistaken in thinking that I was shy of physical work – I built the voice imitator in Avaddon's flat myself. But I installed this secret hatch for amusement, not for use. I would sit here with a visitor, talking about this and that. With him in the place of honour in the armchair, and me at the desk, toying with the lever. And I would think to myself: "Your life, my little pigeon, is in my hands. Just a little turn, and you'll disappear from the face of the earth. It's very helpful for your self-respect, especially if the visitor is haughty and pompous, like our Japanese prince who has just met such an untimely end. I never thought that my little toy would come in so useful.'

I sat there turned to stone, listening to this bloodcurdling speech, and feeling more afraid with every moment. I had to run, to get away from there immediately! He would never let me go alive – he would throw me down the well too.

I was about to make a dash for the door, but then my eye fell on the Bulldog, still lying on the edge of the desk. Prospero would grab the gun and shoot me in the back.

Well then, I had to get the gun myself!

The desperate nature of the situation lent me courage. I jumped up and reached for the gun, but Blagovolsky proved quicker and my fingers landed on his hand, which was already covering the revolver. A moment later we were struggling with each other, both clutching the gun with both hands. Taking small steps, we skirted round the table and then started jigging on the spot, as if we were performing some macabre dance.

I kicked at him and he kicked back, hitting me on the ankle. It was very painful, but I didn't open my fingers. I jerked the gun towards me with all my strength and we both lost our balance and went tumbling to the floor. The Bulldog slipped out of our hands, slid across the gleaming parquet floor and stopped halfway over the edge of the hatch, swaying uncertainly. I scrambled towards it on my hands and knees, but I was too late. As if it had finally made up its mind, it tumbled over the edge.

A few dull thuds, growing fainter. Then silence.

Taking advantage of the fact that I had my back to him, Prospero grabbed me by the collar with one hand and by my coat-tail with the other and started dragging me across the floor towards the pit. Another second and it would all have been over, but by good fortune my fingers struck the leg of the desk and I clung to it with a grip of iron. My head was already hanging over the hole, but Blagovolsky could not move me another inch, no matter how he tried.

I was straining every muscle so hard that it was a while before I looked down into the hole – and in any case my eyes needed time to adjust to the darkness. The first thing I saw in the gloom was a vague rectangular shape that I only recognised a few seconds later as the chair, turned on its side – it had got stuck in the shaft, after falling less than a sazhen. And then I noticed two white spots below the chair. They were moving, and I suddenly realised that they were white shirt cuffs protruding from Genji's leather sleeves! I couldn't see his hands, but the starched cuffs were clearly visible through the darkness. So Genji had not gone plunging to the bottom, he had managed to grab hold of the chair when it got stuck!

This discovery emboldened me, although there did not really seem to be any real reason to rejoice: if Genji was not helped, he could only hold out like that for two or three minutes, and then he would fall in any case. And who was going to help him? Certainly not Blagovolsky!

Thank God, the Doge couldn't see into the hole, and he had no idea that his main adversary was still alive, although quite helpless.

'Horatio, do you play chess?' Prospero's faltering voice gasped behind me.

I thought I must have misheard.

'In chess this kind of situation is called a stalemate,' he

went on. 'Unfortunately, I am not strong enough to shove you into the well, and you cannot let go of the leg of the desk. Are we going to go on lying on the floor like this for ever? I have a better suggestion. Since force has not produced the desired result, let us return to a state of civilisation. By which I mean, let us negotiate.'

He stopped pulling on my collar and stood up. I also hastily jumped to my feet and moved as far away as possible from the hatch.

Both of us looked very much the worse for wear. Blagovolsky's tie had slipped to one side, his grey hair was dishevelled and the belt of his dressing gown had come untied; I was no better, with a torn sleeve and missing buttons, and when I picked up my spectacles, I discovered that the right lens was cracked.

I was completely bewildered and did not know what to do. Run out into the street to get the police constable standing on Trubnaya Square? It would be ten minutes before I got back. Genji could not hold on for that long. I glanced involuntarily at the hole in the floor.

'You're right,' said Blagovolsky, tying up his dressing gown. 'That gap in the floor is distracting.'

He took a step forwards and turned the bronze figure anti-clockwise. The cover of the hatch slammed shut with a clang, making things even worse! Genji had been left in total darkness.

'Now there are just the two of us, you and I,' said Prospero. He looked into my eyes, and I felt the familiar magnetic influence of his gaze enveloping me and drawing me in. 'Before you make any decision, I want you to listen carefully to your own heart. Do not make a mistake that you will regret for the rest of your life. Listen to me, look at me, trust me. The way you used to trust me, before this outsider invaded our world and spoiled and perverted everything . . .'

The sound of his clear baritone voice flowed on and on, until I no longer understood the meaning of the words. I realise now that Prospero had put me under his hypnotic influence, and very successfully too. I am highly suggestible and easily submit to the will of a stronger person, as you know very well from your own experience. And in addition, it is in my nature to take pleasure in my subservience – it is as if I dissolve into the personality of the other individual. While Genji was with me, I obeyed him unquestioningly, but now I was in the power of the Doge's black eyes and mesmerising voice. I write about this bitterly, but soberly, in the full awareness of the more shameful aspects of my own nature.

It took very little time for Blagovolsky to transform me into a mesmerised rabbit, unable to move in the gaze of the python.

'The superfluous third party is no longer with us, no one will disturb us,' said the Doge, 'and I shall tell you how everything really was. You are intelligent, you will be able to distinguish the truth from lies. But first you and I will have a drink – for the peace of the uninspired soul of Mr Genji. And in accordance with Russian tradition, let us drink vodka.'

And so saying, he walked into the corner, where there was a huge carved wooden cupboard standing in a niche. He opened its doors and I saw large bottles, carafes and goblets.

Now that I no longer felt his spellbinding stare on me, my mind seemed to awaken and start working again. I looked at the clock on the wall and saw that less than five minutes had gone by. Perhaps Genji was still holding on! However, before I could come to any decision, Blagovolsky came back to the desk and trained his black eyes on me, and once again I was overcome by a blissful apathy. I was no longer thinking about anything, only listening to the sound of his masterful voice. We were standing on opposite sides of the desk. The disgraced roulette wheel was between us and its nickel-plated rays glinted and sparkled.

'Here are two glasses,' said the Doge, 'I don't usually drink vodka – I have a sick liver, but after a shock like that I could do with a pick-me-up. Here.'

He set the glass on one of the pockets of the Wheel of Fortune (I remember it was a black one), gently pushed a little lever, and the crystal vessel described a semicircle as it slowly moved towards me. Prospero halted the roulette wheel and set the second glass down on another black pocket in front of him.

'You will trust me and only me,' the Doge said, speaking slowly and ponderously. 'I am the only one who sees and understands the workings of your soul. You, Horatio, are not a man, but half a man. That is why you need to seek out your other half. You have found it. I am your other half. We shall be like a single whole, and you will be calm and happy . . .'

Just at that moment there was a sharp cracking sound from under the floor and we both shuddered and turned to look. One of the parquet blocks on the door of the secret hatch had split in half and there was a small round black hole in the middle of the crack.

'What the devil . . .' Prospero began, but then there was another bang, and then another – five or six in all.

Several more holes appeared beside the first. Chips of wood were sent flying, two parquet blocks jumped out of the floor, and white crumbs of plaster showered down from the ceiling. I guessed that Genji must be firing into the cover of the hatch. But what for? How would that help him?

I soon found out. There were several dull blows against the underside of the hatch: one, two, three. And then, on the fourth blow, several parquet blocks stood up on end and I could hardly believe my eyes when I saw a fist emerge from the hole. It was incredible, but Genji had managed to punch through the cover of the hatch with his bare hand – at the spot where the bullets had made holes in it!

The fist opened, the fingers grasped the edge of the hole that had been made and began pulling the cover down, overcoming the resistance of the spring.

'He's the devil himself!' Prospero exclaimed, flinging himself across the desk on his stomach and seizing the inkwell.

I had no chance to stop him. Blagovolsky turned the heroic folklore figure and the hatch swung shut. I heard a groan and a dull blow, and a moment later an ominous rumbling sound receding into the distance.

The impact of the Doge's sudden movement shook the desk: the roulette wheel trembled and turned through another half-circle. A few drops of vodka splashed out of the glasses into the pockets of the wheel.

'Ooph,' Prospero exclaimed in relief. 'What a persistent gentleman. And all because we didn't drink in time for the peace of his soul. Drink it down, Horatio, drain your glass. Or else he'll climb back out again. Come on!'

The Doge knitted his brows menacingly and I meekly picked up my vodka.

'We drink on one, two, three,' Blagovolsky told me. 'And damn my sick liver. One, two, three!'

I tipped back the glass and almost choked as the fiery liquid seared my throat. I should say that I am no lover of the Russian national beverage and usually prefer Moselle or Rheinwein.

When I wiped away the tears that had sprung to my eyes, I was astounded by the change that had come over Blagovolsky. He was standing absolutely still, clutching his throat with one hand, and his eyes were staring out of his head. I am unable to describe the expression of boundless horror that contorted the Doge's face. He wheezed, tore at his collar and doubled over.

I couldn't understand a thing, and events began following each other so rapidly that I could barely turn my head fast enough.

First there was a knocking sound and when I looked round I saw a hand grab the edge of the hatch. Then a second hand did the same, and a moment later Genji's head appeared out of the hole – his hair was dishevelled and his scowling forehead was covered with scratches. A few moments later this amazing man had already climbed out and was brushing the white dust off his elbows.

'What's wrong with him?' Genji asked, wiping his grazed and bloody fingers with a handkerchief.

The question referred to the Doge, who was rolling about on the floor and howling desperately. He kept trying to get to his feet, but could not.

'He drank some vodka, and he has a sick liver,' I explained stupidly, still not recovered from my stupor.

Genji stepped across to the desk. He picked up my glass, sniffed it and put it down again. Then he leaned down to the roulette wheel and looked at the spot where Blagovolsky's glass had stood. I saw that the spilled drops of vodka had left strange white marks on the black pocket.

Genji bent over, looked at Prospero writhing convulsively on the floor and remarked in a low voice: 'It looks like "royal vodka", a mixture of nitric and hydrochloric acid. It must have completely burned away his oesophagus and stomach. What a terrible way to die!'

I started shaking when I realised that the villainous Prospero had intended the poison for me, and only a lucky chance – the jolt that had turned the Wheel of Fortune – had saved me from a hideous fate.

'Let's go, Horatio,' said Genji, tugging on my sleeve. 'There's nothing more for us to do here. The unfortunate Radishchev d-died in exactly the same way. There is no way to save Blagovolsky. And no way to ease his suffering either – except by shooting him. But I shall not render him that service. Let's go.'

He walked towards the door and I hurried after him, leaving the dying man howling in agony behind us.

'But . . . but how did you manage to climb out of the well? And then, when Blagovolsky closed the hatch again, I distinctly heard a rumbling sound. Didn't you fall?' I asked.

'It was the chair I was standing on that fell,' Genji replied, pulling on his massive gauntlets. 'I shall miss my Herstahl very badly. It was an excellent revolver. You can't b-buy them anywhere, they have to be ordered from Brussels. Of course, I could climb down the well and look for it on the bottom, but I really don't feel like going back into that hole. Br-r-r!'

He shuddered, and so did I.

'Wait about a quarter of an hour and then phone the p-police,' he said when we parted.

As soon as he was gone, an unexpected thought struck me like a bolt of lightning. The Doge of the suicide club killed himself! There's higher justice for you! So God does exist!

This idea now occupies my mind more and more. I am even willing to concede that all the shocking events of the recent past had only one purpose: to bring me to this revelation. Ah yes, but that is no concern of yours. I have already written far more than necessary for an official document.

In summary of the above, I testify on my own responsibility that everything happened as I have described it.

Sergei Irinarkhovich Blagovolsky was not killed by anyone. He died by his own hand.

And now goodbye.

With every assurance of my most sincere disrespect,

F.F. Weltman, doctor of medicine

P.S. I considered it my duty to inform Mr Genji of the interest shown in him by yourself and the 'highly placed individual' of your acquaintance. He was not in the least surprised and asked me to tell you and the 'highly placed individual' not to trouble yourselves with any further searches or attempts to cause him any unpleasantness, since to-morrow (that is, in fact, today) at noon he is leaving the city of Moscow and his God-fearing homeland and taking his friends with him.

It was for this reason – in order to give Mr Genji time to travel beyond the bounds of your jurisdiction – that I did not telephone the police from the scene of last night's events, but waited for the whole day and am sending you this letter in the evening, not by courier, but via the ordinary post.

Genji is not at all like Isaiah, but his prophecy concerning me appears to have come true: the strong has come forth out of the weak.